Books by G.A. McKevett

Just Desserts
Bitter Sweets
Killer Calories
Cooked Goose
Sugar and Spite
Sour Grapes
Peaches and Screams
Death By Chocolate
Cereal Killer
Murder á la Mode
Corpse Suzette
Fat Free and Fatal
Poisoned Tarts
A Body to Die For
Wicked Craving
A Decadent Way to Die
Buried in Buttercream
Killer Honeymoon
Killer Physique

Published by Kensington Publishing Corporation

Killer
PHYSIQUE

G.A. McKevett

Killer
PHYSIQUE

A SAVANNAH REID MYSTERY

KENSINGTON BOOKS
www.kensingtonbooks.com

KENSINGTON BOOKS are published by

Kensington Publishing Corp.
119 West 40th Street
New York, NY 10018

All Kensington titles, imprints and distributed lines are available at special quantity discounts for bulk purchases for sales promotion, premiums, fund-raising, educational or institutional use. Special book excerpts or customized printings can also be created to fit specific needs. For details, write or phone the office of the Kensington Special Sales Manager: Kensington Publishing Corp., 119 West 40th Street, New York, NY, 10018. Attn. Special Sales Department. Phone: 1-800-221-2647.

Kensington and the K logo Reg. U.S. Pat. & TM Off.

Library of Congress Card Catalogue Number: 2013920820

ISBN-13: 978-0-7582-7654-4
ISBN-10: 0-7582-7654-0
First Kensington Hardcover Edition: April 2014

eISBN-13: 978-0-7582-7656-8
eISBN-10: 0-7582-7656-7
First Kensington Electronic Edition: April 2014

10 9 8 7 6 5 4 3 2 1

Printed in the United States of America

For Kristian

*So young, and yet already known for his
wisdom, compassion, and his love of peace.*

*Blessed are the peacemakers, Kris.
We're so blessed to have you among us.*

I want to thank Leslie Connell, who has worked tirelessly for the Moonlight Magnolia team year after year. She provides not only invaluable proofreading services, but love and support at times when they are most needed. Her greatest gift has always been her friendship.

I also wish to thank all the fans who write to me, sharing their thoughts and offering endless encouragement. Your stories touch my heart, and I enjoy your letters more than you know. I can be reached at:

sonja@sonjamassie.com
and
facebook.com/gwendolynnarden.mckevett

Chapter 1

Standing at her bathroom sink, staring at the disgruntled, newly married woman in the mirror, Savannah Reid rehearsed the speech she intended to give the jury at her murder trial. It would be during the sentencing phase, no doubt, because she fully intended to plead guilty.

She was certain that if there was even one semipersnickety female on the jury, she'd escape the needle.

"You have to understand, ladies and gentlemen, that I spent three and a half long weeks redecorating that bathroom—all in anticipation of his parents' visit. I'm pretty sure I messed up my back permanently by hanging those fancy ceiling tiles . . . the ones that used to be white but are now all globbed up with dribs and drabs of blue shaving foam. How in heaven's name does a grown man get shaving foam on the ceiling?"

She glanced around at the carnage of her freshly renovated bathroom and added in her thick, Georgia drawl, "I reckon the same way he got it all over the sink, the faucet handle, the light switch, and the mirror. My dear jury members, you haven't lived till you've tried to scrub that stuff off a mirror. It's blue cement.

You can take a razor blade and fingernail polish remover to it, and it won't budge."

A brisk knock on the door interrupted her plea for mercy.

"You in there?" inquired a deep, annoyed male voice.

"Yeah," she barked back.

"You comin' out soon? Or am I gonna have to go downstairs again to do my business?"

She jerked the door open and stood—nose to nose, give or take a few inches—with her beloved new husband. "Boy, you and your thimble-sized bladder are irritatin' the daylights outta me."

He shrugged and grinned down at her with a sexy smirk that would have set her bloomers atwitter, were it not for the devastation behind her.

"Hey," he said, "when the dragon needs drainin', what's a guy to do?"

He waited, giving her plenty of time to chuckle, or at least grin. But all he got was an icy blue stare. It was the glacial glare that had made former cop, now private detective Savannah Reid infamous among suspected murderers, robbers, embezzlers, and jaywalkers. Evildoers of all shapes and sizes, including husbands who left the toilet seat up and burped loudly in fancy restaurants, had been on the receiving end of those cobalt lasers.

Rolling his eyes, Dirk moaned and said, "Oh, man. I'm always in trouble. What did I do *this* time?"

Stepping to one side, so that he would have a clear, unobstructed view of the crime scene, she waved an arm to indicate the extent of the damages. "That," she said. "That's what you did. Again."

He gave the room a cursory glance and frowned, obviously confused. "What? What's the matter? Did I fold the towel in half instead of perfect thirds? Did I leave the cap off the toothpaste?

Am I gonna get shot at sunrise or hanged from the neck until dead?"

She decided not to tell him that she had, indeed, been fantasizing about an execution only moments before. Her own. Society's recompense for premeditated, first-degree homicide.

As she watched his eyes dart around the room, registering absolutely nothing amiss, by his own lax nonstandards, her ire rose. "Does this room look neat and tidy to you?" she asked.

"I've seen worse," he replied.

"Yes, I'm sure you have. But not in *my* house. Look at those toothpaste spit specks all over the mirror."

"Hey, happens when I floss. You don't want a husband with lousy dental hygiene, do you?"

"And why did you leave your deodorant, shave cream can, and jock itch powder there on the sink again? I asked you to put them back in the medicine cabinet when you're done with them."

He looked genuinely perplexed. "But why should I go to all that work when tomorrow I'm just gonna have to drag 'em out so's I can use 'em again?"

"Al-l-l that work? Dra-a-ag 'em out? You act like I'm asking you to pick a bale o' cotton in the hot Georgia sun."

He gave her a sappy, condescending smile that was, no doubt, intended to smooth her ruffled feathers, but in fact accomplished exactly the opposite. "If I put those three tiny little things away," he said, "will that make my beautiful new bride happy?"

"I reckon," she grumbled. "And maybe you could wipe off the mirror once in a month of Sundays, since it's you who gunks it all up four times a day."

Sighing deeply, he trudged past her into the room, picked up his offending toiletries, and with great ceremony placed them in the medicine chest. He fussed with the containers for what seemed like forever to Savannah, making quite a show of spacing them perfectly, evenly, among their neighbors, turning the labels straight outward, then readjusting ad nauseum.

With that delicate mission accomplished, he strode to the toilet, unrolled a giant handful of tissue, and returned to the sink. Still grinning like a goat munching sand burrs, he flipped on the sink faucet and wetted the paper.

As Savannah's blood pressure soared, he calmly, casually, smeared the sodden wad all over the mirror, leaving bits of soggy mess behind. Unfortunately, the blue blobs of shaving cream remained undisturbed.

Standing behind him, her face turning redder by the moment, Savannah looked around the room for potential murder weapons and wondered if it were possible to inflict a fatal wound with a Lady Gillette aloe-moisturizing bikini line shaver.

"There," he exclaimed, proudly displaying his handiwork. "Happy now?"

"Plum ecstatic," she muttered.

"Good. And now that I'm in here, I'm gonna choke the chicken. So unless you've got some picky-ass directions about how I oughta do that, too, you might wanna skedaddle."

With her chin a few notches higher than usual and a grim look on her face, Savannah marched stiffly to the door. She paused there for a moment as a hundred or so of Granny Reid's admonitions about "living in harmony with the man the good God gave ya" and "overlookin' the better part of a husband's transgressions bein' the path to domestic tranquillity" danced through her head.

She could take the high road and just walk out without saying another word. That would be noble, virtuous.

Blessed are the peacemakers, and all that good stuff.

Dirk was, after all, a decent man. He loved her. He'd put his crap away with a smile—okay, a smirk—on his face and kinda, sorta cleaned up when she'd asked him to. What more could a woman ask, really?

Yes, she would put away her anger and choose the path of peace.

Virtue, after all, had its own reward . . . mostly in the form of self-righteous gloating.

Then she heard a sound behind her that made every muscle in her body kink into a knot. A merry little tinkling sound.

Not the sound of liquid hitting water. Oh, no. It was the un- mistakable merry little melody of pee hitting tile.

She whirled on him with a vengeance. "Dammit all, Dirk! At the shooting range, you score forty-nine out of fifty shots from twenty-five yards—standing, kneeling, *and* prone! But you can't hit a dadgum toilet that's two feet away?"

He stood—chicken partially choked, dragon half drained—a look of shock and confusion on his face. "What?"

"If I were to paint a bull's-eye on the bottom of the bowl, do you reckon it'd improve that piss-poor aim of yours?"

He thought about it. Long and hard. Then, having given it all due consideration, he solemnly nodded, smiled, and said, "It could. Yes, I think it might at that. Good idea, babe. You get on that right away."

"You . . . ! You . . . ! I oughta . . . ! A-a-u-u-gh!"

She stomped out of the room and slammed the door behind her, rocking the house to its foundation.

As she strode down the hallway, she could hear her groom laughing his butt off on the other side of the bathroom door.

Yeah, well, at least somebody's enjoying all this wedded bliss, she thought.

"Laugh it up, fuzzball," she muttered as she went into the bedroom to get dressed for their big night out. "I'll getcha back. One way or the other."

Granny Reid had told her many times, "Don't let the sun set on your wrath, Savannah girl. No matter how bad the squabblin's been that day, come nighttime you always make it right 'tween you and your man before you lay your head on your pillow to sleep."

Savannah had no problem with that sage advice. It would be at least seven hours before they retired for the evening. Surely she could arrange some soul-gratifying form of revenge before then.

Nope, she had no intention of going to bed angry. Come nighttime, she intended to be giggling on that pillow and rubbing her hands with glee.

Chapter 2

As Savannah rode down the Ventura Freeway in the rear seat of the beautiful old Bentley—on her way to a major Hollywood movie premiere, dressed to the nines in her best, sapphire silk dress—she couldn't help thinking about that tiny, rural town where she had grown up.

McGill, Georgia, was, and remained, little more than a wide spot in a rough, pothole-ridden road.

Thanks to Granny Reid, who'd raised Savannah and her eight siblings, Savannah had many pleasant childhood memories. But she had even more grim ones from the days before Granny had taken custody of her grandchildren. And at times like this, when her life was full to overflowing with the abundant blessings of basic needs fulfilled, loving friends, and the occasional adventure, like this one, she thought about the child she had been in McGill.

Sometimes she enjoyed the irrational but healing fantasy of the adult Savannah returning to yesteryear, scooping up the ragged little girl she had been, setting her on her lap, and telling the child, "Things are gonna get a whole lot better, darlin', when you grow up. You just hang in there and it'll happen, sooner than you think. You're just a little caterpillar now. But when you grow up, you're gonna be a big, beautiful butterfly."

It would have helped, she had no doubt. Because if anybody in the world could have benefited from a crystal ball that showed a sparkling future, it was a poor kid from McGill, Georgia, struggling to make it through a tough childhood in a dark place with limited hope.

As Dirk reached over, took her hand, folded it between his large, warm ones, and squeezed, her earlier irritations with him melted away. She gave him a sideways glance, then a wink, and a grin that deepened her dimples. She had to admit he looked darn good in a tux. The end results were almost worth the trouble of having to hog-tie him first to get him into it.

He leaned his head down to hers and nuzzled her dark curls with his nose. She prepared her heart for the sweet nothing he was about to whisper in her ear.

"See?" he said. "I didn't have to wear this stupid penguin outfit, after all. The damn tie's choking me so bad I can't even swallow my own spit. Any minute now I'm gonna start drooling down the front of this sissy shirt."

Okay, she thought. *Which will it be? Kill him with kindness? Or just open the car door and push him out?*

She decided to be nice. "Nice" was the programmed, default mode for Southern belles. Though she could flip the switch into "cantankerous" when the situation warranted it—when "nice" wasn't getting her what she wanted.

Long ago, she had decided that Dixie gentility had more to do with effectiveness and efficiency than any code of ethics. And being a pragmatist, she had no problem with that.

"But, darlin'," she cooed, "you look so handsome in a tuxedo. Sorta like James Bond, Clint Eastwood on Oscar night, and Elvis—all rolled into one."

"Now, when did you ever see the King wearing a tux?"

"I don't know. He probably did when he and Priscilla got married."

Dirk nodded toward the front of the car, where their good friends, Ryan Stone and John Gibson sat—John at the wheel and Ryan in the passenger seat. "Yeah, well, you were wrong about the formal wear crap, about me having to wear this stupid thing to this stupid shindig. They're not wearing tuxedos. Hell, Ryan's not even got a tie on. I feel like an overdressed idiot. And that's the worst kind—gussied up *and* uncomfortable."

Savannah considered telling him the truth, which was: When you look like Ryan Stone—tall, dark, gorgeous hunk that he is—you didn't need a tie.

With a body like Ryan's, he would've looked good in a barrel or, better yet, in Savannah's humble opinion, a loincloth.

"He may not be wearing a tuxedo," she whispered. "But that's an Armani suit he's got on. I'm pretty sure that John's is Prada."

She glanced up, and her eyes met John's in the rearview mirror. Obviously having heard what she'd said, he was giving her one of his warm, kindhearted smiles.

"Before you complain too bitterly, old chap, about your formal attire," John said, his British accent thick and lush, like his silver hair and mustache, "remember that when this evening's festivities are over, you're the only lad in this vehicle who'll be going home with that lovely lady sitting next to you."

Dirk gave a little sniff. "It ain't like the two of you wanna go home with her, or any other lady for that matter."

Savannah gave him a warning pinch on the thigh. But Ryan turned in his seat, a grin on his face, and gave Dirk a long, deliberate, head-to-toe look. "If I were you, and I wanted to update my look, I'd ditch the tie, open the collar, and muss up my hair a bit."

Savannah cringed, knowing how well that suggestion would go over. Mussed hair looked a lot better on a guy like Ryan, who had plenty to muss. Dirk, on the other hand, worked long and hard on his hair to make the most of every precious strand. To a guy with so many bare spots to cover, "mussing" was simply not an option.

True to form, Dirk scowled and grumbled something semimenacing under his breath as he peeled off the tie, shoved it into his pocket and unfastened his top two studs.

Savannah decided she'd better turn things around, before her hubby's mood plummeted into the Dirk Abyss. In the space of two hours, he had been yelled at for messing up the bathroom, then squashed into a tuxedo that he now realized he didn't have to wear, and told to muss up hair that he didn't have.

She recognized the signs; their evening steeped in Hollywood glamour was circling the toilet. A full-fledged flush was imminent.

"I hear the special effects in this movie are amazing," she said a bit too brightly. "And they say that Jason Tyrone's been bulking up like crazy. Looks even better than he did in his last film."

A sideways glance at Dirk told her that this road might not be the one to take either.

"And the gal who plays the heroine looks fantastic, too," she added quickly. " 'Fills out her barely there costume exactly like a super-hot Celtic goddess should.' I believe that's what *The New York Times* reviewer said."

Dirk rewarded her efforts with a broad grin.

Ryan and John chuckled.

"Indeed," John said, as he guided the Bentley off the 101 and onto the Hollywood Freeway, heading toward Los Angeles. "I believe those were the reviewer's words verbatim."

"At least if it's got Jason Tyrone in it, you know there's gotta be some ass-kicking action," Dirk said. "It ain't gonna be one of those girlie flicks where everybody's just sitting around talking to each other, and the audience blubbers their faces off at the end."

"Heaven forbid," Ryan said, with a smile and a wink for Savannah. "I think you two will enjoy it. The production values are top rate, the special effects are awesome, and the acting and the script are pretty good, considering that it's a superhero action film."

"But above all else," John added, "we're looking forward to introducing you to Jason. He's a fine lad. Hasn't let all this fame and fortune go to his head."

"That's true." Ryan nodded. "We've known him since he was a kid, washing dishes in the bars and restaurants on Sunset Strip and working his way to the top in bodybuilding competitions."

"Didn't he do some modeling, too?" Savannah asked. "I think I remember seeing him and all of his muscles on billboards."

"Yeah, wearing nothing but his skivvies." Dirk gave a sniff. "You'd never catch me posing for something like that, showin' the whole world what I got."

"Oh, yeah?" Savannah gave him a poke in the ribs. "I seem to remember a certain policeman hunks charity calendar, where you were Mr. December. And if it wasn't for a well-placed Christmas package, you would've been showing off a certain package of your own."

Ryan whipped around in his seat. "What's this? A *hunk* calendar? First we've heard of this."

"Indeed!" John added. "We require details, details."

Dirk growled and shot Savannah a You-Started-This-Crap look. "It was for a good cause, and the present I was holding was extralarge. That's all the details you two need. What were we talking about before?"

"Jason Tyrone and how hot he is right now," Savannah said. "Even Granny Reid knows who he is. Every week, he's on the cover of the tabloid she reads. To her that's the epitome of success."

"A success, to be sure," John replied, as he brought the Bentley to a halt on the congested street. "Look at this bloody mess, and we're still blocks from the theater."

Ryan took out his phone, did some research, and said, "They have Hollywood Boulevard blocked off between Highland Avenue and Orange Drive. Parking may be a bit of a challenge. Are you two up to a hike?"

Savannah thought of the movie trailer she had seen—multitudes of scantily clad, bronzed bodies with rippling muscles as far as you could see. She glanced over at Dirk and saw his grin and the lusty twinkle in his eye. Her womanly, wifely intuition told her he was thinking something similar about buxom Celtic goddesses overflowing their costumes.

"Oh, yeah," she said. "We're up for a bit of a jaunt, ain't we, darlin'?" She nudged Dirk.

He chuckled. "Absolutely. Park anywhere you can. We'll hoof it from here."

Jaunts in three-inch heels were highly overrated. And so was wearing a long-sleeved, wraparound, silk dress on a warm Southern California day. Or so Savannah decided after six blocks of jostling through the rambunctious crowds en route to their destination.

Savannah and her three favorite fellows passed through numerous security checkpoints as they fought their way to the center of the festivities. But each time, Ryan presented the magic tickets—even before Dirk could take his badge out of his pocket—and they were graciously motioned past.

"Kinda nice being treated like royalty, huh?" Savannah said, nudging Dirk with her elbow.

"I get this every morning at my local 7-Eleven where I buy my lottery ticket. Or at least I used to, before I became a married man and had to give up all my vices."

"Oh, yes, all those decadent vices of yours: leaving the toilet seat up, dropping your dirty drawers on the bedroom floor, littering the place with empty beer bottles."

"Rituals that are near and dear to the male heart. Abandoned, all for the love of a woman."

"I never told you to stop playing lotto."

"But now that I don't live by that store, I can't buy my tickets there."

"Buy them somewhere else. There's a convenience store two blocks from my house."

"Nope. It's gotta be my lucky store or nothin'."

She looked up at him, gave him a flirtatious grin, and whispered, "I didn't hear you complaining about all these changes in your life last night when I was abusing you something fierce between the sheets."

He chuckled. "This marriage stuff isn't without its benefits. That brand of mistreatment I can handle."

"Manly man that you are."

"Exactly."

As they drew nearer to Grauman's landmark theater with its Chinese pagoda façade and famous hand- and footprints captured for eternity in cement, the celebratory pandemonium around them increased exponentially.

In front of the gigantic columns that flanked the ornate, gilded double doors stood twenty-feet-tall, cut-out figures of Jason and his co-star, Alanna Cleary. They wore the brief leather-and-bronze costumes of their supernatural, superhero characters, Dagda and Caolainn.

Savannah wondered what it must feel like, to be a mere mortal and look up at those figures and see your face and body. In society's eyes, they were the epitome of mankind and womanhood.

Like most people who weighed more than the charts recommended, Savannah was quite aware that she didn't live up to the culture's ideal. But unlike most people, she had managed to stop giving a hoot.

Her body was strong, healthy, and, most important, it provided a place for her to hang out here on earth and enjoy life's most basic pleasures. So she was thankful for it and loved it. Every pound and inch of it.

And she felt no envy at all, staring up at Alanna Cleary's taut, tanned belly, with its exaggerated six-pack.

Okay, maybe just a smidgen of envy, she admitted, before turning her attention away from the advertised and unattainable. *But not nearly jealous enough to ruin such a good time.*

As she looked around at the rowdy crowd, she was glad she wasn't in charge of security at this wild event. Temporary barricades barely restrained the hoard of fans hoping to catch a glimpse of their superheroes. Even within the areas restricted to the press alone, seasoned reporters jumped up and down like crazed teenagers at a rock concert and chanted the names "Jason" and "Alanna."

Each time a celebrity exited one of the gleaming black limousines and stepped onto the red carpet, hundreds of cameras flashed, twinkling like fairy starlight dusted over the crowd.

Savannah decided that, in spite of all the derogatory remarks she had heard about Hollywood, she considered herself very fortunate indeed to be here, enjoying this bit of never-never land, this fairy-tale fantasy coming to life in the real world.

"I gotta admit, this doesn't suck as bad as I thought it would," Dirk whispered as he squeezed her hand.

She smiled. Fluent as she was in Dirk-language, she knew that translated into "I'm having the time of my life!"

"Understate whenever possible" was Rule Number One in the *Manly Man Handbook*. And she knew, if there had been room, Dirk would have had that booklet tattooed on his left buttock, so strongly did he believe and uphold its precepts.

At that moment, a particularly large and especially shiny black limo glided into view and stopped at the end of the red carpet. Security guards, disguised in chauffeur livery, stepped forward and opened the rear door.

A dainty foot with a five-inch, high-heeled strappy sandal emerged, followed by an impossibly long and shapely leg—then its mate and yards and yards of shimmering, emerald green satin.

Cries of "Alanna! Alanna! Hey, look this way! Alanna, come here! Come over here! Alanna, over here!" erupted from the crowd.

Ryan turned to Dirk and with a quirked eyebrow said, "There you go, buddy. Alanna Cleary in the gorgeous flesh."

Dirk appraised her, head to lovely toes, for a moment, then he shot Savannah a quick, guilty glance. But as Savannah watched the magnificent goddess in green satin glide down the red carpet, her waist-long copper hair flowing, her toned arms and legs glowing—an exquisite, Celtic beauty beyond compare—Savannah couldn't blame him for gawking. Every eye was on Alanna Cleary, as she moved along, the picture of composure and grace, offering a warm, open smile to everyone she passed.

"Hey, where's her date?" Savannah whispered to John.

"Yeah," said Dirk. "You wouldn't expect a woman like that to come alone."

"Sh-h-h," John replied. "Let's just say there've been rumors."

"We'll fill you in later," Ryan added.

No sooner had Alanna disappeared inside the theater than another limo arrived. The rear door was opened, as before. But this time, when the passenger emerged, the cheering from the crowd was peppered with the occasional hiss and jeer.

Savannah was surprised at the fans' reactions, until she saw the face of the newcomer. It was none other Vladik Zlotnik, the villain of the film. Standing at six-foot-four, his long, black hair slicked back and hanging limply to his collar, his skin pale to the point of having a faint bluish cast, the Russian movie star looked more like a vampire than the dark, Irish god of the underworld that he played in the film.

"Creepy guy," Dirk said. "No wonder he always plays an evil dude."

"Vladik's not so bad," Ryan answered. "In fact, he can be the life of the party if you get enough vodka in him."

John added, "If you're an actor who looks like he does, you're not going to get a lot of opportunities to play the hero."

Nodding, Savannah said, "I guess if little children cry when they see you, and dogs bark and run away, you might as well use it to your advantage."

"I'd rather play the villain any time," Dirk said. "It's gotta be more fun, snarling and doing dastardly deeds. At least until the end when you get your comeuppance."

A petite blonde who was more than a foot shorter than Vladik was helped from the limo, and the two of them walked hand in hand up the carpet.

To Savannah, Vladik's date looked more like a teenager arriving at her first prom than a seasoned society girl. She tugged at her all-too-revealing black gown and wobbled awkwardly on her high, high heels.

As they made their way briskly along the crimson path, she glanced up at Vladik with an almost appealing look on her fresh, young face, as though seeking some approval or reassurance from him. But none was forthcoming. Vladik walked a step ahead, all but dragging her along. And Savannah didn't need anyone to tell her this "date" was an arrangement of convenience.

At least for Vladik.

But before they entered the golden doors, another limousine arrived, and with its entrance, absolute chaos erupted. All the attention shifted from Vladik to the new arrival. The crowd went crazy, everyone pushing their neighbors aside, trying to get closer to the front, while screaming, "Jason! Jason! Jason!"

Dirk leaned his head down to Savannah's and shouted in her ear, "Gee, I wonder who it is."

"Some detective you are. I'd say it's the star of this whole she-bang, but that's just a hunch."

Once again, the security guards snapped to attention. Even before the big Cadillac limo was completely stopped, one had reached for the handle, while his partner slid into position just behind him.

A tall, burly chauffeur jumped out of the driver's seat and quickly wedged himself between the guards and the automobile. He gave the surrounding area a long, scrutinizing look before opening the door.

At that moment, the noise rose to a level that Savannah could hardly believe. She had never been in a crowd whose energy and enthusiasm even approached this frenzy.

She had seen videos of the Beatles arriving in the United States during the sixties and clips of Elvis performances where women shrieked, wept, and fainted. But this was the first time she had witnessed such a brouhaha herself.

"Mercy," she said, though she knew no one would be able to hear her. "Just imagine . . . such a commotion over one measly feller."

In her opinion, any woman who passed out at the mere sight of some guy—who put his britches on, one leg at a time, like any other man—had to be a few pecans short of a Sunday dinner pie.

Then she saw him. And she understood what the hoopla was all about.

Jason Tyrone was absolutely, heart-stopping, take your breath away, cause you to drop dead in your tracks and go straight to heaven gorgeous.

Standing at least six foot, six inches tall, shoulder and arm muscles bulging against the fabric of his tuxedo, and with thick, wavy blond hair that was fashionably shaggy, the bluest eyes she had ever seen, and a jawline that had sold copious amounts of Tyrone Nights cologne and aftershave—Jason lived up to all the hype and more.

As he strolled along the red carpet, drawing nearer to where she and her three guys were standing, she could feel her own knees literally getting weak. She had to work at not wobbling on her high heels.

Yes, maybe she'd judged those Elvis and Beatle fans too harshly, after all.

Jason was the picture of elegance as he moved along, nodding to one, waving to another, pausing to shake hands briefly here and there.

Though Savannah did notice that beneath it all—in spite of the graceful, masculine presence he projected—there was something else that she couldn't quite put her finger on. Something unsettling.

Maybe it was the way his eyes occasionally darted around the crowd, as though he were on guard, searching for someone or something. Perhaps an unwelcome, unfriendly presence of some kind?

Dirk poked Savannah in the ribs. "When do we get to meet him?" he said, his mouth against her ear. "Ryan and John are supposed to be his good buddies. Are we just gonna stand here with our thumbs up our—?"

"Sh-h-h!" She gouged him back. "Just wait and see."

A moment later, Jason was even with them, only a few feet away. And that was when he spotted Ryan and John.

Instantly, his face lit up, and his whole demeanor changed. "Hey!" he shouted, rushing over to them. He grabbed Ryan in a bear hug, then managed to fold John, as well, into the hearty embrace. "Man, I was hoping you guys would make it!" he said, as pleased as a kid whose out-of-town dad had arrived at his last baseball game of the season.

"Are you kidding? We wouldn't have missed this for the world," Ryan replied, thumping him soundly on the back.

"Wild horses couldn't keep us away," John added. "But these crowds nearly did. You've collected quite a bevy of fans for yourself here, lad."

Ryan turned to Savannah and Dirk. "And here's a couple of them," he said, pulling them closer. "Jason, we brought two of our favorite people in the world to meet you and see the show. This is Savannah and Dirk."

As though in slow motion, Savannah watched and recorded every micro-second of the experience she knew she would relive ten thousand times before she got to be Granny Reid's age. At least.

Jason Tyrone stepped toward her. His eyes met hers . . . his world-famous eyes that were the same sapphire blue as her silk dress. The world around them disappeared—the raging crowd, Ryan and John, and even poor Dirk.

For just a moment she felt terribly guilty. Here she was only a few weeks married, and her knickers were a'jingle over a couple of blue eyes. And a mane of golden hair. And six and a half feet of solid muscle.

Okay, she didn't feel all that guilty. But she did make a mental note to cut Dirk some slack later if she caught him ogling Alanna.

Jason Tyrone, his whole gorgeous self, reached for her hand, and enfolded it in his. His enormous, strong hands—that she couldn't help noticing were just a little bit moist.

In fact, if they had been anyone else's hands, she might have called them clammy. But you didn't use a word like "clammy" when describing a Celtic god/sex symbol. It just seemed inappropriate somehow.

"I'm so happy to meet you, Savannah," he said, as though they were the only two people in the world, hundreds of cameras weren't snapping their pictures, and a thousand or more people weren't waiting impatiently for Jason to make his way inside so the real festivities could begin.

"And I'm just so proud to—"

Bang!

Just over her right shoulder, a loud popping sound. It went through her nervous system like an electric jolt.

Someone in the crowd shouted, "Gun!"

In an instant, Ryan, Savannah, and John had grabbed Jason. Dirk had Savannah. And they were rushing en masse toward the theater doors.

Chapter 3

Savannah, Dirk, John, Ryan, and Jason had just reached the giant cutout figures, when Savannah heard a sound behind them—a strange sound, considering the circumstances.

Laughter.

She took a second to glance over her shoulder and saw a young woman holding a giant bouquet of sparkling gold and silver, helium-filled balloons.

Several people around her were laughing, poking at her, as she stood there red-faced and giggling nervously.

One of the guys standing closest to her held up one hand and addressed the crowd. "Balloons, everybody! Balloons! It was just a couple of balloons popping! Everybody settle down!"

Savannah looked at Dirk. They both turned to Ryan and John.

All four processed this new information in half a second and realized the "threat" had passed.

Savannah gave a nervous little chuckle and said, "Now, wasn't that just a barrel of fun. Let's do it again."

"That kind of fun I can do without," Dirk growled.

"Me too," Ryan replied.

"Ah, well," John said, with a sigh of relief. "As long as it all works out in the end. No harm done."

In unison they turned to look at Jason, and Savannah nearly gasped when she saw the pallor of his previously bronzed complexion. He was sweating profusely and breathing much harder than she would've expected, considering that he had run only a few feet.

John reached over and put a comforting hand on his friend's broad shoulder. "Are you okay, old chap?"

"Sure," Jason replied.

Savannah wondered if she had ever heard a less assuring "sure" in her life.

Jason Tyrone—Dagda, mystic king of the Tuatha De Danann—looked like he was about to faint, right in front of his fans, a thousand cameras, and the twenty-foot cutout of his glorious self.

"Let's get him inside," Savannah whispered to Dirk. "Quick."

"Gotcha."

Dirk grabbed Jason by one arm. Savannah held the other. And Ryan and John cleared the way, as they hurried him into the theater.

No. If Jason Tyrone's friends, old and new, had anything to do with it, this crowd was not going to watch their superhero fall flat on his face.

Savannah's downstairs hall clock was chiming one-thirty as she and Dirk pulled back the beautiful quilt that Granny Reid had made them for a wedding gift and climbed into bed. She relocated one of the two black mini-panthers that she called house cats from her pillow down to the foot of the bed.

"Sorry, Di," she told the disgruntled Diamante. "Mommy had a big day. She's tired and doesn't feel like having your furry butt in her face all night."

Dirk, on the other hand, pulled his favorite, Cleopatra, against his bare chest. Murmuring sweet nothings to her, he snuggled her close and began to rub that magic "cat spot" behind her ears.

Disgusted with "Mom's" treatment, Diamante left Savannah's side of the bed and found a place next to her sister where she could claim her share of the Dirk pets.

"You're spoiling those cats rotten," Savannah said. "Before you moved in, they'd only eaten cat food."

"Get real. I've seen you feed them ice cream off the end of your finger, and they've even licked the bowl when you're done."

"Okay, mostly just cat food. But now that you've introduced them to the wonders of a made-for-humans tuna sandwich, I can't leave my lunch unattended without finding black fur and a bite gone when I come back."

"Oh, stop your gripin' and be glad you married a guy who likes cats." He pulled Diamante up under his chin and kissed the top of her head. "They're the nicest part of marrying you and moving in here—getting to pet them any time I want."

"Really? That's the very best thing?" she asked, lying down and rolling onto her side where he could get a full, unobstructed view of the abundant cleavage her new lace gown revealed.

He grinned broadly. "Okay, the kitties are the second best."

She flounced around a bit, like a hen making her nest. Once her pillow had been adequately fluffed and the sheet properly tucked, she turned the bedside lamp off.

Even with the lights off, the moonbeams streaming through the lace curtains provided enough light for her to see his face. It was a face that had grown progressively dearer to her over the years—handsome in a rugged sort of way, its streetworn roughness softened by the dim light.

Then there were the cats. Being black, they were nearly invisible, but their purring filled the late-night silence.

That sound, combined with Dirk's deep, male murmurings of

"There ya go, Di. I didn't forget you, baby" would have normally put Savannah's spirit at ease. But tonight something was nagging at her. And she wasn't sure exactly what it was.

"Now that we aren't around Ryan and John," she said, "what did you think of the movie?"

"It was pretty good. Better than I'd thought it'd be," he admitted. "When that monster thing came up out of the sea and ate all those guys—that was awesome. You know, with all the blood spurting, and the guts and body parts flyin' all around. It was pretty real-looking."

She rolled her eyes. "Oh yes, that was the high point for me, too."

"And the acting was okay. That Alanna gal was pretty convincing when she called all those mean, smoky spirits up outta that wishing well."

"Wasn't that the scene where her top blew off?"

"Yeah."

"Convincing acting, indeed."

He snickered. "Hey, held my attention."

"I imagine it did."

He rearranged the kitties so that he could lie against Savannah. Slipping his arm around her waist, he pulled her close. "I saw all those looks you were giving Jason. You were watching him, instead of the movie, the whole night."

"Not for the reason you think," she said. "Oh, I was impressed with his looks and all that at first. But it didn't take long for me to start wondering what was up with him."

"Oh, then it wasn't just me. I thought he seemed sorta jumpy, too. But I figured it was that balloon-popping thing."

"No. He was skitzy before, too. As soon as he got out of the car, he was looking around like he was expecting somebody to jump outta the bushes and pounce on him."

He reached over and with one finger, brushed a curl out of her eyes and tucked it behind her ear. "I guess he's better at swinging a sword at sea monsters than he is fighting off crazy female fans who wanna throw him on the ground and ravish him."

"A few male fans, too, it seems."

"Yeah, I had no idea he was gay until Ryan said so on the way home. Wonder how many of those women would get over him fast if that was public knowledge?"

"Not that many."

"But what's the point in fantasizing about something you're never gonna get?"

Savannah giggled. "Oh, yes. Men are so much more practical. They would never fantasize about—oh, say—a lesbian."

"Um. Yeah. Right." He cleared his throat. "But speaking of things you *can* have . . ."

His hand began to move beneath the covers. But before he could zero in on any warm, soft spots, the cell phone that Savannah had left on her nightstand began to buzz.

He sighed. "Or should I say things you might be able to have if the damn phone wasn't ringin'?"

She reached for it, her pulse pounding. No phone call that came at one-thirty in the morning was ever good news. Though she had never admitted it, even to herself, Savannah feared that with an octogenarian grandmother, a middle-of-the-night phone call could signal the end of her world as she knew it.

With a shaking hand, she picked up the phone and read the caller ID. "Ryan Stone." *Oh, okay*, she thought. *Maybe this won't be so bad, after all.*

Ryan probably assumed they were still awake, since he had only dropped them off a short time before.

"It's Ryan," she told Dirk. "What did you do, leave your sunglasses in their car again?"

"I resemble that remark," he said, as he turned his attention back to Cleo's left ear. "He better have a good reason—interrupting my foreplay like that."

25

She punched the "talk" button. "Hello, darlin'," she said. "What's shakin'?"

"Savannah, I'm sorry to disturb you so late," he said, his voice tight, his words clipped.

She sat straight up in bed and shot Dirk a worried look. "That's okay, hon. What's up?"

She heard him gulp, then there was a moment of silence as though he was gathering his composure.

Yes, this was going to be bad.

"It's Jason," he said, his voice breaking.

She didn't have to ask. She knew.

Ryan Stone was a cool, collected sorta guy. Some might even say stoic. He hadn't called them in the middle of the night because Jason Tyrone had gotten himself a parking ticket.

"Is he . . . ?"

She thought of the big, handsome, charismatic man they had just spent the evening with—so vibrant, so full of life.

"Yes, he's gone."

"Oh, no! But how? When?"

Dirk sat up, grabbed Savannah's arm and squeezed. "What is it? Who . . . ?"

"Jason," she whispered, then returned her attention to the phone. "I'm so sorry, Ryan. Tell me what happened."

She heard him take a deep breath. "Remember, we told you he'd asked us to come by his hotel, the Island View, after we'd dropped you two off?"

She recalled them mentioning that during the car ride home. Something about Jason having an early-morning flight to New York and him wanting to talk to Ryan and John privately before he left.

"I remember," she said. "He said he had something he needed to talk to you about."

"Something important, he said."

Instantly, Savannah flashed back on the whole balloon-popping event there on the red carpet—the haunted look in Jason's eyes. "Did you get a chance to talk to him, to find out what it was?"

Again, there was a long, painful silence on the other end. Then, "No. When we got to the hotel, we found him. I mean, his body."

"Are you still there at the Island View?"

"Yes."

"Hang tight, darlin'," she said. "We're on our way."

Chapter 4

On the few occasions when Savannah had strolled through the lovely lobby of the Island View Hotel, she had thought it would be a charming place for a romantic rendezvous. But until recently, romance hadn't been high on her list of priorities. Mostly because . . . to be high on the list, it would have to actually *be* on the list. And until things had taken a pleasant turn with Dirk, her list had been mostly romance-free.

Unfortunately, now that a passion-filled overnight might be a possibility, she couldn't afford to spend one here. The five-star hotel—with its sunlit atrium and meandering stone walkways that led visitors beside sparkling fountains, koi ponds, and exotic tropical plants—didn't come cheap. A drink at the bar and a kiss beside the fountain was the best they could do.

As they emerged from the elevator, Savannah and Dirk could already hear the commotion down the hallway to their right—excited male voices and a couple of worried female ones, mixed with the scratchy static of walkie-talkies.

"Oh, man," Dirk said, "I hope they haven't stomped all over the crime scene already."

"Crime scene? Why are you already calling it a crime scene?"

"You were with him less than two hours ago. Did he seem to you like a guy who was about to keel over from natural causes?"

"Well, no, but . . ."

For everyone concerned, she wanted desperately to argue with him. The loss of such a beloved person as Jason Tyrone was going to be bad enough, without adding homicide to the tragedy.

But she couldn't help thinking back to those moments on the red carpet: the apprehension in his eyes, the tension in his big "superhero" body, his near-panic at the simple sound of a balloon popping.

The negative, frightened energy she had felt radiating from him had to have been more than simple opening-night jitters.

"Hopefully, somebody thought to tape it off," she said, admitting in her own way that Dirk was probably right. They were most likely on their way to the scene of a homicide.

They rounded a corner, and the room in question was only a few yards down and to their left. She knew without even noting the numbers on the doors. Because that was where the crowd had assembled.

Two EMTs stood in the hallway, near an empty gurney and several cases bulging with medical equipment. They were whispering excitedly to each other. Savannah couldn't help thinking what a sad claim to fame this would be for them. She could just see them tonight on the eleven o'clock news. "Yes, we were the first responders who tried to save Jason Tyrone," they would say, without risking their careers by giving away too many salacious details.

Nearby stood three cops, hands on their hips, looking most officious. One held a clipboard and a pen. Instantly, Savannah recognized him as Mike Farnon, one of her favorite members of San Carmelita's finest. Back in the day when she herself had been a police officer with the SCPD, Mike had assisted her on more than one case. And she had always found him to be personable and professional.

He saw them approaching and cut a path through the mob of hotel employees, who wore maroon blazers with the hotel logo embroidered on the pocket.

"Hey, Savannah. Good to see you, girl."

"You too, Mike."

He turned to Dirk. "Evenin', Sarge. Oh, and congratulations, you guys. Haven't seen you since the wedding. How's it going?"

"It goes better when I don't get called out the middle of the night," Dirk grumbled.

"You caught this case?"

Savannah slipped her hand around Dirk's arm and gave it a little squeeze. "It's more like we're here in a personal capacity," she said.

Mike held out his clipboard to Dirk. "I started a log, Sarge. You want it, or should I hang on to it?"

"Yeah," Dirk said, reaching for it, "I'll take it." He pointed to the yellow crime-scene tape that was stretched across the partially open door. "Did you string the tape, too?"

"No, that big, tall guy inside the room did it. I think he's with the FBI or something."

"That'd be Ryan," Savannah said. "He used to be with the bureau."

"Once a fed, always a fed?" Mike chuckled.

"Cops never stop being cops—no matter what's printed on the badge," Savannah agreed.

Dirk nodded toward the EMTs. "They couldn't revive Tyrone?"

Mike shook his head. "No. They worked on him quite a while. But I think they were mostly doing it to cover their own asses—you know, him being a famous person and all. One look and you could tell he wasn't coming back."

Overhearing their conversation, one of the EMTs joined in. "We were going to transport him to the hospital," she said, "but this guy here said we should just leave him for the coroner." She gave a nod toward Mike.

"That's right," Mike admitted. "I already called Dr. Liu. She's on her way with her team."

"Yeah, okay," Dirk muttered. "I guess you guys didn't screw it up too bad."

Anyone else might have been offended by such lackluster praise, but Savannah saw a small grin flicker across Mike's face. He'd worked with Dirk long enough to know that was a glowing compliment, coming from Detective Sergeant Dirk Coulter.

"Excuse me," said a woman who was wearing one of the maroon blazers. She wedged herself between Dirk and Mike, then poked Dirk on the chest with her forefinger. "Are you some sort of policeman or something? I'm the manager here, and I have to tell you I'm not happy about being locked out of one of my own rooms—the executive suite, no less."

Dirk reached down, grabbed the tip of her finger, and then bent it backward, just enough to make her wince and snatch it away. Then he reached inside his leather bomber jacket and pulled out his badge. He flipped it open right in front of her nose.

"Yes, Ms. Manager. I most certainly am some sort of policeman or something. And once we find out what's going on inside your executive suite, you'll be the first to know—or the second, or third, or fourth, or . . . We'll letcha know. Okay?"

In typical, Dirk linebacker style, he shouldered his way through the small crowd. Savannah followed in his wake.

The door was open about a third of the way. Inside Savannah could see John Gibson pacing the length of the room, his silver head bowed, his hands thrust deep in his pockets.

Dirk loosened one end of the tape and swung it aside so that Savannah could enter. She pulled the end of her sweater sleeve down over her hand and gave the door a gentle nudge. Carefully she avoided the doorknob area and any fingerprints that might have been left there.

Dirk followed her inside the room and gently closed the door behind them.

When John saw them, a look of relief flooded his face, and he rushed over to Savannah. He threw his arms around her, hugging her tightly, pressing his face into her shoulder.

"Oh, love," he said with a half-sob, "I'm so very happy you're here. I can't tell you how awful it was, finding him like that."

She held him until he finally broke the embrace. "I can't even imagine," she said. "I only knew him a few hours and can't picture him gone. But you and Ryan finding him—I'm just so, so sorry."

Dirk cleared his throat, then reached over and gave John a couple of thumps on the back that were, no doubt, meant to be gestures of consolation. "By the way, where is Ryan? And the, um, Jason?"

John nodded toward a door in the back of the room, beyond the suite's kitchen and dining area. "Back there, in the bedroom," he said. "Ryan wanted to stay with him until you guys got here. But I just couldn't."

"I understand," Savannah said, kissing him on the cheek. "You go sit over there on the sofa and rest yourself a while. You've had a powerful shock to the system. Don't wanna go taxing yourself at a time like this."

"That's true," Dirk said. "Take a load off while we check stuff out."

"Thank you," John replied, as he did as he was told and collapsed onto the sofa. Once settled, he propped his elbows on his knees and buried his face in his hands.

33

Savannah walked to the bedroom door and found it ajar. Again she pulled her sleeve down over her hand, then pushed it open.

Taking a step inside, she glanced around the strangely quiet room and saw Ryan. He was sitting in a comfortable reading chair to the right, against the floor-to-ceiling glass wall. Normally, that window would have revealed the spectacular panorama of the Pacific Ocean in all its grandeur. But tonight the view revealed only the blackness of the sea.

And to Savannah that seemed appropriate under the circumstances.

Like John in the other room, Ryan was leaning forward, his elbows on his knees, his hands over his face. It was as though both of them were trying not to see the sad truth they had just witnessed.

"Ryan," she said softly. "It's us, honey. You okay?"

He jumped to his feet and hurried toward her. "Savannah, I'm so glad you're here." He saw Dirk right behind her. "And you too, buddy. You have no idea how glad."

Even as Savannah gave him a hearty hug, the former cop in her couldn't resist the urge to glance around the room.

And there he was.

At least, there was Jason Tyrone's body—stretched out on the floor beside the bed, wearing only a pair of jeans. His feet were bare and so was his massive chest.

Dirk had already walked over to the corpse and knelt beside it. "Sorry about this, man—him being your friend and all."

"Thanks," Ryan said. "Ordinarily John and I, we'd be better at handling something like this. But when it's someone you know, somebody you care about. . . . It's really hard to think at a time like this."

"You don't have to explain anything to us," Savannah said, as she gave him a comforting pat on the back; then she left him to join Dirk.

"That's for sure," Dirk added. "When Savannah got hurt so bad, you should've seen me. I was a basket case."

Savannah looked down at her newlywed husband, kneeling beside the body on the floor. She remembered all too well what a rock he had been the night she had been shot and nearly killed. Were it not for him and his ability to function in terrible circumstances, she would be as dead as poor Jason here.

She knelt next to Dirk and, along with him, began to give the body a cursory inspection.

Jason Tyrone, superhero to the masses, the brightest star in Hollywood's sky, was dead all right. His beautiful, blue eyes stared sightlessly up at the ceiling. That famous, masculine jaw sagged downward toward his chest. And it occurred to Savannah, not for the first time, that the Grim Reaper was particularly unkind in the way he robbed elegant and graceful people of their basic dignity in the end.

It seemed terribly unfair, especially since human beings place such importance on the first time they meet someone and the last time they see them.

She knew this terrible vision would be the one Ryan and John would see in their mind's eye every time they remembered their dear friend in the years to come.

Instinctively, she reached over, closed his eyes, and gently eased his mouth closed.

Of course, the county coroner, Dr. Jennifer Liu, would have objected to any manipulation of the body she had yet to examine. But the Crime Scene Investigation team wasn't there yet, and Savannah figured that what Dr. Jen didn't know wouldn't hurt her. And, more important, it wouldn't hurt Savannah.

Having done the "decent, humanitarian" deed, Savannah made the conscious effort to turn off her emotions and flip the switch into inspector mode.

A quick, overall appraisal told her little. She saw no fatal wound. No wound of any kind, for that matter. Nothing amiss. Nothing to indicate any type of violence, foul play, egregious accident, or obvious illness.

The body on the floor was the picture of robust, masculine health. The golden skin and well-defined musculature exemplified raw, male power—Adonis in the flesh.

Except for one thing.

Unlike the perfect, blemish-free pectorals that she and the rest of the audience had gaped at for two hours in the theater, the real Jason Tyrone's chest had an all too human malady—acne.

Terrible, deep, red, and raw . . . the skin even looked infected in places.

"Wow," Dirk whispered to her. "Get a load of those pimples. Have you ever seen zits like that in your life?"

"Can't say that I have," Savannah replied, keeping her voice low, for fear Ryan would hear.

And he did.

"The steroids will do that to you," Ryan said, a sad note in his voice. "That and a lot of other bad stuff, too."

She looked up at him as he walked over and stood at his friend's feet. "Jason took steroids?" she asked, somehow knowing the answer. Perfection, like that stretched out on the carpet before her, seldom came naturally.

"Sure he did," Ryan replied. "To get a body like that, you have to do more than just lift weights and eat a ton a steak every day."

"I wondered about that," Dirk said, "when we were watching the movie. There's muscle, and then there's . . . this. A guy like me could work out twenty-four hours a day for a year and not even come close to this."

Savannah got up from her kneeling position and began to walk slowly around the room. On the nightstand next to the bed, she saw at least a dozen bottles of various sizes and colors. As she read the labels, she recognized a few as nutritional supplements that she had seen in her own local health food store. But most of them she had never heard of, and some of them had no label at all, which piqued her curiosity.

Among the bottles was a small, cardboard box with the word "Lido-Morphone" printed on the side. The lid was open, and inside she could see numerous blue envelopes, each about four inches square.

Beside the box was a plastic container filled with empty syringes.

Savannah couldn't help flashing back on numerous death scenes she had examined as a police officer where syringes were customary, an all-too-frequent component of a drug overdose.

She glanced back at the corpse on the floor and wondered if Jason Tyrone had gone down that road himself. He wouldn't have been the first Hollywood star to tumble from the sky following a particularly decadent bout of self-indulgence.

He hadn't exhibited any telltale evidence of drug addiction at the premiere. But experience had taught Savannah that you couldn't always see the signs. She had certainly been fooled before. A heroin-addicted district attorney had taught her that lesson. And he hadn't been the last.

But as she wandered around the room, studying every bit of personal property Jason had scattered about, she saw no signs of any illegal drugs or paraphernalia. Judging from the dirty clothes tossed onto the dresser and the empty cans of energy drinks on the floor next to the bed, Jason might have been accused of being a messy guy. But she could find no solid evidence that he abused drugs or alcohol.

She did another quick scan among the supplements to check for insulin. Nothing.

"Was Jason diabetic?" she asked Ryan.

"Not to my knowledge," he replied, joining her by the nightstand. "Why?"

She pointed to the syringes.

"Oh, those," he said. "He injected his steroids."

"Wow. Really?"

Ryan nodded. "Some say if you inject steroids, you'll have fewer side effects than if you take them orally." He shrugged. "At least, that's what he told me when I saw him doing it once and asked him why."

Dirk left the body and walked over to them. He squatted down next to the nightstand and squinted at the labels on the assorted bottles and boxes. "Is there any chance that this junk," he said, as he waved a hand, indicating the plentiful stash, "might have contributed to that over there?" He nodded toward the body on the floor.

"It's certainly possible," Ryan replied. "We all warned him—all of his nonbodybuilding buddies, that is—that he could ruin his health with this stuff. But, of course, for every one of us, he had ten friends at the gym telling him it was okay. You'd be surprised how many guys pop this stuff like candy."

"They aren't worried about the dangers?" Savannah asked. "This junk can't be good for you."

Ryan sighed and ran his fingers wearily through his hair. "What they're worried about is not being big enough."

"Big enough?" Dirk asked, as he pulled a surgical glove from his inside jacket pocket and put it on. "Big enough for what?" He lifted the box marked "Lido-Morphone" and looked it over carefully before setting it down and picking up one of the bottles.

"Big enough to be considered 'manly,'" Ryan replied. "It's a major thing now—guys thinking they'll never be large enough, muscular enough. For some of them, it's like a mental illness. And because of it, they do things that endanger their health to beef up."

"That's so weird," Savannah said. "I thought it was just us women who got hung up on stupid stuff like that. It just doesn't seem possible that a man who looks like that could be unhappy with his body."

Ryan knelt beside his friend, then reached over and lightly touched Jason's hand. "It is strange, almost impossible for the rest of us to understa—"

His voice caught in his throat, as tears began to roll down his face.

In a gesture that both surprised and touched Savannah's heart, Dirk walked over to Ryan and placed a comforting hand on his shoulder. "Sorry, man," he said softly. "This really sucks, for you and for John. And of course, for him. If that turns out to be the cause of death—wow, what a waste."

Ryan took a linen handkerchief from his pocket and wiped his face. He stood, looking down at his once vibrant, much beloved friend. "You know, Jason had a body that women swooned over. He was the envy of every man in that theater audience tonight. And yet I've watched him work out in the gym and obsess about every tiny muscle. Everyone else thought he was the perfect he-man. But when Jason looked at himself, all he saw were imperfections. He thought of himself as an object, something that was flawed. And no matter how hard he tried, he'd never be able to fix it."

Savannah thought of all the women she'd known who saw themselves that way, and it broke her heart. But she had always considered body dissatisfaction to be a female affliction.

No, she thought. *Now it seems that hating the flesh you live in is an equal-opportunity torment.*

"You said he asked you and John to come here because he had something he wanted to talk to you about," Savannah said. "Do you have any idea what it was?"

"None at all," Ryan replied. "He said it was important—that he had a problem, and we were the only ones he could trust with it."

"Sounds ominous," Dirk added.

"No kidding," Savannah said. "So you came here and found him. . . . How did you get into the room?"

"That was the first sign that something might be wrong." Ryan walked into the adjacent bathroom and took a clean towel from a shelf near the sink. Walking back to the body on the floor, he said, "The door was ajar. And Jason was very security-conscious. With his level of celebrity, he had to be. He never would have left it open like that when he was in the bedroom."

He knelt beside his friend and reverently covered his face with the towel. As he rose, he said, "I know, you aren't supposed to do that—cross-contamination and all."

"I understand," Savannah said. "It'll be okay."

But she wasn't thinking about the towel or worrying about how Dr. Liu would react to having her scene "compromised."

She was wondering what Jason had needed to discuss with Ryan and John. And she was thinking that it was a terrible shame that he died before sharing his secret.

Because, regardless of overdose or steroids or whatever evidence there might be that suggested this was an accidental death, she didn't believe it. Her instinct told her there was foul play.

Homicide had a certain feel, a distinct, dark energy about it that Savannah could sense a mile away.

And to her, this particular death stank. It smelled like murder.

Chapter 5

Hours later, after Dr. Jennifer Liu and her forensics team had removed the body and processed the room, Savannah and Dirk exited the hotel to find that it was fully daylight. Night had come and gone, and Savannah could feel the missed hours of rest and rejuvenation in every cell of her body.

Years ago, she would have sprung back from a sleep-free night. She would have hardly even felt it.

But not now.

"I'll be ruined for days over this," she said, as they made their way across the parking lot to Dirk's ancient Buick. "Plum worthless. You wait and see. And I've got a ton of work to do with your parents comin' and all."

He slipped his arm around her shoulders and gave her a hearty, sideways hug. "Oh, don't worry your pretty little head about that. You know I'm gonna help you out with the house and the yard and all that. We'll have everything shipshape before they arrive. You wait and see."

Help me out with the house? she thought. *Get everything shipshape? Yeah, like that's going to happen. I'll be lucky if he doesn't track mud all over the freshly shampooed front-room rug and doesn't throw his dirty underwear on the kitchen counter.*

"How's about you and me go grab some coffee and donuts over at the Patty Cake Bakery?"

Ah, she told herself. *See there. I judged him too harshly. He can be a real sweetie pie when he's a mind to be.*

And she was pretty proud of herself that she had followed Granny Reid's advice and not gone to bed mad at her husband. Of course, she lost a few "Wife Points" since they hadn't actually been in bed more than a minute or two. But she still felt pretty proud of herself. Maybe she'd be able to get the hang of this marriage thing, after all.

Dirk looked down at his watch, smiled, and nodded. "Yep, this is the perfect time to drop by Patty's. She'll be gettin' ready to toss last night's coffee and startin' to box up the day-old donuts for the homeless shelter. With any luck we can score some of both. Won't cost us a plug nickel."

He gave Savannah an extra squeeze and a kiss on the top of her head.

Yes, there was nothing in the world that made Dirk Coulter happier than free food. And when her husband was happy, Savannah was happy, and all was right with the world.

More or less.

"I hope Dr. Liu rules this death an accident," she said, as he opened the car door for her.

"Hope all you want," he replied dryly. "You and me both know it wasn't no accident. It's got 'hinky' written all over it."

As Savannah got into the Buick and Dirk closed the door, she wondered: What could be worse than accidentally killing yourself for pure old vanity?

She closed her eyes and, for the sake of her dear friends and all of Jason's adoring fans, wished with all her might that this situation was as bad as it was going to get.

Because, sad as an accidental death might be, it was a heck of a lot better than murder.

Anything was.

When Dirk drove the Buick up to the front of their house, Savannah saw a hot pink, vintage Volkswagen Beetle parked in the driveway, next to a pre-restored 1969 Dodge Charger.

"Gee, Tammy's here, and so is Waycross. I'm positively shocked."

Dirk chuckled. "Every time we leave home, your baby brother makes up some flimsy excuse to park his butt over here."

"Oh, I don't think he needs an excuse, flimsy or otherwise. I reckon before we even clear the driveway, she's on the phone, inviting him over."

"And how does Big Sister Savannah feel about having Baby Brother Waycross cavorting with the help?"

Savannah smiled. "Two of my favorite people in the world finding happiness together—that's like a double-dark fudge brownie with a big ol' scoop of Granny's homemade vanilla ice cream on top. What's not to love about it?"

As they got out of the Buick and walked past the Charger, Savannah noticed a new coat of gray primer on the front right fender.

"Hey, look at that. He got the front end all straightened out," she said.

"You know, when he first bought this old pile of junk, I thought he was nuts," Dirk replied. "But it's comin' along."

"Never underestimate Waycross. He's always been a hard worker—an ambitious kid. He'll turn that 'old pile of junk,' as you call it, into a General Lee before you know it."

"Rebel flag and all?"

She laughed. "Honk the horn and it'll play 'Dixie.' You can take the boy out of Georgia, but—"

"But his neck's still gonna be red?"

"Something like that."

When they reached the front door, Savannah took her time and made quite a lot of noise as she unlocked it and stepped inside. Dirk followed, just as noisily.

But even with all of their precautions, it was a red-faced, breathless, and embarrassed couple they found snuggling on the sofa.

Giggling and trying to smooth her beautiful, long blonde hair back into place, Savannah's assistant, Tammy Hart, looked like a kid who had gotten nailed with her hand in the proverbial cookie jar.

Though one look at her younger brother's half-opened shirt told Savannah that it probably wasn't a cookie jar that Tammy was exploring.

Waycross's cheeks were flushed, nearly the same ginger color as his thick, curly hair. "Hey there, Sis! Brother Dirk!" he said, far too cheerfully.

They both jumped up from the sofa in unison, like a pair of synchronized jack-in-the-boxes.

"Wow, you two were out and about early!" Tammy exclaimed. "I couldn't believe you guys were already up and gone when I got here."

Tammy scurried to the rolltop desk in the corner of the room and flipped on the computer. "I paid some bills," she said, "and answered a few of your e-mails for you."

"Thank you, darlin'," Savannah replied, grinning.

"That's the least you could do," Dirk added, "considering the big bucks she pays you."

Tammy looked surprised. "She pays me big bucks?"

"I pay her bucks?" Savannah raised one eyebrow. "And here I thought she did it all for the betterment of mankind."

"I do it," Tammy said, as she sat at the desk and began to play with the computer, "because I'm a natural-born sleuth. I can't help myself. Detecting is in my blood."

"In other words, she read too many Nancy Drew books when she was a kid," Savannah said, as she sank into her comfy rose-chintz chair, propped her feet on the ottoman, and cuddled the cats who immediately jumped onto her lap.

"How was that movie thing y'all went to last night?" Waycross asked, discreetly rebuttoning his shirt.

Savannah glanced over at Dirk and saw her own sad, dark emotions registered on his face.

"The premiere was great," she said. "Unfortunately, the night went downhill after that. Way, way downhill."

"Oh! Oh, no way!" Tammy was staring, wide-eyed, at the computer screen. "Oh, this is awful! You're not going to believe this but—"

"Jason Tyrone is dead," Dirk said, as he walked past the desk and toward the kitchen. "Yeah, we know."

Tammy spun around in her chair to face Savannah. "Is that where you guys were?"

Savannah sighed and nodded, stroking Cleopatra's silky head. The cat's affectionate nuzzling of her hand somehow touched an aching spot in Savannah's heart and brought tears to her eyes.

"Yes," she said softly, "that's where we were. Ryan and John found him dead in his suite at the Island View Hotel."

"Mercy! That's plum terrible!" Waycross said. "Ryan and John must've been mighty upset."

"To say the least," Savannah replied.

Dirk paused at the kitchen door and looked back at Savannah. "I'm gonna make us some more coffee," he said. "Patty's throw-outs weren't enough. You want decaf or regular?"

"Regular's fine. Thanks, darlin'."

He turned to leave, then hesitated. "I thought we were gonna hit the sheets and try to get a little sleep. You sure regular won't keep you awake?"

Savannah closed her eyes for a moment, feeling the sting of fatigue in her eyelids. "Right now, sugar, I could take me a ten-hour nap in the middle of a runway at LAX. And as soon as I drink that coffee and fill these nosy bodies in on all the gory details, that's exactly what I aim to do."

"Me too," Dirk replied. "Except for the LAX runway business. We've got an un-slept-in bed upstairs that'd be a helluva lot more comfortable."

"I can't sleep."

"I told you we should have decaf."

"It ain't the coffee."

"I know."

Savannah rolled onto her side to face Dirk, who lay next to her on his back, staring up at the ceiling.

Cleopatra was sprawled across his bare chest, snoring. Diamante slept between them, one paw curled over her face.

At least the felines of the household are getting some sleep, Savannah thought. But then, they hadn't seen a handsome young actor sprawled lifeless on the floor—a friend of two of their dearest friends. Disturbing, to say the least, and not the least bit conducive to rest and relaxation.

"I have a bad feeling about this whole thing," she said.

"You sense skullduggery afoot?"

"Well, that sounds more like something Tammy would say, but yeah—something stinks about all this."

"I'll say, it does. Like a block of Limburger cheese left on Somebody You Hate's manifold on a hot summer day."

"Now *that* sounds a lot more like you."

"Thank you."

"You're welcome."

She reached over and laid her hand on his chest. For just a moment she put the troubles of recent events aside and marveled at the pleasure that simple intimacy provided.

This business of having a husband, one she could just reach over and touch, one who touched back—and very nicely, too—was far, far sweeter than she had expected it would be.

But the moment didn't last long.

The memory of Ryan's and John's faces chased it away.

"What do you think Dr. Liu's gonna find?" she asked, laying her cheek on his shoulder.

"I don't know." He kissed the top of her head as he ran his fingers through her curls. "I don't know whether to hope she finds something or just rules it an accident or natural causes."

"Of course, it'd be better if it was the latter."

"It would?"

"Sure."

"If she says everything's okay, you're gonna believe it? Gonna feel good about it?"

She didn't have to think that over for very long at all. "No," she said. "I know something's wrong."

"Then let's hope she finds out what."

"Exactly."

They lay quietly a few minutes more. Then Dirk broke the silence. "You figure she's done with that autopsy yet?"

"Done? She's probably just begun."

"Figure she needs some help?"

Savannah laughed and poked him in the ribs. "Oh, right. Doctor Jen just loves it when you drop by the morgue to 'assist.' "

"She doesn't mind so much when I have you with me."

"True."

"And when we bring chocolate."

"I've got an unopened two-pound box of Godiva truffles in my stash."

"It's not like we're really gonna get any sleep anyway."

"Let's go."

Chapter 6

If Savannah had to guess what Hell's waiting room would look like, she would imagine a drab, gray building like the county morgue.

"This place is so ugly and depressing," she told Dirk, as they walked across the parking lot to the front door, passing flower beds that held only wilted and dying plants.

The town of San Carmelita was suffering a double whammy—economic issues and a drought. So the city elders had decided that turning off the landscape sprinklers on the municipal properties would help cure the community's ills.

As a result, children played on parched brown lawns in the town parks, the courthouse grounds looked like a desert, and even the drought-resistant plantings around all the public buildings were giving up their little botanical ghosts.

It only strengthened Savannah's conviction that the morgue was a site of doom and gloom. Who would expect marigolds and California poppies to thrive in Purgatory?

"Yeah, I know what you mean," Dirk said. "It's not like anything good ever happens here."

Savannah thought that over for a moment, then reconsidered. She remembered something Dr. Liu had told her a long time ago.

When Savannah had asked the coroner how she could stand to do her job since her duties were so sad and grim. Dr. Liu had chuckled—one of those dry, semi-bitter laughs with no humor in it. Then she'd said, "How ironic that you should ask me that question. I just said the same thing last night to a friend of mine who's an emergency room physician. I don't know how he stands it, all the sadness, the pressure. I have the easy job. But the time they arrive here, the worst has already been done. Anything I do will only make things easier."

"But sometimes you have to tell family members such terrible things."

"I tell them the truth. And no matter how painful it might be for them at the time to hear it, in the end, truth always makes things better."

And now, as Savannah and Dirk entered the building, she re-examined her attitude about the place and the things that happened inside those gray walls. The truth might not always be pretty, but it had the power to heal a lot of pain.

"And speaking of pains," she muttered, as she caught a glimpse of Officer Kenny Bates, the oversized receptionist, sitting in his undersized desk behind the reception counter.

"Don't worry about that numbskull," Dirk told her. "You're my wife now. If he gives you any trouble at all, I'll knock his teeth so far down his throat he'll have to sit on a sandwich to eat it."

"What? And ruin all my fun? Whuppin' the tar outta ol' Kenny once a year is the high point of my social calendar."

Dirk opened the door for her. "Don't forget, they installed a camera after that last incident."

"You mean when I smacked the crap outta him with a rolled-up girlie magazine?"

Dirk chuckled. "That was a low blow, you gotta admit. Beating a man nearly to death with his own porn. The guys still rag him about that at the Fourth of July barbecues."

As they entered the lobby and walked to the counter, Bates looked up from the video game he was playing on an electronic tablet he was half-hiding behind a stack of files on his desk.

The moment he saw Savannah, a mixture of lust and loathing crossed his ugly mug, making him, if possible, even less attractive.

She did find it amusing, though, to see him reach up and readjust his toupee—sprawled like a roadkill raccoon across his head. And as he stood and walked to the counter, he brushed some wayward corn chip dust off the front of his two-sizes-too-small uniform shirt.

"Now, Officer Bates, you don't need to go getting all spiffied up just for little ol' me," she told him.

"Yeah, it won't help," Dirk added. "She'd still hate you, even if you took a honeysuckle bubble bath and brushed that green, fuzzy guck off your teeth."

"Just sign the sheet," Bates said, shoving a clipboard across the counter at them.

Savannah caught a whiff of his breath as he tossed a pen, as well. *Hmm*, she thought. *Apparently, a bag of nacho cheese chips is now the breakfast of champions.*

She scribbled a signature and time, then passed the board to Dirk.

He snickered when he read what she'd written: U. S. Tink.

In the years that she'd been signing Bates's sheets, she'd written far worse. But today she was feeling charitable. Lack of sleep had softened her crusty exterior.

"How's married life treatin' you, Savannah?" Bates asked, as she and Dirk left the desk and headed for the hallway. "If Coulter there needs to put another man on the job, I'm available."

Dirk turned on his heel and headed toward the counter. But Savannah grabbed him by the arm and pulled him back.

"One of these days, you lop-eared peckerhead," she told Bates, "I'm gonna turn this man of mine loose on you. And when I do, he's gonna stomp a mud hole in your backside big enough for Tom Hill's pigs to waller in."

Leaving Bates to contemplate the future of his backside, Savannah and Dirk continued down the hall toward the autopsy suite in the rear of the building.

Dirk asked Savannah, "Was there ever really a pig farmer named Tom Hill, or did you just make him up on the spot back there?"

"Of course there was. He was Sam Hill's brother. You know, as in, 'What in Sam Hill are you . . . ?' "

Dirk stopped in the middle of the hall and stared at her blankly, shaking his head. "I have no idea what the hell you're talking about, woman."

"You have no idea what in Sam Hill I'm talking about. Get 'er right, boy."

"What?"

She laughed and laced her arm through his companionably. "Yankee boy, you're married to a Southern woman now. You have just *got* to learn the language."

They opened one of the double swinging doors that led into the autopsy suite just a crack and peeked inside. Sure enough, there was the county coroner, Dr. Jennifer Liu, standing beside a stainless steel table. And stretched across the cold, sterile table lay the body of Jason Tyrone in mid-autopsy.

Though Savannah hardly recognized him, because his torso was spread open with the ugly, customary coroner's Y incision.

Even the top of his head had been removed, and Dr. Liu was holding the brain in her gloved hands.

Savannah was grateful that neither Ryan nor John were here to witness this. She could hardly stand to see it herself.

Forcing her eyes away from the body on the table, she concentrated on Dr. Jennifer Liu, San Carmelita's first and only female coroner.

Over the years Savannah had become accustomed to Dr. Liu's unorthodox on-the-job apparel. The tall, slender, exquisite Asian beauty frequently performed her duties while wearing a barely-past-her-shapely-bottom miniskirt or skintight pants and four-inch stilettos.

But Savannah had never seen the leather short-shorts before. Or the glittery, acrylic platforms.

This was a bit much, even for the good doctor.

"Wow!" Dirk whispered.

"Yeah. No kidding."

Long ago, Savannah had decided not to be jealous when Dirk ogled Dr. Jen. After all, if Savannah, a heterosexual female, stood with eyes wide and mouth agape at the sight of this femme fatale in all of her overtly salacious glory, how could she expect him not to drool—at least a little.

"Do you think she wears those getups when she's cleaning house?" he mused, as they continued to peep.

"I've wondered about that myself. Or maybe, after hours, she's always at one of those sex clubs, then comes straight to work without going home to change first."

Dirk grinned lasciviously. "Hey, I like your theory better. I mean, I was into the fantasy of her bending over to dust in one of those short skirts, but your scenario's way more—"

She gouged him in the ribs. "Hey, watch it. You're a married man now."

"Fantasies are free."

"If you share too many details with your old lady, you might find yourself paying the price."

She had raised her voice a bit too much, and Dr. Liu had heard. She laid the brain she was holding onto a nearby scale, then turned to them and gave them a scowl.

"What are you two doing here?" she barked.

Savannah opened the door a couple more inches and shoved the box of chocolate through. "Delivering some goodies?"

Savannah watched the battle registering on the doctor's pretty face—the battle of chocolate addiction versus her indignation at having her work interrupted by a couple of notorious buttinskies.

Finally, she asked, "Are they truffles?"

Savannah laughed. "Of course. Do you think we'd show up this early with anything less?"

"Get in here."

Ah-ha, Savannah thought, resisting the urge to cackle triumphantly. *PMS-induced carbohydrate craving wins again.*

She knew it would. She and Dr. Liu had been friends for a long, long time.

When she and Dirk reached the table, the doctor wasted no time before ripping off her surgical gloves and snatching the box of chocolates out of Savannah's hand.

Oh no, Savannah thought. *She's gonna eat them right here, right now.*

No matter how many times Savannah saw the coroner consume edibles and potables in the presence of a corpse, she would never get used to it. It just seemed so . . . wrong.

Way, way worse than eating in a bathroom, Savannah had decided—since nibbling chocolates and sipping wine in a candlelit bubble bath was one of her favorite pastimes.

Choosing a mocha cream, the doctor placed the whole piece in her mouth, closed her eyes, and chewed, with a look of orgasmic pleasure on her face. When she finished, she carefully licked a tiny bit of chocolate residue from the flaming red nail polish on her index finger.

Savannah took a sideways glance at Dirk, saw the gleam of male interest in his eyes, and decided she did not want to know what sort of fantasy he was spinning at the moment.

"You know, of course," Dr. Liu said, as she reached for a second truffle, "I've never fallen for this ridiculous chocolate-delivering ruse you guys use when you drop by."

"You just got a suspicious streak," Dirk replied, his attention now fixed on the chocolate. He was, if nothing else, a man with his priorities in order.

Savannah gave the coroner her sweetest, down-in-Dixie smile. "Why, darlin', you know we come in here just to see you. To brag on you and tell you what a good job you're doing."

"Yeah," Dirk added, "just think of us as your cheerleaders, standing on the sidelines, shakin' our pom-poms."

Dr. Liu grinned in spite of herself and shook her head. "No, thanks. That's a mental image I can do without—especially if you're the one with the pom-poms, Dirk."

She walked over to a cupboard, opened its door, and stashed the box of candy high on the top shelf.

Then she turned back to them, pulled a fresh pair of surgical gloves from the pocket of her white smock, and donned them.

"You know, you're wasting your time and your chocolates," she told them. "I'm not even close to finishing this autopsy."

She walked back to the body on the table and the brain she had just placed in the scale. "If a 'hurry-it-up' call from the chief of police, another one from the mayor, and yet a third one from an Oscar-winning movie director couldn't speed me up, you two don't have a chance."

"We just came by to help," Dirk said.

"And deliver the chocolates." Savannah cleared her throat. "And of course, help in any way we can."

"Help? Until I determine if this is natural, accidental, or homicide, you two shouldn't even be in here."

Savannah grinned, thinking how many times she had heard that. Having once been a popular and respected member of the San Carmelita Police Department, she was granted easy access to the scene of nearly every crime committed in the town. And though, years ago, she had been fired from the force, the brass who had canned her did little to curtail her activities.

She knew this had little to do with her dimples and Georgia accent. She understood it was because she and her detective agency had solved some of their most difficult cases.

As Granny Reid would say, "They know what side their biscuit's buttered on."

"You know, Doc," Dirk said with a smirk, one eyebrow raised a notch, "we're honeymooners. We could be home in bed foolin' around right now. Or better yet, sleeping—which we haven't done for more than twenty-four hours straight."

"Not that we haven't tried," Savannah added. "It's just that we were lying there, wondering about this case, thinking about our friends, Ryan and John. You know Ryan and John and what great guys they are."

Savannah waved a hand in the direction of the body on the table. "Jason here was a good friend of theirs. They knew him way back when. And now they're worried sick, wondering what happened to him. You can't blame us for trying to find out."

Dr. Liu said nothing for a long moment, as her dark eyes studied Savannah's. Finally she said, "Okay, I'll tell you what I've got. But I don't think you're gonna like it."

Savannah steeled herself for the worst as she and Dirk walked to the other side of the table opposite the doctor. She tried to forget that she knew the person who lay on the table between them. At moments like this, she had to put her heart on hold and switch into a purely cerebral mode.

"As you can see," Dr. Liu began, "this is a young male, I'm told in his early thirties, with highly developed musculature. And as I'm sure you guessed, he didn't get all those muscles strictly from lifting weights."

"Steroids?" Dirk asked.

"Definitely. Heavy, long-term usage."

"Then what happened?" Savannah asked. "Did he OD on steroids?"

"Not exactly." Dr. Liu drew a deep breath. "Actual steroid overdose is rare. The damage that performance-enhancing substances do to the body is more gradual."

She pointed to a stainless-steel pan on a nearby countertop that contained numerous body organs.

"But the signs of abuse are all there," she said. "An inflamed liver, the enlarged kidneys, and the heart—the heart is a mess. Not only are there inflammation cells inside the heart muscle, but connective tissue had started to form between the cells."

"Did he die of a heart attack?" Savannah asked.

"No." The doctor walked over to the scale and lifted the brain. "He died of cerebral hypoxia."

"What the hell's that?" Dirk wanted to know.

"The brain suffered oxygen deprivation."

"Do you mean, like someone choked him?" Dirk asked.

Dr. Liu shook her head. "No. There are no bruises on the neck, and no petechial hemorrhaging in the eyes."

Savannah looked up and down the enormous body with its bulging muscles. "I can't imagine that anybody was able to pin him down and hold a pillow over his face to suffocate him," she said.

"Or tie a plastic bag over his head," Dirk added. "So what would cause his brain to die from lack of oxygen?"

Dr. Liu shrugged. "He stopped breathing."

"That's it?" Savannah asked.

"That's enough," Dr. Liu replied dryly. "A body stops breathing, that will do it every time."

"But what caused him to stop breathing?" Savannah asked.

Shrugging her shoulders, Dr. Liu placed the brain in the pan with the heart, liver, kidneys, and other organs that, until recently, had kept Jason Tyrone alive.

"Well," she said, "that's the million-dollar question, now, isn't it?"

Chapter 7

Usually, when Savannah arrived at the luxury condos where Ryan and John lived, she was in an excellent mood. A visit to this lovely bit of property, perched on a hillside with a panoramic view of the ocean, usually included a scrumptious, gourmet meal, lovingly prepared by the handsome twosome, a snifter of the finest brandy, and scintillating conversation galore.

What wasn't to love?

But today her heart was heavy.

Feeling the pain of others had always been a burden to her—an overly active sense of empathy instilled in her, no doubt, by her dear grandmother. Tenderhearted Granny Reid would sob her face off over a plaintive tale about her neighbor's kitten, left outside on a cold winter day without saucer of milk. By the same token, Gran would happily smack the puddin' out of that negligent pet owner with a twelve-inch cast-iron skillet while lecturing him on the importance of providing proper care for the Good Lord's innocent creatures.

Gran was a complex, multifaceted sorta gal.

Yes, Savannah had been taught the fine points of sympathy, as well as the art of retribution. And as a result, she felt the heartaches of those around her keenly . . . even if, occasionally, she was the one inflicting their pain.

"I wish we had more to tell them," Savannah said to Dirk, who was walking beside her, his head down, his hands shoved deep into the pockets of his old, battered bomber jacket.

"No kidding," he replied. "That visit to Dr. Liu brought up more questions than it answered."

They passed the pool and wound their way along the stone paths, through the lushly planted landscaping. Overhead, palms rustled as a midday breeze stirred their fronds. And in the perfect, cloudless blue sky, snowy gulls dipped and dove, squawking to each other, complaining about all sorts of birdie drama—perhaps an unshared tree limb, a hawk circling too closely nearby, or maybe a purloined French fry.

Having lived so long in an oceanside resort community and having grown accustomed to noisy, disgruntled seafowl, Savannah ignored them as she and Dirk made their way to the building at the far corner. The prime spot in the rear of the complex provided the most privacy and the best ocean view.

Ryan and John had called this beautiful place home for years, and Savannah had always envied them, just a little, and wondered how it would feel to live on top of the world.

But today she didn't envy them. In fact, she wouldn't have traded places with them for all the ocean views in the world.

Fancy condos, Pacific sunsets, and sea breezes meant little on a day when one of the people you loved died. And especially so if it was under suspicious circumstances.

When Dirk knocked on their door, Savannah couldn't help noticing that he did so far more softly than usual. Normally, he had a tendency to knock so hard that a house shook on its foundation—a consequence of spending too many years on the police force.

He had also refrained from doing his shave-and-a-haircut routine.

She was grateful for small favors. Maybe she was having a civilizing effect on him, after all.

It took a while before anyone answered the door. So long, in fact, that she was beginning to think maybe no one was home. But eventually the door opened, and John was standing there in a dove-gray, satin-brocade smoking jacket, his meerschaum pipe in his hand. He looked relieved and happy to see them on his doorstep.

"Ah, 'tis the two of you," he said, opening the door wide and ushering them inside. "Ryan will be so pleased you've called, and so am I. Do come in and take a seat."

He led Savannah to a club chair near the large, ocean-view windows on the opposite side of the living room. She sat down and marveled, not for the first time, at the ultrasoftness of the leather against her hands as she slid her palms across the armrests.

The heavy, masculine furniture in this room always welcomed her, like a friend's warm hug, every time she visited. And, surrounded by bookshelves filled with leather-bound classics and walls hung with traditional art in gilded frames, Savannah felt she was visiting the library of an elegant, British manor house, instead of a California condo.

John walked over to an exquisite bar made of carved mahogany and topped with hammered copper. "I know it's a bit early in the day to imbibe," he said, "but could I interest you in a particularly nice Spanish sherry, Savannah?"

Long ago, Savannah had adopted the policy of never refusing any refreshment offered by John Gibson or Ryan Stone. Life was simply too short to deny yourself pleasures so sweet.

"Absolutely," she said. "It's never too early in the day for a glass of your sherry."

She watched as John poured a generous amount into a tiny and delicate Waterford sherry glass.

Reaching behind the bar, into the mini-refrigerator, he pulled out a frosty bottle of Dirk's favorite beer.

As he walked over to them and placed the drinks in their hands, Savannah thought how far John's and Ryan's friendship with Dirk had come. In the beginning their relationship had been rocky, at best.

The streetwise Dirk and the urbane twosome could not have been more different in every way. Dirk listened to country music; John and Ryan were opera aficionados. Dirk's idea of a good time was sprawling on a sofa and watching a boxing match on TV. The other two would top off a day at the golf course with an evening at a dinner theater. John and Ryan wore Armani, while Dirk fervently hoped he would someday be buried in his decrepit bomber jacket and his jeans with the threadbare knees.

But the three men had one thing in common—they adored Savannah.

So, over the years, they had tolerated each other with as much good grace as they could summon. And eventually, they had discovered other areas of shared interests. The greatest of which was the challenge of a tough case and the joy of nabbing a bad guy.

Savannah had noted, with a great deal of personal satisfaction, when the male bonding had become complete. She knew the day had arrived when John and Ryan began to stock Dirk's favorite beer in their home bar, and Dirk started to bring a bottle of chardonnay to Savannah's backyard barbecues, along with his six-pack.

Yes, it was the ultimate sign of tolerance. Maybe even acceptance.

"Where's Ryan?" Dirk asked, as he unscrewed the cap from his beer.

"Having himself a shower." John picked up his pipe and stuck it in the corner of his mouth, though Savannah knew he wouldn't light it in her presence, out of respect for her nonsmoking status.

Then there was Dirk, who had recently given up his cigarettes and was doing a pretty good job staying smokeless. Considerate chap that he was, John wouldn't have wanted to be responsible for anyone tumbling off the cigarette-free wagon.

"A shower won't help," Dirk said, after taking a long swig of beer. "Believe me, I know."

Savannah didn't have to ask what he meant. She couldn't count the times when she had hurried home and jumped into the bathtub, hoping to somehow wash away the sorrow and the horror of what she had witnessed that day on the job.

She had seen far too much, too many things, that had made her older than her years—things that could never truly be washed away, no matter how much rose-scented bath gel she used.

Unfortunately, the human soul couldn't be cleansed as easily as the body.

"He's taking it pretty hard then?" she asked.

John gripped the bowl of his pipe. "Actually, I don't think it's fully hit him yet. This sort of thing takes a while to sink in. You know what I mean?"

"I sure do," Savannah replied. "Death is such a strange mystery. As much of it as I've seen, I still can't get over how a person, a human being, can just . . . end like that."

"Me too." Dirk nodded. "You can't really believe it. Especially when it's someone you were just talking to."

John wiped his hand across his face, and Savannah thought, for the very first time ever, that he looked his age. In fact, he looked like an elderly man—gray-skinned and dull-eyed.

She realized that he and Ryan, like she and Dirk, had missed an entire night of sleep. Added to the shock of their friend's passing, this had to be hard on the older man.

She took a sip of the sherry, held it on her tongue for a moment, and allowed herself to enjoy its fortifying warmth. When she swallowed, she felt its fire tracing a path to her belly. In a matter of moments she delighted in the sensation of it spreading throughout her body, soothing and comforting.

Of course, the solace that alcohol provided was artificial, an illusion at best. It was no substitute for true, spiritual peace. But at a time like this, she'd take whatever she could get.

Hearing someone coming down the hall to her right, she turned and saw Ryan enter the room, wearing white shorts and a white polo shirt. His hair was wet and uncombed. He looked preoccupied, his expression despondent, until he saw them. And then he brightened slightly.

"Oh, hi. I didn't realize you guys were here. But I'm glad you are." He glanced around at the drinks in their hands. "And I see we've started happy hour a bit early. Good idea."

He walked over to the bar and poured himself a glass of chardonnay. Then he joined them, sitting on the end of the sofa nearest Savannah.

"What's new?" he asked. "What did Dr. Liu have to say?"

Dirk gave him a crooked smile. "What makes you think we've been to see Dr. Liu?"

"I know the two of you," Ryan replied, running his fingers through his disheveled hair. "And I knew you wouldn't rest till you took a trip to the county morgue to find out what she's got."

"I should have thought of that," John said. "But then, Ryan's mind is far more devious than mine." He turned to Dirk. "What *did* she say?"

"Not a lot," he replied. "She said the cause of death was brain hy . . . hyp . . . something."

"Hypoxia," Savannah supplied.

"He suffocated?" Ryan said, his face registering even more distress. "I'm surprised."

"I'm surprised you knew what hypox . . . that word . . . meant," Dirk replied. "Yeah, that's what she said. He died because he stopped breathing."

"Well, not to be callous, but don't we all in the end?" John said. "I wish she had been a bit more specific."

Savannah took another drink of the sherry and then spoke the news she had dreaded sharing. "She did mention that there were problems inside his body—damage that suggested the long-term, heavy use of steroids."

"Sad to say, I expected as much." John laid his pipe on a nearby end table. "I was afraid it would turn out to be something like that—the result of some bad lifestyle habits and not some unavoidable medical condition."

Ryan sighed. "Personally, I was hoping for a congenital heart condition or something like that."

"At least," Savannah said, "there's no obvious sign of foul play. I was relieved to hear that, because I was wondering if, you know . . ."

Dirk cleared his throat. "Yes. We were all wondering. We all had a feeling." He looked at Ryan, then John. "Didn't we?"

At first they said nothing. Then John finally broke the awkward silence. "Yes. And I'd wager we all still do. We have that sinking sense that something's amiss."

"Then let's go over it together," Savannah said. "Last night at the premiere, when the two of you were alone with him, did anything happen that was out of the ordinary? Does anything stick out in your mind?"

"Yes," Ryan said right away. "When he asked us to come by the hotel later."

John nodded. "That was strange, indeed. Even at the time, I

could feel a bit of a shiver down my back. I knew he wasn't asking us over just to have a pint and chat about the old days."

"Exactly when and where did this happen?" Savannah asked. She could hear her own voice change as the old cop's investigatory tone replaced the personal, down-homey one.

Once an interrogator, always an interrogator.

"It was right after the movie ended," Ryan replied. "We'd gone into the men's room in the VIP lounge. John and I had finished our business and washed our hands. So had Jason. But he was taking a lot of extra time, washing his face and combing his hair. Then he took forever, fiddling with one of those pain patches he wears sometimes—taking it off, putting it back on, repositioning it. I think he was deliberately stalling."

"Yes," John agreed. "It was as if he was biding his time until everyone else in the WC had left."

"And finally," Ryan said, "when it was just the three of us, he bent over and glanced up and down the line of stalls, like he was looking for feet. When he was sure we were alone, he said, 'Listen, guys. I'm gonna ask you for a big favor. I'd really appreciate it if you'd come by my room at the Island View tonight after you drop off Savannah and Dirk. I know it'll be late, but there's something I really need help with. And you two are the only ones I can trust with something like this.' "

"No wonder your antennae went up," Savannah said.

"He didn't give you any idea at all what he was talking about?" Dirk asked.

"Not a clue." John shook his head. "No sooner had he said that than a couple of blokes walked in, and that was the end of the conversation."

"Do you think it might've had something to do with you dudes being bodyguards?" Dirk suggested.

"Yes," Ryan answered. "I remember that's what I thought at the time. He sounded sort of nervous, a bit scared. And I thought maybe he intended to hire us for security. Not that we would've taken his money."

"Most certainly not," John added. "He was family to us . . . like the two of you."

Savannah smiled. "You say he was wearing a pain patch?" she said, changing the subject.

Ryan nodded.

"I've seen him use those many, many times," John said. "With his training regimen he was always pulling or straining something. He said they didn't take the pain away completely, but they made it a bit more bearable for him."

"Where was the patch?" Savannah asked.

"About here," Ryan said, pointing to the center of his own chest. "He complained of a condition called costochondritis—inflammation of the breastbone. He'd come down with a severe case of it years ago, when he was a bodybuilding champion."

"Aye," John added, "the physicians told him to give it a rest and allow it to heal. But, of course, he wouldn't. He was that sort. Driven. That was Jason."

Savannah thought back to the hotel room—to the young man's body sprawled on the hotel floor. "He wasn't wearing a patch on his chest," she said. "When you found him, his chest was bare."

Ryan looked at her, considered her words, and nodded. "That's true."

"Maybe he took it off," she suggested.

"He might have. He wouldn't have put it on unless the pain was really bad. He wouldn't even take an aspirin unless he absolutely had to."

"That's true," John added. "He wasn't like a lot of those bodybuilder chaps. Stayed away from medications as much as possible—though sometimes the pain got the best of him, and he had to use things like those patches and over-the-counter pills."

"After he messed with the patch, what happened then?" Savannah asked.

"We walked out of the lounge," Ryan replied. "And then we left the theater."

"You walked him to his limousine?" Dirk asked. "And you actually saw him get in?"

"Yes, we stuck close by," John said. "It seemed like he was still a bit nervous. Had been ever since the balloon-popping affair. And then with that mysterious thing he said in the lounge— we thought he might feel better if we stuck close."

Savannah recalled the moment she had seen Ryan and John put their friend into the limousine. Jason had seemed jumpy, eager to get into the vehicle as soon as possible.

She had seen that sort of behavior, that frightened demeanor, many times before. But usually the skittish person was a female, often one who was trying to escape a stalker.

"He acted like someone was after him," she said under her breath, more to herself than to the others.

But they heard her.

"Yes, he did," Ryan replied. "He was acting like somebody who'd had a death threat."

"And a credible threat at that," John added. "If I live to be a hundred, I'll be haunted by the thought that he needed our protection, and we didn't keep him safe."

Ryan's eyes filled with tears. "No kidding," he said. "That's what we do for a living. But we couldn't even save our friend. I'm never going to get over this."

Savannah looked at them both, seeing two of the dearest people she had ever known. In her life, she had borne more than her share of guilt over situations that were quite similar.

She thought about what Dr. Liu had said: "The truth makes things better, even when the truth is painful."

And in that moment Savannah silently promised her friends and herself that, one way or another, she was going to find out what had happened to Jason Tyrone. Even if it's ugly, truth is truth. And without it there would be no justice and no freedom from guilt.

Nothing could be done to bring Jason back. Dead was dead. But maybe, just maybe, she could provide a bit of healing to the living.

Chapter 8

The forensics lab was in the industrial part of town—where graffiti was the only form of paint on the buildings' gray cement-block walls, and the weeds that sprouted from between cracks in the asphalt road provided landscaping.

Unlike the morgue, which contained grieving family members, dead bodies in various stages of decomposition, and, worst of all, Officer Kenny Bates, Savannah didn't mind the forensics lab so much. In fact, she had often thought it would be an interesting place to work.

Not a fun place, because of Eileen. But interesting.

Eileen was an enormous woman, oversized in every way. She was at least six feet, two inches tall, and she had a sizable girth, a booming voice, and the personality of a Marine drill sergeant whose hat and boots were two sizes too tight.

Eileen's personal work ethic was impeccable. She did things the way they were supposed to be done and when they were supposed to be done, if not sooner. And as head of the lab, she demanded equal dedication from every employee unfortunate enough to work under her.

She didn't suffer fools. She didn't particularly like people, especially men. And she hated anyone who wasted a minute of her precious time while she and her team were processing materials from a crime scene.

Therefore, she loathed Dirk.

Although she hadn't found enough evidence to convict him of being a "fool," he was far too masculine for her female sensitivities. And probably more than anyone else in the SCPD, he had wasted her time by bugging her every five minutes when she was trying to find the much-needed answers to questions about his cases.

Long ago, Dirk had been banned from the lab premises. But fortunately for him, Eileen was quite fond of Savannah and would usually tolerate his presence if he brought along the fairer member of the Van-Dirk team.

Apparently, he was thinking about this as he pulled the Buick into the parking lot near the simple white door that bore a small county seal.

"Do you have any idea how demeaning it is," he said, "to have to bring you along every time I come here?"

Savannah shot him a look. "Do you have any idea how demeaning it would be to walk around for the next week with a black eye and a fat lip?"

"You know what I mean." He sniffed. "I got me twenty years on the job, a gold detective's shield, and a fully loaded Smith and Wesson against my ribs, but that woman in there won't even answer the damned door unless I've got you along for the ride."

Savannah chuckled. "That's because she's under the delusion that I keep you under control at all times. She figures that if I'm around you won't curse, handle the evidence, pass gas, or spit on the floor."

"What's the matter with that? *She* does all that stuff and more. She is one scary broad, if you ask me."

"It's her lab. She's big. She's mean. And she knows how to murder you at least a hundred ways. And get away with it."

"Don't think I haven't thought of that," he said, as they got out of the car and walked up to the door. "She's probably got vials full of acid and nasty crap that she could just spill a drop or two on you, and you'd fall down and crumple up into a wriggly, snotty, slimy heap and die right then and there. You know, like a slug when you sprinkle salt on it."

Savannah gave him a weird, sideways look. "Sounds like you've given this a lot of thought," she said. "Way more than you probably should've."

She punched the doorbell button. From inside they could hear a loud, irritating buzz that must have resounded throughout the building, like a ten-foot-tall, angry mosquito.

"Maybe that's why Eileen's so cranky," she said. "I'd be cranky too, if I had to listen to that thing all day long."

"*Who's* cranky?" came a loud, annoyed voice from the speaker mounted over their heads.

The door was yanked open and there stood Eileen. All of her. Topped off by a thick mane of curly silver hair that Savannah had often thought could have provided coverage for at least half a dozen regular folks.

She was convinced that was one reason why Dirk didn't like Eileen. Anybody who daily counted the hairs on top of his head wasn't likely to look fondly upon someone with so much to spare.

"Did I just hear you call me 'cranky'?" Eileen barked.

"Cranky? You?" Savannah deepened her dimples and batted her eyes. "Why, darlin', would I say something like that about you? In all the years I've known you, I don't recall the two of us sharing a single cross word between us."

Eileen raised one bushy, silver eyebrow that had never once been visited by a pair of tweezers. "Well," she said, "we haven't had any differences that a bag full of your homemade chocolate chip cookies wouldn't resolve."

She looked down at Savannah's hands but saw only a purse. "Apparently, you're here on a peaceful mission, and this guy you've dragged along with you isn't going to piss me off by asking if I've already processed everything I took out of that hotel room."

Dirk gulped, and Savannah had to repress a giggle. It amused her to see how scared he was of Eileen. Oh, he would yell at her and get in her face if she got his dander up. But as tough as Dirk thought he was, he had a healthy respect for feisty females and more than a smidgeon of fear.

And Savannah was very happy she was included in that number.

Chivalrous as Dirk was, he felt the need to pull every punch when dealing with the fairer sex, which left him at a disadvantage. With another guy he could go at it, tooth and claw, holding nothing back. But with a woman, Dirk always played the gentleman.

Savannah loved that about him and never, ever used this lovely quality against him.

Eileen, on the other hand, had no such standard.

"I mean it," Eileen was saying, her hands on her ample hips as she glared at Dirk. "If you think you're going to come into my lab, and pace up and down my floor, and look over our shoulders, and ask every five minutes, 'When are you gonna be done?' then you can just get back into that pile of crap you call a car and go find somebody else to bother."

Dirk's hair-thin thread of patience snapped. Nobody insulted the Buick and got away with it. "I would like to have it noted for the record," he said, "that I have just been standing here with my teeth in my mouth, minding my own business, while you ladies talk between yourselves. I haven't asked one question or made one demand. But in spite of my restraint, my basic character was criticized and my vintage vehicle disrespected."

Eileen seemed to think that over for a moment, and some of the harshness faded from her face. She gave him something that Savannah might have called a smile, had someone else been wearing it.

"Okay," the CSI said in a half-friendly tone, "what can I do for you two today?"

Savannah considered her next words carefully. A gentle peace had been established; it had to be preserved at all cost. How could she ask the question and yet preserve this new spirit of co-operation?

Unfortunately, she didn't think quickly enough.

Dirk had time to jump in. "We wanna know what you found there in that hotel suite. You processed the scene . . . what . . . oh . . . about eight hours ago? You oughta know by now whether you've got something good or not."

The next thing they knew, they were staring at a closed door—a simple door, a white door, the door with the county seal on it.

Savannah supposed there was at least one thing to be grateful for. If Dirk's nose had been even an inch longer, it would've been broken.

"Boy, you just beat all," she said. "You take one step forward then slide face first in the mud half a mile back'ards."

Dirk shook his head sadly. "And I thought we were doing so well there for a minute."

"We were. Then you had to go open your trap and be your ornery, cantankerous self." She turned and socked him on the arm. "You know what this is going to cost me, don't you?"

"Yeah, I know. It means we have to stop at the grocery store on the way home for the chocolate chips. Lots and lots of chocolate chips."

"It sure does," Savannah said. "And I gotta tell you, after missing out on a whole night's sleep I'd much rather spend my afternoon snoozing than baking a monster batch of homemade cookies."

"Maybe she'd settle for store-bought."

"Eileen? No way. She can totally tell the difference."

"I'm sorry," he said.

He looked and sounded like he meant it, so she decided to take pity on him. "It's okay. I forgive you. But you have to stir the dough . . . and you can't gobble down a bunch of it either, like you usually do."

They turned to leave when they heard a voice—a decidedly cranky voice—coming from the speaker over the door. "This time, throw some macadamia nuts in there, too."

"How can anything that smells so good be so bad for you?" Tammy said, as she watched Savannah take a heavily laden cookie sheet from the oven.

Savannah smiled, accustomed to Tammy's outspoken campaign against all things nonnutritious. "Once in a while, you have to eat something that's good for the soul, as well as the body," Savannah told the younger woman. "You don't do it every day."

"*You* do it every day," was the ready response. "Several times a day."

Savannah donned her best pseudo-self-righteous look. "I do not make chocolate chip macadamia nut cookies every day."

"That's true. Sometimes it's peanut butter fudge or blackberry cobbler or German chocolate cake."

"Then don't falsely accuse me, girlie. You gotta get your facts straight before you convict."

As Savannah used the spatula to deftly flip the cookies off the sheet and onto the cooling rack, she heard the front door open and her brother's soft voice as he called out, "You gals in here?"

"In the kitchen," Savannah shouted back.

"Boy, howdy," he yelled back, "I can smell them cookies all the way in here."

"Just follow your nose." Savannah lowered her voice and said to Tammy, "If you intend to keep on keeping company with my little brother, you're gonna have to reconsider your dietary habits. He's a good ol' boy, and Georgia menfolk don't thrive on lettuce leaves and celery stalks."

Tammy sighed. "We've already talked about that. If it hasn't mooed or clucked lately, he doesn't consider it food."

"And it's gotta be swimmin' in gravy, too."

"I know. You Southerners seem to consider gravy a beverage."

"And don't you forget it."

Waycross entered the kitchen. He had orange paint on his hands and arms and a generous smear of it on his left cheek.

"Looks like the Charger's getting a new orange dress," Savannah said.

"Not yet. I'm still workin' on the engine. But no reason it can't be as bright as a new penny, too."

Savannah looked at the tall, skinny redhead, and her heart melted. Of her eight siblings, Waycross was, by far, one of her two favorites. Cheerful, kind, and without a lazy cell in his body, he was a pure joy to be around.

She was thrilled he had decided to stay in California for a while. Dirk had been kind enough to let him move into his old mobile home that sat in a trailer park on the edge of town. Waycross was a skilled auto mechanic who also did excellent body and paint work, so she'd had no problem finding him work at a shop that specialized in restoring classics.

Between the California sunshine and the beaches, a manly man trailer to live in, and the company of a sweet, beautiful girl like Tammy, Waycross was simply thriving like weeds in a watermelon patch. And Savannah couldn't be happier about it.

He started to reach for a cookie, then stopped, his bright orange hand hovering over the cooling rack stacked with goodies. Turning to Tammy, he said, "My hands are a mess, sugar. Could you please get me one o' them?"

Tammy giggled, grabbed a cookie, and fed it to him—so slowly and sensuously that Savannah felt like she needed to go take a cold shower by the time the deed was accomplished.

"By 'one o' them,' I meant 'two,' " he told her, licking a bit of chocolate off his lower lip.

Tammy watched the simple action, totally entranced. Eventually, she snapped to attention and said, "Oh, sure. Of course."

Savannah decided to look away as the whole erotic scene replayed and gave them a bit of privacy.

It was so strange, seeing them together like this. In love. And, yes, in lust—but so cute about it.

She couldn't help wondering if she and Dirk appeared that silly to other people. Probably not. They were so much older and far more mature.

Then she recalled, only a few days ago, when they had been exchanging kisses on the town pier. A ragged old curmudgeon who was fishing off the end had packed up his equipment with a vengeance, shot them a disapproving grimace, and grumbled as he stomped away, "Get a room, will ya?"

Okay, maybe they made fools of themselves, too. Apparently, you never got too old for True Love to make a fool of you.

As Waycross chewed on his second and then third cookie, Tammy asked Savannah, "Is there anything we can do to help you out with this case? Not that it's really a case yet, because you don't even know what happened, but, well, you know what I mean."

"I know what you mean." Savannah began to place some of the cookies that had cooled into a plastic container. If she didn't, with Waycross around, the batch was likely to meet an untimely death. "It's sort of a case. After all, a seemingly perfectly healthy young man fell down dead. A lot of people are wondering why."

"Like you?" Tammy said with a little smile.

"Absolutely. You can't be in the detective business without having a mile-wide streak of curiosity."

"You mean, without being a nosy busybody," Waycross said around his half-chewed cookie.

Savannah reached over and gave him a bop on his curly head. "Don't talk with food in your mouth," she said. "And don't forget that you're a Reid, too. So, genetically speaking, you've got a lot of 'nosy' in your DNA along with the rest of us."

"Nope. The womenfolk in our family are the only ones who carry that nosy gene thing. Along with wide backsides and generous fronts," he added with a chocolate grin.

"Oh, boy . . . now you really are asking for it!"

He reached for another cookie. She slapped his hand. And they struggled with the container for a while before she relented and tossed one at him. He snatched it out of the air and popped it whole into his mouth.

"Does he eat like that when he takes you out to restaurants?" Savannah asked Tammy.

"No," she replied, giggling. "He saves his worst behavior for you."

Savannah sealed the lid of the container, set it on top of the refrigerator, and said, "There are exactly twenty-four cookies in there. If, later on, I find I'm one short, Waycross Reid, I'll be draggin' you behind the barn for a hickory limb switchin'."

He snickered. "Since you don't have a barn or a hickory tree, you'll have to forgive me if I ain't exactly quakin' in my boots."

"Are you two gonna help me with this case that ain't a case, or are you gonna eat me outta house and home?" Savannah asked, mildly miffed.

She was losing her good humor as she thought about Dirk upstairs, snoozing away in bed, while she slaved away in a hot kitchen, preparing bribes for people he had offended.

Life was frequently unfair.

"Sure." Waycross dusted his hands together, ridding them of imaginary cookie debris. "What can we do?"

"Find out everything you can about Jason Tyrone, but concentrate on the scandalous stuff."

"Dig up the dirt," Tammy said with a smile.

"Exactly. Especially anything having to do with a recent romantic breakup."

"He's a gay feller, ain't he?" Waycross said. "I think I read that in one of Granny's newspaper magazine thingies."

"Yes," Savannah said, "it was all over the tabloids that he recently split up with a partner he'd been with for a long time. Find out what that was all about, if you can."

Tammy nodded knowingly. "Always check out the significant others first—especially if there was a recent parting of the ways."

"And run a financial check on him, too, while you're at it," Savannah said. "Find out if there were any problems in that area."

"We'll see if we can root up any of the usual naughtiness— foolin' around on your honey, gamblin', drugs . . ." He glanced up at the top of the refrigerator. ". . . stealing goodies from your big sister when she ain't lookin'."

"I kid you not, you knucklehead. You touch those, I'll throw a duck fit."

She turned to go into the living room with the intention of heading upstairs for a bit of beauty rest beside her snoring husband. But instead, she ran into Dirk at the bottom of the stairs.

His hair was tousled, his face bed-crumpled and wearing an expression that was most disgruntled.

"The cookies are done," she said. "I was just coming upstairs to join you."

"Too late," he replied, as he tucked his shirt into his jeans and ran his fingers through his hair. "I just got a call from Dr. Liu. She wants us to meet her right away."

"Oh? Okay. I don't really want to make another trek out to the morgue, but if she's got something that's—"

"Not the morgue," he told her.

"What? Where then?"

"The pier."

"The pier? Why? There's not another crime scene, is there?"

He shrugged. "I don't know. She called me on my cell, told me to meet her at the pier and to bring you. She also said not to tell anybody about it."

Savannah was totally taken aback. Since when did the totally open and honest Dr. Liu play cloak-and-dagger games?

"Did she say why it's a big secret?" Savannah asked, as she strapped on her weapon holster, inserted her Beretta, and reached for her purse.

"Nope."

"And you didn't ask her?"

He grabbed his bomber jacket out of the closet. "Nope."

"Why not?"

"Because she sounded like she was in a mood. And not a good mood, if you know what I mean."

He opened the door and held it as she passed through.

But she couldn't let it drop. "It's just plum not like you," she insisted, "not to ask. You're the one person on the planet who's even more nosy than I am."

"Yeah, that's true. But if you really have to know—the one person I'm even more afraid of than Eileen is Dr. Liu." He took a deep breath, and Savannah could swear that she saw him shudder a little. "I'm afraid of her even on a good day," he added, as though confessing some deep, dark character flaw. "Let alone when she's having a bad one."

Chapter 9

Most of Savannah's memories of trips to the town pier were happy ones—including her last visit with Dirk, when they had been reproved by the old fisherman for their public display of affection.

Built in 1842, the San Carmelita pier was the second-largest one in California. And it was Savannah's favorite, mostly because of the lack of typical tourist attractions. The pier was home to only one modest seafood restaurant, a tiny bait-and-tackle shop, and a bicycle-rental kiosk.

There were no tacky souvenir stores, palm readers, kite vendors, or ice cream shops. In the pier's heyday, it had serviced giant steamships. But now it was a simple and peaceful haven for those who wanted to catch a fresh fish for dinner. And a nice place to make out with your new husband, if there were no crotchety fishermen around to object.

At least once a week Savannah would come down to the pier for a long walk and allow the fresh sea air to blow through her hair and carry her troubles away—at least for a few minutes. The sounds of the gulls, crying out to each other as they swooped and dove overhead, and the music of children's laughter as they played on the swings and slides on the sand below were a soothing balm to her soul.

As far as she was concerned, a day that included a visit to the pier was almost always a good day.

But today . . . today she wasn't so sure.

A secret audience with the county's medical examiner didn't sound like a fun time. Over the years, Savannah had formed the opinion that—other than those having to do with Christmas presents and surprise birthdays—the word "secret" was usually spelled "t-r-o-u-b-l-e."

This trip, Savannah had insisted on driving her Mustang. Beautifully restored years ago by Waycross, the bright red 1969 'Stang was her baby, her pride and joy.

She could take only so much riding around in Dirk's Buick before she had to mention that far nicer transportation was available to them.

That always went over well.

Along with her insistence that she, not he, drive.

Therefore, he was in a semipouting mood when she pulled into the parking lot near the pier and cut the ignition.

"I don't see her anywhere," she said, a little too cheerfully, as she looked up the beach, then down.

He simply grunted and got out of the car.

She followed him, slipped her arm through his, and nudged him. "Why so grumpy?" she asked. "I've been driving us around for years. It's never been a big deal."

"It's kinda a big deal," he said. "After all, we're married now."

"What's that got to do with anything?"

"It's got to do with everything. I'm your husband. Wives let husbands drive their cars. I mean, California's a community property state. That means the Mustang's kinda half mine."

She stopped in mid-stride and stared up at him, mouth open, for a long time. Finally, she found her voice. "Git outta here. No way. If we followed your logic I'd own half of that old jalopy of yours."

He brightened hopefully. "That's right! Half of the Buick is yours and half of the Mustang's mine. Fifty-fifty."

"No, no, no. You get one hundred percent of your Buick. I get one hundred percent of my Mustang. And that's fifty-fifty."

He grumbled under his breath but reached for her hand and gave it a little squeeze. "I think your math is a little faulty there, gal."

She chuckled. "And if you think that a measly marriage certificate entitles you to any part of the Red Pony . . . then your cornbread just ain't quite baked in the middle."

As they mounted the steps leading up to the pier, Savannah spotted Dr. Liu about halfway down the dock. And had Savannah not been looking for the coroner, she probably wouldn't have recognized her at first glance.

Gone was the overtly sexy attire—the ultra-high heels, the short skirt or the tight pants. Jennifer Liu was wearing a simple pair of jeans, a white tee-shirt, and a Dodgers baseball cap. Oversized sunglasses hid nearly half of her pretty face, and her long, black hair was pulled into a ponytail.

She was walking slowly away from them toward the end of the pier, her head down, her hands thrust into her jeans.

"Wow," Savannah said, "she really *is* in a bad mood. Looks like she just lost her best friend."

"No kidding," he replied. "Wonder what's up."

"Maybe it's bad news about the case. Maybe she found out it was homicide, after all."

"Since when would something like that bother Dr. Liu? If there's anybody who's used to all that blood and guts and murder crap, it's her. A ruling of homicide never bothered her before."

"That's true. Oh, well, we'll be finding out soon enough."

By the time they had caught up to the doctor, all three were at the far end of the pier. She was standing with her hands on the railing, staring out at the horizon, where thick storm clouds had gathered, obscuring the distant islands and staining the sea a dark indigo.

Savannah shivered, feeling a slight chill that had little to do with the brisk ocean breeze.

"Hey there," she said, as they approached the coroner. "Fancy meeting you out here, instead of back there at the old coal mine."

Dr. Liu turned to face them. She glanced around and, seeing no one else nearby, she took off her sunglasses. Her eyes looked troubled as they locked with Savannah's.

"I'm meeting you here," she began, "because, well, I'm not really meeting you. Got it?"

"Are you saying," Dirk replied, "this little impromptu rendezvous never happened?"

"Something like that."

"No problem," he said. "You got it."

"What's up?" Savannah asked.

Dr. Liu leaned back against the railing as though she were exhausted. Savannah registered the fact because she couldn't recall a time when she had ever seen the doctor weary. Savannah had always thought of her as a person with boundless energy.

"It's this autopsy," she replied. "I've never had one like this before."

"Like what?" Savannah asked.

"Like one that has me totally stumped." She closed her eyes for a moment and shook her head. "I have at least half a dozen parties breathing down my neck, pushing me for an answer, and I have nothing to tell them. I've finished the autopsy, we got the lab results back in record time, and still, I have absolutely no idea what killed Jason Tyrone."

She turned to Dirk and poked him in the chest with her forefinger. "And if you tell anybody what I just said, I will get you. I mean it. I'm a medical examiner, and you don't mess with a medical examiner, because they know fifty ways to kill you and get away with it."

"A lot like a CSI lab tech," he mumbled, reaching down and gently moving her pointing finger aside. "I hear ya. Don't worry about it. On your bad side is the last place I wanna be, believe me."

Savannah thought of what he had said back at the house about being afraid of Dr. Liu, and she nearly laughed. But she sensed that the coroner wasn't in the mood for humor of any kind right now.

"I thought you said he died of brain hypoxia," Savannah offered, trying to help.

"He stopped breathing, and his brain died of oxygen deprivation, that's true. But I can't find one reason why he would stop breathing. And there has to be a reason. There has to be one, and dammit, I can't find it."

Dr. Liu turned to face the ocean once again, her elbows on the railing. Savannah and then Dirk did the same, taking similar positions on either side of her.

Savannah looked down at the turbulent waters that were crashing against the barnacle-encrusted pilings below. She sensed the same kind of agitation in the spirit of the woman standing next to her and felt bad for her longtime friend.

Dr. Jennifer Liu was an amazing coroner. Everyone knew it, including the good doctor, and she took great pride in her well-earned reputation.

"Doesn't that happen once in a while?" Savannah asked. "Aren't there cases, from time to time, that nobody can solve?"

"It doesn't happen to me!" Dr. Liu shot back, her dark eyes flashing. "Not to me!"

"There's a first time for everything. Maybe your luck just ran out," Dirk said gently. He reached over and put a comforting hand on her wrist, but she shook it off and folded her arms across her chest.

"It's got nothing at all to do with luck. It has to do with hard work and dedication and the fact that I'm damned good at what I do."

"Of course you are," Savannah told her. "You've always done an awesome job for the people of this county. If this case is a problem for you, it would be for anybody."

She paused, letting her words soak in for a moment before she continued. "Tell us what you've got and—"

"—and the two of you are going to figure it out, when I can't figure it out myself?"

"No-o-o," Savannah said, forcing herself to sound patient, whether she felt it or not. "Of course the two of us won't be able to figure it out, if you can't. But maybe while you're explaining it all to us, you might think of something you haven't before."

To Savannah's surprise, Dr. Liu's eyes filled with tears. "I'm sorry, you guys. I know I'm out of line. You're just trying to help, and I appreciate it, whether I'm acting like it or not."

Once again Dirk reached over and put his hand on her arm. And this time she didn't brush it away. "Don't worry about it, kiddo," he said. "It's a difficult case, all the way around. And we're all running on little or no sleep, so we're entitled to be a little out of sorts."

Savannah patted her on the back. "Tell us what you do have."

Dr. Liu drew a deep, shuddering breath, and the negative emotions seemed to slide off her face and were replaced with a stoic, neutral expression.

Savannah watched and felt encouraged. The doc was in "professional mode" now. And that was a great improvement—as Savannah knew, all too well, from personal experience.

When your emotions were too high, you couldn't think. And a situation like this required clear, rational thought.

"Jason Tyrone was basically a healthy young man," Dr. Liu began. "Other than the things I showed you—some minor cell damage to the heart and the liver—there were no remarkable pathologies. Nothing was really all that wrong with him."

"Then what's your ruling going to be?" Savannah asked.

"Officially, I'm determining the manner of death to be accidental. The cause of death: cardiovascular complications as a cumulative result of lethal polypharmacia."

Savannah ran the words through her head, but couldn't make sense of what she'd heard. "What's polly-farm . . . whatever you said?"

"Heart damage from too many years of taking too many drugs—anabolic steroids, diuretics, painkillers."

"Could it have been another kind of drug overdose?" Dirk asked. "The usual suspects, like cocaine, heroine, meth . . . something like that?"

"The blood work was all negative for recreational drugs. But like I said before, he had plenty of prescription and over-the-counter drugs in his system. His stomach showed some damage, probably due to heavy NSAID painkiller usage. It isn't that uncommon with someone who works out and pushes their body to the extreme the way he did."

Dirk nodded. "All that weight lifting—he was bound to have some aches and pains."

"He also had some carisoprodol in a system," Dr. Liu said.

"What's that?" Dirk wanted to know.

"A muscle relaxant," she replied. "Doctors prescribe it sometimes when a patient complains of muscle spasms and soreness. Again, nothing out of the ordinary, and at that dosage, certainly not lethal."

"What about those pain patches that were on his nightstand?" Savannah suggested.

"You mean the Lido-Morphone?"

Savannah nodded.

"Yes," the doctor said, "that showed up in the blood work, too. But like everything else, the quantities fell within the normal range. There wasn't one single red flag."

"Could it have been an overdose of steroids?" Savannah asked. "Like maybe he just took too many all at one time."

Dr. Liu shook her head. "Like I told you before, overdosing on anabolic steroids isn't that common. Which is not to say that they aren't dangerous. But the damage they do is usually more insidious and occurs over a period of time. I'm sure people have died as a result of abusing steroids. But frankly, they're more likely to be murdered or commit suicide while in the throes of what's commonly called 'roid rage."

Savannah stared out into the turbulent water, considering everything she'd just been told. She could certainly see why Dr. Liu was frustrated. When she thought of Jason Tyrone—a seemingly perfect physical specimen—just dropping dead for no apparent reason, her own sense of justice cried out in indignation.

It just wasn't fair!

Of course, she had learned the lesson many times over that life was far from fair. But she had never learned how to accept the fact with grace.

When bad things happened to seemingly good people—and other life lessons had taught her to always insert that "seemingly" qualifier—she couldn't help herself; she got angry. And if there appeared to be no avenue to justice, or even a rational explanation for the tragedy, she got royally mad.

"This would bother me anyway," Dr. Liu was saying, "no matter how famous the deceased might or might not be. But it doesn't help having everybody from the SCPD to the governor's office breathing down my neck, demanding answers."

"Frankly, it riles me somethin' fierce," Savannah said, "when they make a way bigger fuss over celebrities than regular folks."

Dirk added, "Me too. When did you ever get blood work back that quick?"

"Never. Not once in my career. It's usually days, even weeks. Never hours."

Dirk ran his hand over his face, and it occurred to Savannah that it had been a long time since she had seen him look so weary. And she knew it was more than just the missed night of sleep.

She knew that he, like she, wanted to do the right thing by their friends. And besides the more personal reasons, both she and Dirk had a fierce sense of justice. They would chase a bad guy to Hades—and had more than once—rather than let him get away with some nasty crime.

But she also knew this case had come at a bad time. Dirk was feeling a lot of pressure over meeting his biological parents for the first time. Far more, she was sure, than he was even saying.

She determined, then and there, to get him home and in bed as soon as possible. They were both in desperate need of an extended time in Slumberland.

"This is going to ruin that kid's reputation forever," Dirk said. "Last night he was king of the world, superhero to millions and all that. But as soon as your report gets out, he'll just be a fool who killed himself by doping."

Dr. Liu whirled on him, her eyes blazing. "Dammit, Coulter. Don't you think I've thought of that? Believe me, I don't like this any more than you do."

Savannah turned to Dr. Liu. "What can we do? How can we help?"

The coroner thought her answer over carefully. Finally, she said, "I had to release the body to the funeral home. There's nothing more I can do at this point. Now it's up to you."

"Okay," Dirk said. "I'm not making any guarantees that we're going to come up with anything better than what you have."

"But we'll try," Savannah quickly added. "We'll do our best."

"Thank you."

Dr. Liu reached out, laced her right arm through Dirk's and placed her left hand on Savannah's. "If you think this was a murder—and I know you do, because I do, too—then investigate it as a homicide. See what you can uncover."

"That's exactly what we're going to do," Savannah told her. "Try not to feel so bad about it. You've done your best."

"You just let us take it from here," Dirk said. "And we will keep you posted all the way."

"Thank you, Dirk," she said, as she gave Savannah's hand a companionable squeeze. "I wish I could help you more. I'm ashamed that I can't. And if somebody killed that beautiful young man, and they get away with it, because of my incompetence . . . I'm telling you, it'll haunt me for the rest of my life."

Chapter 10

By the time Savannah and Dirk returned to the forensics lab, Savannah was in the mood to commit homicide herself.

She had no particular victim in mind. She just hated the world in general.

Someone out there was conspiring to ruin her life and doing a darn good job of it. They were preventing her from sleeping, eating a decent meal, and taking a much beloved rose-scented bubble bath, and on a more practical note, they were keeping her from scrubbing her house from top to bottom in preparation for her in-laws' visit.

"I know what we promised Dr. Liu," she told Dirk, as they trudged across the parking lot to the little white door with its county seal, "and of course, we'll keep our word and follow through. But frankly, I don't have time to conduct any kind of serious, full-fledged homicide investigation right now. I need to be painting the downstairs bathroom, washing and ironing the kitchen curtains, and scrubbing the grout on the backsplash tile."

Dirk shot her a worried scowl. She had seen a lot of that particular grimace lately. He donned it any time the topic of home improvement came up.

Too bad, she thought. *Wait till he gets a load of his honey-do list. Then he'll have something to frown about.*

"I doubt my parents are going to notice your backsplash grout," he said, as he punched the doorbell button and rang the obnoxious buzzer.

"Your mom's a retired nurse," she replied. "They're very clean, nurses. I'll betcha her house is spotless. You could probably eat right off her kitchen floor."

"Fortunately, we have plates, so you don't have to sterilize your kitchen floor."

"But this is the first time I've ever had in-laws. The first time I've ever met my in-laws. I want to make a good impression."

He sighed, and for a moment she could see traces of fear, maybe even a bit of terror, in his eyes. "You want to make a good impression? How do you think I feel? Meeting your parents for the first time in your *life* when you're in your forties? No stress there."

She shifted the plastic container containing the cookies to one arm, and with her free hand she reached up to stroke his cheek. "You're gonna do just fine, sugar. Just fine. They're gonna be so proud when they see what a big, strong, good man you've turned out to be."

He grinned, a tremulous little smile, then chuckled nervously. "I hope you're right."

"I'm always right." She gave him a wink. "And if we could just start every argument with that as a given, think of all the time we'd save."

This time Eileen didn't bother to interrogate them over the speaker before opening the door. She even had a bit of a smile—or at least her perpetual frown was less pronounced—when she looked down and saw the container of cookies under Savannah's arm.

"Do come in," she told them, reaching for the goodies. "It's hot out there, and I wouldn't want you to melt."

"Since when did you worry about us melting?" Dirk asked.

"She always worries about *me*," Savannah said, giving him a nudge. "And she wouldn't want the chocolate chips to get all runny."

"Like either one of you gals would turn up your noses at any kind of chocolate, runny or otherwise," Dirk said, as he followed Savannah inside the air-conditioned laboratory.

Even on Southern California's hottest, summer day—when the dry Santa Ana winds swept in from the east, replacing the usually cool ocean breezes—the lab was kept at a constant 77°F and 50 percent humidity. And on more than one Fourth of July Savannah had invented reasons to visit Eileen in her perfectly controlled environment.

Chocolate chips were safe from melting within its comfortable confines. . . . And so were perimenopausal Southern belles.

Plus Savannah found the laboratory, Eileen, and her assorted CSI techs fascinating. While she would never have wanted to trade jobs with them, they had her undying admiration for their scientific expertise, and her deep appreciation for all the times they had helped her solve a case.

She harbored no misconception that she could perform their duties. They were a strange and wonderful combination of law enforcement officers and scientists rolled into one.

And although Savannah could interrogate a perp and squeeze a confession out of him as efficiently, or more so, than anyone on any police force, she would have never made it as a lab tech. The math and chemistry alone would've been her downfall, had she even started down that path.

Any dreams she might have harbored of becoming a woman of science had perished in the third grade with the introduction of long division.

But in the end, she had decided that was okay with her. When all was said and done, she preferred to stare straight into the bad guy's weaselly, evasive, ugly little eyes until he squirmed like the gooey little worm he was, rather than study his blood-spattered shirt under a microscope for hours.

Fate had arranged everything, just as it should be.

She and Dirk followed Eileen through the lab's office area, which included four utilitarian, gray cubicles with gray desks, gray file cabinets, and black leatherette desk chairs. Apparently the "decorator" had decided to take a chance and be daring with the chair color.

Eileen's cubicle was slightly larger than the other three. Over her desk hung an Elvis calendar.

Long ago, Dirk and Eileen had bonded over that calendar, as both were ardent fans of the King. The bond had held until Dirk's next abrasive comment—ten seconds later.

Theirs was a short-lived friendship.

"I suppose you came by to see what we've got," Eileen said, as she pulled the lid off the container of cookies and dove into the contents.

Sensing that a sarcastic reply from Dirk was forthcoming, Savannah gave him a warning look and said, "No, we just came by to give you the cookies. But, of course, if you want to share what you've got, we'd be mighty keen to hear all about it."

Dirk eyed the cookies. "And if you wanna share a few of those chocolate chippers—"

"Get real," Eileen said around a half cookie that was in her mouth. "You're married to this woman now. Which means you have access to food like this twenty-four/seven. Whereas I, on the other hand, have to wait for somebody to get murdered before I get a Savannah-made treat."

Savannah's ears perked up, like Granny Reid's bloodhound, Beauregard, when he heard a squirrel rustling around in the henhouse. "Murdered? You think somebody got murdered?"

"I think it's a possibility, and so do you two, or you wouldn't be here." She gave them a wry smile. "I don't believe for a moment you're here just to poke cookies into my pretty face."

"You're a suspicious old broad," Dirk told her with a wink.

"Watch who you're calling 'old,' you half-baked cracker," Eileen said with a sniff.

"Half-baked cracker?" Savannah said, chuckling. "Sometimes, girl, I wonder if you've got a down-in-Dixie rebel or two on your family tree."

Eileen smiled. "Yes. There's a Confederate or two lurking in my pedigree. Why do you think I appreciate your good Southern cooking the way I do?"

"You can't go by that," Dirk said. "Everybody who sits down to Savannah's table becomes a son or daughter of the old South— at least for the time they're sitting there."

"I believe it."

Eileen led them to the back of the building and into the laboratory. Much larger than the office area, it was a wide, open space with numerous examination tables upon which lay copious files and folders, boxes, and evidence bags.

Against the walls were more tables, desks, filing cabinets, and countertops covered with beakers, microscopes, meters, and measurers of all sorts that Savannah had never seen outside of this room.

The place looked and smelled a lot like her high school chemistry room, where she had slaved so hard for that measly C–. Only the lab was much larger. And Eileen was far more intimidating than her teacher, Mr. Dorsch, had ever been.

"We've already finished processing the evidence from Tyrone's hotel room," Eileen said. "And, of course, we've already put everything away. Which makes your visit here all the more annoying," she added, shooting Dirk a nasty look.

"Hence the cookies," he replied.

"Exactly." She walked to a counter in the back of the room and picked up a cardboard box with a chain-of-custody label on it.

She carried it to a table in the center of the room, took a pen from her pocket, and scribbled her name, the date, and the time on the label before opening the box.

Well-trained in crime lab protocol, Savannah and Dirk had already fished pairs of surgical gloves out of their pockets and donned them.

"Here it is," Eileen said. "Not that there's anything new here that you hadn't already seen at the hotel."

Savannah heard the accusation in her voice but decided to ignore it. Eileen habitually complained about anyone examining a crime scene before she and her team arrived.

"We didn't touch anything," Dirk told her, his tone more than a little defensive.

"Yeah, sure," Eileen shot back. "That'll be the day, when Dirk Coulter leaves the crime scene untouched."

Savannah couldn't resist jumping into the affray. "We were wearing our gloves. And we left everything exactly where we found it. Really. What do you think we are? A couple of country bumpkins?"

Eileen gave Dirk a contemptuous look and opened her mouth to reply. But Savannah beat her to it. "Don't answer that. Have another cookie."

Dirk reached into the box and began to take out various items. All were tagged with identifying numbers and letters. Some things were in brown paper evidence bags—like the amber prescription medicine bottles.

"You guys checked all this stuff already?" Dirk asked.

Savannah could practically see the feathers on the back of Eileen's head ruffle.

"I'm sure they did, Dirk," Savannah said gently.

"Process evidence? Us?" Eileen said, her voice dripping with sarcasm. "Of course not. The only reason we come to work every day is so that we can soak in the charming ambiance of this place. Lovely, isn't it?"

She waved a hand, indicating the vast room in all its steel-gray, industrial splendor. "After all, who wouldn't want to spend sixteen hours a day in a joint like this?"

Dirk held up his hands in surrender. "All right, all right. You processed everything in your usual thorough, professional manner. What did you find, if anything?"

Eileen sobered, her eyes traveling from one item on the table to the next. She sighed and said with a somewhat defeated tone, "Nothing. That's what we found. Nothing out of the ordinary. Except for an unusual amount of pharmaceuticals and vitamin supplements, it was just your usual guy's hotel room."

One by one, she pointed to the various items. "You've got your standard toiletries, three or four changes of clothing, a best-selling novel, a couple of bodybuilding magazines—one of them had him on the cover—a cell phone, an electronic tablet. And surprisingly enough, the tablet isn't even top-of-the-line. You'd think a rich movie star, like him, could afford the best."

Dirk took offense. "Hey, some people just don't want to waste a ton of money, upgrading all the time."

"Let me guess," Eileen said with a snicker. "You've got the same phone you've had for ten years."

"And there's not a damned thing wrong with it either," was Dirk's retort.

Savannah laughed. "Hey, I had to twist his arm to get him to buy that one. Had to pry him away from his soup cans with the string attached."

"Speaking of electronics," Dirk said, "did you get anything off his cell phone or that tablet thing?"

"We scanned through his calls and texts," Eileen replied. "Only one thing stood out."

Savannah asked, "What's that?"

"He got a bunch of texts yesterday from somebody named Thomas Owen."

"How much is a bunch?" Dirk wanted to know.

"Enough to be considered harassment, if you ask me. I think there were between fifty and sixty in the afternoon alone. For a while, he was sending one per minute."

"That'd be enough to get my dander up, for sure," Savannah said, as she picked up the phone and turned it on.

She brought up one text after another and read the short, unfriendly messages aloud. "Call me. Dammit, call me. I can't believe you're doing this. You can't go without me. I'm sitting here all ready to go. You better send somebody for me. Jason, do the right thing. You'll be sorry for treating me like this. I'm not going to forget this."

Savannah turned off the phone and replaced it in its evidence bag. "Sounds like a pissed-off, stood-up lover to me."

"No kidding," Dirk replied. "That's the kind of messages a husband would get if he forgot to take his wife out for their anniversary. And heaven help him when he got home."

"Exactly." Savannah thought hard, trying to remember something she had heard about Jason and his partner breaking up. Had Ryan and John mentioned it, or had she read it on the front of a tabloid cover while waiting in line at the grocery store?

She made a mental note to call Ryan the moment they left the lab.

"Since you probably don't want me to take that phone with me," Dirk said, "I need a list of all the calls on it."

"Can't you subpoena the phone company for that?" Eileen said. "We've got two robberies and a domestic assault to process before the day's over. And thanks to the chief and the mayor leaning on us about this case, it's the only thing we've accomplished in the last twelve hours."

Dirk gave her his most "patient" look. It was a look that he frequently used to annoy slow waitresses in every cheap eatery in town.

"And if I have to get a subpoena and go to the phone company," he said, "that'll take forever, and you know it. Where you, on the other hand, could ask one of those bozos out there in a cubicle to print it right out for me."

Eileen just stared at him for what seemed like forever, then she turned to Savannah. "You married this guy?"

Savannah laughed and shrugged. "I did. Seemed like a good idea at the time."

"You actually let him put a ring on your finger, and you promised to stay with him for the rest of your life?"

"No, just till death do us part."

"Ah, gotcha."

Savannah glanced down at the cell phone. "So is that it?" she asked. "An avalanche of pissy texts from a disgruntled lover? Is that the most scandalous thing we have from the scene?"

Eileen nodded. "That's it. We analyzed everything in the medicine and supplement bottles. They contained exactly what the labels said they did."

"How about the pain med patches?" Savannah asked.

"Lido-Morphone and the gel that it's suspended in. That was all. I'm telling you, the only thing we found in any of those substances is exactly what the manufacturer says they put in them."

Eileen began to replace the items into the box. "And we got word, just before you two got here, that Dr. Liu is ruling it accidental. The result of him taking too many body-enhancing drugs for too long." She shrugged. "We've all seen the pictures—him standing there, posing, muscles bulging everywhere. Let's be honest, it's no big surprise. He cheated and doped his way to that big body of his. And he paid for it. The ultimate price, as it turns out."

Moments later, as Dirk and Savannah left the laboratory and walked across the parking lot to her Mustang, she turned to Dirk and said, "You realize, that's how he's going to be known from now on. A doper and a cheater."

"Yeah, I know," he said, glancing down at the names and numbers on the printed list he had finagled out of Eileen—with the promise of more baked goods from Savannah's kitchen. "Unless we prove that it's something even worse. Something . . . shall we say, more sinister?"

She thought that over for a moment, then nodded. "True. A doper, a cheater . . . or a murder victim. What a lousy set of choices."

Chapter 11

"**M**an, oh, man, this being married business has some major perks," Dirk said, as he started up the Mustang and drove her out of the CSI lab's parking lot.

"Us being married has nothing to do with it," Savannah said, as she settled into the passenger seat, a grouchy look on her face. "It has everything to do with me being a good citizen and letting you drive so that I can make a phone call."

"Whatever," he said, his foot a bit heavy on the gas pedal.

"No. There's no 'whatever' about it. This is a once-in-a-lifetime thing. So enjoy it while you can."

He responded by screeching around the corner and laying down a bit of rubber—rubber from her newly purchased, classic, red-wall tires.

She growled, reached over, grabbed his knee, and gave it a painful squeeze. "Don't enjoy it that much, boy, or you'll be pulling her over to the shoulder and giving me back those keys, pronto."

He laughed, but he took the next corner a bit more slowly.

Satisfied that neither her life nor her vehicle were in danger, she pulled her phone from her purse and called Ryan.

He answered almost instantly, his usually relaxed, deep voice tight with tension. "Savannah, what's up?" he said, dispensing with his normal pleasantries.

"Nothing, honey," she told him. "Absolutely nothing."

"I called you at home," Ryan said, "and Tammy told me you'd gone to meet with Dr. Liu."

"Yes, we did. She's finished the autopsy, and she's ruling it an accident."

There was a long silence on the other end. Finally, he said, "An accident? But how can that be? There was no sign that he'd fallen or hurt himself."

Savannah swallowed hard and took a deep breath. "Not that kind of an accident," she said. "More like he accidentally took too many different kinds of medications for too long and damaged his heart."

"He died of a heart attack?"

"No, I think she called it cardiovascular damage. Something like that. And the problem with his heart caused his brain not to get enough oxygen. And that caused him to . . . well, you know. That's why."

"I guess that's good news," Ryan said halfheartedly. "I mean, it's a terrible thing if he abused steroids and medicines, and it cost him his life. But I'm glad to hear that Dr. Liu doesn't suspect foul play."

Savannah clutched the phone and tried to decide, in that fraction of a moment, whether to be honest with her friend or not.

She had been close to Ryan for a long time, and they had always been open with each other. And yet he had just lost a dear friend. Was there any advantage in telling him the whole truth? Maybe it would be better to wait a few days and see what she and Dirk could dig up.

But she took a few too many seconds to make that decision. And Ryan Stone was astute, if nothing.

"Out with it," he said. "We want to know everything."

"Okay, here goes." Savannah took a deep breath. "Dirk and I, we aren't ready to rule out foul play just yet. And Dr. Liu said that, even though she couldn't find any evidence of homicide, she isn't completely comfortable with her ruling. And that, my friend, has to stay strictly between the four of us. Understand?"

Again there was a long, heavy silence. Then he said, "I don't like it. If that isn't why Jason died, I don't think the world should be told that it was."

"I feel the same way. That's why we're going to go ahead and investigate it as a murder until we know otherwise."

"That's good of you. I appreciate it."

"And speaking of—what can you tell me about a Thomas Owen?"

"Until a week or two ago, he and Jason were a couple. They'd been together for years. Why?"

"Just wondering. Who broke up with whom?"

"From what I understood, from the short phone conversation Jason and I had about it last week, it was Jason who ended it."

"Do you know why?"

"No, he just said he'd put it off as long as he could, out of concern for Thomas's mental health. And he said Thomas wasn't taking it well. Again, why are you asking?"

"There were a bunch of texts from Thomas on Jason's phone yesterday. I'm guessing, but it looks like Thomas was expecting to accompany Jason to the premiere."

"That's possible. If they'd still been together, Jason would have taken him—with or without his agent's blessing."

"His agent didn't approve of his relationship?"

"His agent didn't approve of Jason's orientation. Apparently, it's harder to find roles for a gay superhero than a straight one."

"Maybe we should put his agent on the list of interviewees."

"At the bottom, if at all. I met him. Mellow old guy. Listen,

Savannah. You and Dirk don't have to do all the legwork, you know. This investigation of yours . . . count us in."

"Always, darlin'. Always."

She hung up and sat there, her heart heavy, feeling the weight of her friend's burden.

Over the years, she had lost track of how many times Ryan Stone and John Gibson had come to her aid in one way or another. They truly had been her knights in shining armor on so many occasions. And right now, there was nothing she wanted more than to help them in this situation.

And how are you going to do that, Savannah girl? she asked herself. *By proving their friend was murdered?*

If that's what it takes, a quiet, rational voice deep inside replied. *You're going to uncover the truth. And Dr. Liu says the truth makes any situation better.*

Slowly, Savannah pulled her mind away from the troubling phone conversation and back into her surroundings. Dirk was no longer racing around, putting the Red Pony through her paces. In fact, they had been sitting at a stop sign for a long time.

As though from far away, she heard it—a deep, rumbling sound. It was a bit like a freight train, a little like a Georgia tornado.

She turned to look at Dirk and saw that her new husband's eyes were closed.

He was sound asleep at the wheel. And snoring like a British bulldog with a barrel over his head.

She glanced around. Fortunately, there wasn't another car or pedestrian in sight.

She reached over, put the car in park, and turned off the key.

Mario Andretti Junior woke with a start. "Hey, whatcha doin'?"

"Get out," she said.

"Why? What's up?"

"We're changing drivers."

"Why? I wasn't speeding. I slowed down like you asked me to."

She laughed. "Oh, you slowed down, all right. Buddy, you were sawin' logs. I'm gonna take us both home and put us to bed. In this state we're a danger to society."

He got out of the car, and so did she. As they passed each other, rounding the hood, she heard him say, "Damn! First time I talk her into letting me drive the 'Stang and I slept through it!"

When Savannah pulled the Mustang into her driveway, she and Dirk saw something that didn't surprise her at all. Her brother, Waycross.

Why would any young man spend time in an old house trailer alone when he could hang out at his sister's house and—more important—pass the time with a beautiful young gal who had the hots for him?

So Savannah didn't find it unusual to see his car in the driveway or him, stripped to the waist, washing it.

She also wasn't surprised that Tammy enjoyed seeing Waycross shirtless. The scrawny little boy who had slipped frogs, snakes, and spiders into her lingerie drawer had grown up to be quite a hunk. Savannah figured that most women between the ages of eight and eighty would take notice of a shirt-free Waycross.

But what did surprise her—and Dirk, too, judging from his, "Oh! Wow!"—was the sight of his Buick, sparkling in the late-afternoon sunlight. The old classic glistened as if it had just been driven out of a showroom.

"Holy cow!" she exclaimed. "Would you look at that!"

"I don't believe it!" Dirk said, bailing out of the Mustang.

"Me either. Underneath all that mud and guck, your Buick is blue! I had no idea."

"Watch it, smart mouth," he told her, as they both hurried up to the gleaming old beauty. "I've never insulted your Mustang."

"The Pony's color has never been in question."

Waycross stood, dripping sponge in hand as they examined his handiwork, a goofy grin on his freckled face. He wiped a bit of soap suds off his cheek with his forearm. "I had a notion there was a good-lookin' ride underneath there somewhere," he said. "And sure 'nough. Lookie there. Purdy as a picture."

Dirk was too pleased and astonished to be insulted. He shook his head in wonderment. "Waycross, my brother, you are somethin' else. How'd you do this?"

Waycross shrugged. "Just applied a bit o' carnauba wax and a whole lotta elbow grease. She buffed right up, like she was hungry for it."

Dirk reached out to caress a sparkling fender, then seemed to think better of it and pulled back his hand. "Man, I don't even want to touch it. That's the best it's ever looked—at least, since I've owned it."

He walked over to Waycross, gave him a hearty slap on the back, and shook his hand. "I don't even know where to start to say thank you," he told the younger man. Dirk reached into his back pocket, took out his wallet, and opened it. "What do I owe you for a job like that?"

"Git outta here. You're family now, and besides, you lettin' me live in your house trailer—that just means the world to me. You'll never know. It's the first home of my own I've ever had."

Savannah felt her heartstrings twang at her little brother's words. She'd never thought about the fact that Waycross had never had a real home all to himself. Like her and their seven other siblings, she and Waycross had lived in their grandmother's house, then moved out when they'd become adults.

But once he was out on his own, poor Waycross had practically lived in the garage where he worked. The owner had allowed him to sleep on a fold-up cot in the attic of the garage—a space that was neither heated in the winter nor cooled during the hot, humid Georgia summers.

He had washed his face and brushed his teeth in the gas station's restroom and showered at Granny's.

So it was no surprise that he considered Dirk's old trailer luxury accommodations.

In one sense, Savannah felt sorry for Waycross that he would be so grateful for such a minimal thing as a roof of his own. But on the other hand, she truly felt he was better off for not being spoiled. It took so little to make him so very happy.

As she walked past him on her way up the drive to the house, she stood on tiptoe and gave him a peck on the cheek. "Thank you," she said. "I owe you an apple pie for doing that."

"You don't owe me nothin'," he said. "But if you have a spare pie runnin' around, makin' a nuisance of itself, I'll dispense with it."

Savannah laughed, left the boys to bond over the refurbished Buick, and walked into the house.

There she found Tammy sitting at the desk, working on the computer. One glance at the screen told Savannah that her assistant was researching Jason Tyrone.

It didn't have to be much of a case for Tammy Master Sleuth to pounce on it. In fact, just the whiff of mystery was enough for her to pull out her virtual magnifying glass via the Internet.

"What did you find out there, Miss Tamitha?" Savannah asked her as she settled into her comfy chair and invited the cats to occupy her lap, which they did in a jackrabbit's heartbeat.

"Nothing that anybody who reads the tabloids or watches the entertainment news shows on TV wouldn't know already."

"Well, I don't do either, so fill me in," Savannah said, as she scratched behind Cleopatra's ear with one hand and stroked Diamante's chin with the other.

"He just broke up with his longtime partner. A guy named—"

"Thomas Owen."

"Wow! You knew that?"

"Ryan told me. What else?"

"There were rumors that the breakup was over Alanna Cleary."

"A gay couple breaks up over a woman?"

Tammy shrugged. "Just telling you what I read."

"Okay. What else?"

"I ran a credit check on him. And as you might suppose, considering the bazillion millions he got for those last two movies, he was sitting pretty."

"Criminal check?"

"Of course. Nothing. Not even an overdue library book."

"Hmmm. Clean as a hound's tooth, huh? Figures."

Tammy turned in her chair and gave Savannah a quizzical look. "I heard Waycross use that phrase the other day. What the heck does it mean? Do hound dogs brush their teeth and floss regularly?"

At that moment, Dirk came through the front door, and Savannah thought about the toothpaste-speckled, pee-pee-sprinkled bathroom upstairs. "Yes," she said, "and they always hit the toilet when they take a leak."

Dirk shot her a suspicious look. "You gals talking about me?"

"No. Not at all."

Tammy chimed in. "We're discussing the dental hygiene habits of well-mannered hound dogs . . . I think."

He walked over to the desk, pulled Eileen's list of numbers from his pocket, and waved it under Tammy's nose. "This is the call history from Jason Tyrone's cell phone. Think you could track down these numbers for us?"

She snatched the paper out of his hand, her eyes gleaming with an avarice women usually reserved for sparkly jewelry or cold, hard cash. "Gimme that," she said.

A second later, she was typing like a maniac on the computer keyboard, her eyes trained on the monitor.

"Since the kid's occupied now," Savannah said, as she set the cats on the ottoman, "let's go catch some winks. My eyeballs crossed an hour ago, and the only thing that's gonna uncross them is a nice, long nap."

"Sounds good," Dirk said, heading for the stairs.

"Before you go, Dirko," Tammy called out, still typing and staring at the screen. "There's a message for you on the machine. I listened, but saved it."

"Who is it?"

Tammy tore herself away from the computer long enough to give him a sweet smile. Then she said, "Your dad."

Savannah poured herself a glass of lemonade and gave Dirk some private time upstairs to retrieve his message before she joined him in the bedroom.

Some minutes later, she found him sitting on the side of the bed, staring at the phone.

"Everything okay, sugar?" she asked, concerned.

He nodded.

"What did your dad have to say?"

Shrugging, he said, "I don't know. I haven't listened to it yet."

She held the glass of lemonade out to him, but he shook his head.

"Do you want me to leave you alone again," she asked, "so's you can listen to it alone?"

"No. I was waiting for you to come up. I wanted you to be here when I . . . you know . . . hear whatever it is."

Touched, she put the lemonade on the nightstand and then sat beside him on the bed. "Oh, okay. And here I was trying to give you some privacy."

He looked surprised. "You're my wife now. I don't need privacy from you."

She reached out and took his hand. "That's sweet."

"No. It's just true. Believe me, after all these years of being alone, I've had all the privacy I need."

Savannah thought of what he had told her about being given up at birth and raised in an orphanage. As a teenager, he had been adopted by a ruthless man who had used him for slave labor.

So other than one short-lived, ill-fated marriage, Dirk had been alone his whole life. And like Waycross, who had been denied some of life's most basic needs, Dirk was deeply grateful for what he had.

Her heart warmed toward him as she reached over and slipped her arm around his waist. "Pick up your message, darlin'," she said. "There's no reason to think it'd be bad news."

She ached for him, noticing that his hand was trembling as he reached for the phone on the nightstand.

Dirk was a big guy, a brave guy, a manly sorta man.

Ruthless criminals didn't make him shake. Neither did most dangerous situations. He handled whatever life and the job brought his way with unwavering courage and determination. Sometimes, afterward, he might feel the need for a cold beer and a quiet moment to decompress. But nothing shook him.

Except this.

He had been so pleased when Tammy had found his biological parents on the Internet. He'd been happy to discover that they'd been searching for him for decades. And he was ecstatic to find out they were as eager to meet him as he was to see them for the first time.

But now that the meeting was scheduled—imminent even— he was getting more and more nervous by the moment.

So nervous that Savannah was worried about him.

She watched as he punched the appropriate numbers to activate the message replay. He even put it on speakerphone so they both could listen.

Their silly, playful message ran, "Hi! It's us, Savannah and Dirk. Leave a message or else. Don't make us hunt you down . . ."

A pause, a beep, and then a deep, masculine voice that sounded eerily like Dirk's said, "Hi, son, and Savannah, too. It's Richard. Hope you guys are okay. We're getting packed up and all that. I had the car serviced today, and we talked to the neighbor kid about feeding the cat, so we're about ready to go. We're real excited." He took a deep breath. "Well, I'm excited. Your mom, she's . . . well, she is in a little bit of the dither. Actually, she is in a lot of a dither. It's not that she doesn't want to see you. It's just that she has these bad feelings, you know, about how things turned out and all that."

Savannah glanced at Dirk to see how he was taking this news. The expression on his face looked as worried as his father's voice sounded.

Not good, she thought. *Problems already, and they haven't even arrived yet.*

She reached over, took Dirk's hand, and gave it a comforting squeeze.

"Anyway," Richard continued, "I just wanted to touch base and say that I can't wait to see you, son, and your new wife, too. We'll give you another call once we're on our way."

Dirk replaced the phone on its base. "Well, that was nice of him, to call and all."

Savannah nodded a little too vigorously. "It was. Very nice. He sounds like a nice guy, a good guy."

"Yeah, he does. But what's that business about my mom? What sort of dither? I don't really like females who're in a dither."

He gave Savannah a quick look. "Or guys either," he quickly added. "People in dithers just aren't that great to be around, male or female."

"Good save."

"Thank you. I try."

Savannah stood and nudged him off the bed so that she could fold down the covers. "I think a bit of dithering—or even a lot of it—is to be expected under the circumstances."

"Really?" He stood and peeled off his shirt. He started to toss it onto a nearby chair, then thought better of it, walked to the closet, and pitched it into a hamper she had given him a few weeks earlier—along with detailed instructions on how to use said piece of delicate machinery.

"Lift the lid, toss in the clothes, close the lid."

After numerous spirited discussions on the topic, he had managed to follow the directions fairly well.

Getting him to close the closet door afterward—that was a lesson for another time.

"Yes," she said. "Your mom's entitled to have some misgivings, some trepidation about meeting her son for the first time since, well, you know . . ."

"Since she gave me away?"

"Exactly. I sure wouldn't wanna be in her shoes when she walks up to our front door. Would you?"

"But Tammy said she was forced to, that she was just a kid and—"

"And I believe she'll tell you all about it when she gets here."

"You think?"

"Probably."

Savannah watched him climb into bed. Such a big man. Rugged. A male. So completely, absolutely adult. And yet there was something about his lower lip—the slightly tremulous set of it. Something about the sad and guarded look in his eyes that told her there was a little boy lurking inside that grown-up body. A kid who had spent his childhood in an orphanage and wanted to know why.

"If she doesn't tell you," Savannah said softly, as she climbed into bed beside him, "you might need to ask her. For your own peace of mind."

He snuggled close to her, and for once, he laid his head on her shoulder, rather than the other way around.

"Do you think I should? Would that be okay, you think? If she doesn't volunteer it . . ."

She played with his hair and stroked his cheek as she said, "I think you'll know when the time comes. You think fast on your feet, and you've got really good instincts about people. You'll figure it out as you go."

He thought about it for a long time. So long, in fact, that she thought he might have drifted off to sleep. But then he said, "And if I can't figure it out, I can ask you what you think about it. Right?"

She kissed the top of his head, then pulled him even closer. "Of course you can, silly. You know me. There are two things I never run out of—words and opinions."

"That's for sure."

She swatted him.

He winced. "Ouch."

"Go to sleep, turkey butt."

"Okay. You too."

Less than a minute later, Cleopatra and Diamante came into the room, jumped up on the bed, and found them both sound asleep.

Chapter 12

Heaven, Savannah thought as she fought her way to a slightly higher level of consciousness. *Heaven. Hallelujah, I made it!*

As a rule, private investigators didn't lead a life that could be considered "squeaky clean" by almost anyone's standards. The sneaking around, the breaking in, the listening in, not to mention the bevy of lies told in the course of a single day's work. According to Granny Reid, having those activities on one's resume could present a problem when attempting to enter the Pearly Gates.

At times, Savannah had feared for her mortal soul.

But she had made it! Nothing but Heaven itself smelled like that.

Even before her eyes could focus, her nose was at work, identifying the delicious scents of freshly brewed coffee, sizzling bacon, fried eggs, and right-out-of-the-oven biscuits.

Then a second thought occurred to her. This might not be Heaven itself, but the closest thing to it on earth—Gran's kitchen.

Many of her childhood mornings, she had awakened to this divine aroma. And even though she had never been known as a "morning person," the allure of those delicious smells had coaxed her out of bed.

Opening her eyes, she fully expected to see the bottom of the overhead bunk, where at least two of her sisters would be sleeping. Little sister Alma would be curled against her side, and the baby of the family, Atlanta, would be lying across the foot of the bed. They would all be covered with one of Gran's beautiful, hand-sewn quilts.

But no.

Although it was one of Granny's quilts that covered her, the cozy snuggle-bug next to her side was Cleopatra. And the foot warmer was Diamante.

The other side of the bed was empty, except for a rumpled pair of men's boxer shorts that lay on the pillow. So much for Husband Hamper Training 101.

She squinted, looking at the bedside clock.

7:19.

The stiffness of her muscles and the groggy feeling in her head told her that it wasn't 7:19 PM.

No. It was morning, and she had slept for more than twelve hours.

That had to be a first, even for her.

And as she crawled out of bed and made her way to the closet for a robe, it occurred to her that this being-in-your-forties business had its disadvantages. She was definitely not as spry as she had been in her twenties and thirties.

But as she slipped on her robe and house slippers, she consoled herself with the thought that she was a heck of a lot smarter now than she had been twenty years ago. And she would trade "smart" for "spry" any time.

The cats followed her down the stairs, through the foyer, and into the living room, doing figure eights between her ankles. "One of these days," she muttered, "I'm gonna step on one of y'all and squash your tail. Or worse yet, I'll take a spill and mash you both flatter than a flitter. You wait and see."

As usual, her dire warnings went unheeded by the felines in question. They knew all too well that Mom was a soft touch. None of her threats were ever carried out, and all of her promises were delivered.

They also knew that they would be fed before her morning coffee was even poured, let alone drank. So they continued to intertwine themselves around her legs and rub their faces against her feet, purring the entire time.

Finally, she made it to the kitchen, where she found Dirk sitting at the table, shoving a forkful of eggs into his mouth, chased by a swig from his enormous Bonanza mug that had all three of the Cartwright boys and Pa on the side.

Surely, he wasn't the cook who had filled the house with blissful scents! Could it be she had married a closet chef?

No.

One look in the direction of the stove and refrigerator and she knew that the guilty parties were Tammy and Waycross.

Waycross was flipping eggs in a skillet on the stove. Tammy was taking biscuits from a metal pan and transferring them to a basket lined with a snowy linen cloth.

"Good morning," they all said in unison.

"Sleeping Beauty's decided to join us, after all," Dirk said between chews. "How're you doing, babe? Did you get enough sleep?"

She grunted and made her way to the cat dishes near the back door. "I should say so," she replied. "Another hour and I would've turned into Rumpelstiltskin."

Tammy giggled as she put the basket of biscuits on the table. "Don't you mean Rip Van Winkle?"

"One of those guys with a weird name that starts with an R."

She poured some fresh Kitty Vittles into the cats' dishes and refreshed their water, as well. A moment later, the glossy black faces were buried in the food—ankle circling and Mom-love forgotten in a fit of gluttony.

"When did you crawl out this morning?" Savannah asked Dirk as she walked to the table, planted a quick kiss on the top of his head, and then took a seat beside him.

"Oh, ages ago. Somebody had to get up and get going. We've got a full day's work ahead of us."

Tammy set a jar of Granny's homemade peach preserves on the table next to the biscuits. "Don't let him fool you," she said. "He's only been down here about ten minutes himself. 'Get up and get going,' my butt."

Waycross laughed as he carried a platter laden with eggs and bacon still sizzling from the skillet over to the table and set it in front of Savannah. "Aw, who gives a hooey? Y'all needed some extra sleep after pullin' that all-nighter. Neither one of you's exactly a spring chicken these days."

Savannah shot him a disapproving, big-sister scowl. "You know, I can think depressing thoughts like that 'un all by myself, little brother. I don't need assistance from you in that department."

When she got a good look at the delectables on the platter, she instantly forgave him. "Since when did you learn to do that?" she asked. "Those eggs are beautiful. They don't even have ruffles around the edges."

"Gran taught me," he said proudly. " 'You want the bacon crispy, but not the eggs.' She'd say that ever' time."

A sad look crossed his face, and just for a moment, Savannah thought that maybe this living in California arrangement might not be 100 percent wonderful for brother Waycross. Even Paradise came with a price.

"I miss her, too," Savannah said, giving him a pat on the arm. "In fact, that's the one thing I miss the most about being here on the West Coast. That and seeing the pretty moss hanging from the trees."

"I like that moss stuff, too," Tammy chimed in. "Saw it when we went back to Georgia that time to get Macon out of jail."

At the mention of their brother's name, another less-than-jolly look passed over both Savannah's and Waycross's faces. Among the Reid siblings—some of whom were fairly eccentric and not altogether law-abiding characters—Macon was the one considered most likely to wind up serving a life sentence, making license plates in a Georgia high-security institution.

"How is Macon these days?" Savannah asked.

Waycross shrugged. "Macon's Macon."

"That's too bad."

"Ain't it though?"

Savannah dug into the biscuit basket and picked out a large one. It seemed to weigh nothing at all in her hand. She turned to Tammy. "Did you bake these, Yankee girl?"

Tammy nodded and flushed a lovely shade of pink. She looked slightly embarrassed, like a kid being caught feeding a younger sibling a mud pie. "Yes, I did. It goes against everything I hold sacred, since you have to use white, bleached flour. Of course, at anyone else's house I could have used some sort of whole-grain flour. But since it's your house—"

"Blasphemy! Pure blasphemy! Any second now you're going to get struck dead by a bolt of lightning! Waycross, stand away from her. Divine retribution's on its way!"

Tammy sat down at the table across from Savannah, a glass of herbal tea in her hand. Waycross quickly claimed the chair next to Tammy's and started loading up his plate with goodies.

"What else have you two been up to?" Savannah asked.

Dirk chuckled. "Maybe you shouldn't ask."

"Believe me, I do so with fear and trembling," Savannah replied. She turned to the young couple, who were trading looks that were so lovey-dovey that Savannah was nearly put off her grub. "You can just give me the basics," she told them. "You can keep the gory details to yourselves, considering it's the breakfast table."

Tammy blushed again and tittered. "Well, before you jump to conclusions about our love life—"

"Y'all have a love life?" Savannah interjected. She turned to Dirk. "Our worst suspicions are confirmed. Wait'll I tell Gran. She'll take both of 'em behind the woodshed for a proper switching."

"You tell on me, I'll never wash that Buick again," Waycross threatened.

"Hold on there," Dirk said. "Before this gets outta hand . . ." He shoved both the biscuit basket and the peach preserves toward Waycross. "Tell you what, brother-in-law. If you'll polish that car of mine like you did, say, once every five years, I'll make sure your sister doesn't rat you out to Gran for anything. You can run amuck for all I care and Gran'll never be the wiser."

"And I'll never be the sorrier?"

"You got it. Deal?"

Waycross laughed. "That's a bargain and a half!" He reached over and patted Tammy's hand. "Tell 'em what you came up with, darlin', while they were upstairs snoozin' to beat the band."

Seemingly from nowhere, Tammy produced her electronic tablet and turned it on.

"Did you already run down that list of phone numbers for me?" Dirk asked.

"Oh, I did better than that. I used the info on that list and hacked his account. I've got his calls and texts from months back."

"Don't y'all need some sort of subpoena for that kinda thing?" Waycross wanted to know.

"It's the victim's records," Tammy told him. "Who would we subpoena?"

Savannah cleared her throat. "You only need a subpoena if you're a cop."

"Let's get real here," Dirk said. "You only need a subpoena if you get caught." He took a swig from his cowboy mug. "Or if you intend to use anything you found out in a court of law."

Savannah nodded. "And all we're doing right now is sticking our noses in the air and seeing if we can catch a scent. How else are we gonna figure out which path to go down first?"

Waycross slathered an obscene amount of butter on a biscuit, while Miss Health Nut Tammy pretended not to notice or disapprove. "Don't pay me no never mind. I was just wondering about your methods, not questioning your ethics. I'm sure whatever y'all do, it's on the up and up."

The other three at the table shot each other guilty little looks, before returning their attention to the morning refreshments.

"And what did you find out," Dirk asked, "while you were doing all this high-minded, totally ethical hacking and snooping?"

"I found out that Jason Tyrone didn't have any family to speak of. And for a guy the whole world supposedly loves, you'd be surprised how few friends he had. Or at least, if he did have friends, he didn't communicate with them on the phone."

"Maybe he was just a busy guy who didn't like to chat or text," Savannah suggested.

"Oh, he made calls. Lots of them," Tammy told her. "Calls to his agent. Calls to his manager. Calls to the producer and writers of the movie."

"That's understandable," Dirk said, "for a guy who's in the middle of making a movie."

Tammy nodded. "Exactly. Nothing sinister or unusual there."

"Don't get me wrong," Savannah began. "I appreciate this gorgeous breakfast and all. But . . ." She lifted her nose and pretended to sniff the air. ". . . I don't smell a thing amiss. Nothing you've told us so far would lead us down any particular path. If we're gonna get some meaningful work done today, we need to know who to harass first."

Tammy's fingers flew over her tablet's screen. "If it were me, I'd check out his ex. Here, I made a list of some of the texts that passed back and forth between them this past month. There's been some very emotional, negative energy in that relationship lately. It's no wonder they called it quits. Or maybe I should say, 'Jason called it quits.' Obviously, Thomas didn't want it to end."

Tammy handed the tablet to Savannah, and she scanned the list while sipping her coffee.

Just as Tammy had said, many of the texts were less than cordial. While some were nothing more than the usual domestic squabbles about housework responsibilities and who was going to make the next grocery store run, some were downright bitter.

Three weeks before Jason's death, Thomas had sent him texts of an accusing nature. Apparently, Thomas believed Jason had been sexually intimate with his leading lady, Alanna Cleary.

Shortly after that, Thomas's tone had changed to one of pleading, begging Jason not to end the relationship.

Savannah handed the tablet to Dirk. "Looks like the gossip rags had it right," she said. "It seems they did break up over Alanna."

Dirk read for a while, then said, "Over Alanna or over Thomas's jealousy about Alanna. Just because Jason was being accused doesn't mean he was doing anything wrong."

Waycross gave Dirk a hearty nod of agreement. "That's right, man. Us guys get accused of a lot of malarkey we never did."

"And a ton of it that you did but didn't get caught doing," Savannah said.

Tammy snickered. "Present company excepted, of course."

Savannah choked on her biscuit. "Of course."

Dirk laid down the tablet and picked up his fork. "Thomas did it. All we have to do is prove it."

Tammy's eyes widened. "Isn't that just a little bit judgmental?"

"Yeah," Waycross agreed. "Ain't you sorta jumpin' the gun there, good buddy?"

"Nope. It was Thomas." Dirk chewed on happily. "It's always the husband, the wife, the lover, sometimes just the one-night stand. But if somebody winds up dead, it's almost always somebody they made love to."

Tammy and Waycross both turned to Savannah, questioning looks on their faces.

"What he just said . . . it's absolutely, positively true," she told them. "Sad commentary on the human race, huh?"

Chapter 13

"Hmmm," Savannah said, as Dirk drove the newly polished Buick along a scenic, winding road that led deeper and deeper into a magnificent piece of country property that now belonged to Thomas Owen. "This is a nice little breakup gift, if ever I saw one."

"No kidding," Dirk replied. "Either Jason Tyrone must've been really, really rich, or he felt really, really guilty for calling it off."

"Probably both. This little bit of real estate must have set him back millions." She reached over and gave his thigh a little squeeze. "If you and I ever wind up calling it quits, don't expect a severance package like this one from me."

He gave her a look of alarm. "Hey, don't even kid about a thing like that. There ain't gonna be no severance. This here's a life sentence."

She smiled at him sweetly. "I agree, no divorce. Homicide, on the other hand, is a possibility if you don't stop spittin' toothpaste all over my bathroom mirror. But no divorce."

He looked so relieved that she felt guilty for having made the joke at all. And she vowed to herself never again to be flippant about a topic that would cause her husband such consternation.

She also reminded herself that although she had never suffered through the miseries of a divorce, Dirk had. His first wife, Polly, had run away with a much younger rock guitarist. Savannah wasn't sure which had upset Dirk the most—the kid's youth, or the fact that the rocker had sported at least ten times the amount of hair as Dirk.

They drove over a beautiful rock bridge that crossed a bubbling creek. As the stream flowed along on its rocky bed and disappeared in the distance into a grove of giant oak trees, it made a lovely, soothing sound.

Savannah wished she could somehow reproduce that sound in her bedroom at night. Going to sleep would be no problem when lulled by the music of nature.

To their left was an orange grove. The scent of the ripening fruit mingled with the perfume of the white, starry blossoms, lending the air a fragrance that was as beautiful as the perfect rows of trees themselves.

To the right grew an avocado orchard, its trees much larger and foliage far darker than that of the oranges. Avocados hung on the thick, sturdy limbs in profusion. Apparently, this year it had been a bumper crop.

"You'd think the income from a ranch like this," Savannah said, "would keep old Owen in the manner to which he had become accustomed."

"Ranch? Ranch?" Dirk shook his head and made a tsk-tsk sound. "It just ain't right, them calling a fruit farm a 'ranch.' Ranches have cowboys and horses and steers and manure and manly stuff like that. There ain't nothing masculine about avocados. I mean, they taste good in guacamole, but that's as far as it goes."

"I think 'avocado ranch' is a legitimate term. I've heard it many times."

"Oh, yeah? Did you ever hear of an avocado roundup? Did you ever see any rough, tough cowboys, wearing Stetsons and boots and chaps, lasso a bunch of avocados, throw 'em to the ground, and brand 'em with a hot iron?"

"No, but I might tie a rope around you, throw you to the ground, and stick you with a hot poker if you don't drop this ridiculous conversation."

"Okay. I will, if you just admit one thing."

She sighed, suddenly feeling exhausted, in spite of her long night's sleep. "What's that?"

"You admit that you can't even imagine Pa, Hoss, or little Joe raising a bunch of avocados on the Ponderosa and calling it a 'ranch.' It would have been downright unnatural."

Up ahead, Savannah could see the outlines of a magnificent contemporary home, nestled among some ancient, gnarled oaks. They were nearly at their destination.

It was time to put Dirk out of her misery.

"You are absolutely right, my darlin'," she said. "You couldn't be more right, and I couldn't possibly be more wrong."

He looked confused for a moment, then a bit pleased, then somewhat pissy. "How come it is," he asked, "that even when I win an argument with you, it doesn't feel like I won?"

"You know, sweetie pie, you're absolutely right about that, too. Just as right as rain. You win. You couldn't be any righter if you had to be."

"Oh, shut up."

Savannah knocked twice, and Dirk did the same three times, with hard, determined knocks, before anyone answered the door. But when it finally opened and Savannah saw the bedraggled guy standing there, she instantly knew he was Thomas Owen. She also knew that he was in an acute state of shock and grief.

And even though she felt an enormous wave of pity for him, she also reminded herself that people who had recently committed their first homicide frequently appeared that way.

Fortunately, there weren't all that many hardcore, psychopathic serial killers in the world. Most murders were done by ordinary people in extraordinary circumstances. And the act of killing a fellow human being usually had a devastating effect on the murderer as well.

So Thomas's swollen, red-rimmed eyes, gray pallor, slumped shoulders, and rumpled clothing did nothing to convince her of his innocence.

Dirk might've been a bit of a nitwit when it came to conversations about the Ponderosa's lack of avocado-raising propensities, but he knew more than his share about homicides. And anybody who had conducted even a few murder investigations knew that the victim's significant other was always number one on a detective's list of suspects.

"Thomas Owen?" Dirk asked in his most officious, no-nonsense, cop voice.

The young man ran shaking fingers through his short, mussed, blond hair and nodded curtly. "Yeah. Why?"

Dirk opened his badge and stuck it under the guy's nose. "I'm Detective Sergeant Dirk Coulter with the San Carmelita Police Department."

"And I'm Savannah Reid," she told him. "We're investigating the death of Jason Tyrone."

When Thomas didn't reply, Savannah added a simple, "And we're sorry for your loss."

He gave her the weakest of smiles, then said, "Thank you. How can I help you?"

"We'd like to come in and sit a spell," she told him, "if that's okay with you. We hate to intrude in a time like this, but Sergeant

Coulter here has a few questions to ask you. Strictly routine, of course."

"There's nothing routine about Jason dying." Thomas's eyes filled with tears.

"No, of course not," Savannah said quickly. "We understand that the two of you were close. And I'm sure that his passing must be very painful for you. We won't stay long, really."

She glanced in Dirk's direction and saw that he was beginning to lose the little patience he had. She hoped that Thomas would invite them in without Dirk having to strong-arm him.

She had always found it to be a touchy, delicate situation—the business of interviewing a person who was close to the victim. And that challenge was compounded when he or she was a suspect. If you hadn't yet proven them guilty, you had to treat them with all the kindness, civility, and compassion that you would anyone who had lost a loved one. If they were innocent, the last thing they needed was an overaggressive police officer adding to their stress at one of the worst moments of their life.

On the other hand, you didn't want to coddle a killer. It was a difficult balancing act.

"Okay," Thomas said simply. "Come on in."

He led them into what turned out to be a magnificent home. Though it was contemporary in design and had a lot of steel, concrete, and glass in its construction, an abundance of wood and stonework gave it a natural coziness.

Teak ceilings that soared twenty feet or higher lent the living room a delightful, open feel. Floor-to-ceiling glass walls revealed the magnificent landscaping, bringing the serenity of the outside in.

And gigantic indoor palm trees thrived in all the sunlight the windows provided.

Savannah had to think that so much nature, such an abundance of greenery, had to provide a great deal of peace to anyone fortunate enough to live there.

Unless, of course, someone they loved had just died.

Thomas led them to an inviting sofa made of highly polished bound bamboo and comfortable cushions with a colorful tropical print.

"Have a seat," Thomas said, motioning to the couch. "Do you want something to drink? I've had quite a lot myself the past couple of days."

"No, thanks anyway," Savannah said. "But don't let us stop you, if you want to have something."

Early in her career, she had discovered that interviews were far more productive when the interviewee had consumed a bit of alcohol. Not enough to make him nasty and belligerent, but enough to lower his inhibitions a bit.

Eagerly, almost gratefully, Thomas hurried into the kitchen. He returned thirty seconds later with the glass half full of an amber liquid. When he walked past them, Savannah caught the distinctive smell of scotch whiskey.

She thought he was going to have a seat in a chair near them. But instead he paced back and forth in front of the window, stopping occasionally to stare out at the Japanese garden and take a sip of his whiskey.

Finally, it was Dirk who spoke first. "Nice place you got here. How long have you lived here?"

Of course, Dirk knew how long. Tammy had told them the exact date that Thomas had taken occupancy when she had given them the address. But Savannah herself frequently asked questions to which she already knew the answer. It was a technique that was particularly effective at the beginning of an interview, when you were trying to determine if the person was honest and forthright or just your garden-variety, bold-faced liar. It beat the "Sniffing For Burnt Pants Method" every time.

"I just moved in here. Not even a month ago," Thomas replied. "Escrow hasn't even closed yet."

"That's pretty nice of them, letting you live here before the ink's on the paperwork," Dirk observed.

" 'Nice' has nothing to do with it. Considering how much money Jason put down on it, I'm surprised they didn't move the entire property to the beach for him." He gripped his glass, staring out at the fountain in the koi pond. "Until Jason hit it big with the movies, I had no idea the kind of power that money brings with it. You'd be surprised what people will do for a fistful of cash."

No, I wouldn't, Savannah thought. She had seen people take another person's life for ten dollars or a single line of cocaine.

"From what we understand," Savannah said, "the two of you had been together for about five years. Is that true?"

He gave her a somewhat unpleasant, sarcastic smile. "Gee, you read the tabloids, too. And did you hear that we were going to adopt an alien baby with two heads and three eyes?"

"No, I reckon I missed that issue," Savannah replied evenly.

If Thomas Owen wanted to make a good first impression and get on her good side, this wasn't the way to go about it. Smart alecks had never been high on her list of favorite people.

Thomas seemed to sense her disapproval, and his face softened a bit. He walked over to the sofa and sat down near her.

"I'm sorry," he said, "but you have no idea what my life's been like lately. It's really been the month from hell, preceded by the year from hell. And I can't go into a grocery store or convenience shop without seeing every detail of my hell spread all over the covers of those damned magazines."

Savannah softened as well. "I can't even imagine how hard that must be. Life is difficult enough without the whole world knowing your business."

Thomas set his drink on the glass-topped coffee table. "Knowing your business, having very strong opinions about your business, and making up business that you don't even have and printing it. It sucks."

Dirk seemed a bit less impressed than Savannah, as he looked around at the palatial house. "Yeah, I guess it's hard to get people to feel sorry for you when you live in a joint like this—especially when somebody just handed it over to you, scot-free."

Even as she winced, Savannah saw an anger rise in Thomas's eyes that set off her internal alarm system. Oh yes, Thomas Owen had a temper.

Mentally, she jotted that one down for future contemplation.

"There's more than one way to earn something," Thomas told Dirk. "You put up with a guy like Jason for five years—his obsessive training, his ridiculous diets, his 'roid rages, his fooling around, and his whole manic-depressive crap. And then you tell me whether you should walk away with nothing."

"You didn't exactly walk away, did you?" Dirk said tauntingly. "If those tabloids that you hate so much were right, he gave you your walking papers."

Thomas jumped up, his fists clenched at his sides. His face turned a deep shade of red. "What kind of cop believes everything he reads on the covers of tabloid magazines?"

"Not this one," Dirk replied. "I find that the texts on a victim's cell phone are a lot more valuable, evidentiary wise. And a helluva lot more entertaining, too."

Thomas's face went from red to an ugly purple. Savannah could literally see the veins in his forehead throbbing. If Dirk kept this up, the guy was going to have a stroke on the spot.

Dirk gave her a quick glance, and she realized that he had reached the end of his "bad cop" routine. It was time for her to take over as the "good cop."

"Now, Detective," she said to Dirk in her most condescending voice—the one he just loved, especially now that they were married, "Mr. Owen here has been through a really tough time, and you aren't making it any easier for him, saying insensitive, mean things like that."

"I'm not here to make things easier for Mr. Owen or anyone else, for that matter," Dirk said. "I'm here to find out what happened to Jason Tyrone."

Instantly, Thomas dropped the whole indignant routine. His angry expression disappeared, replaced by intense interest. "What do you mean, 'What happened to Jason?' The medical examiner said it was his heart, that he took too many drugs or something like that. She said it was an accident. It *was* an accident. . . . Wasn't it?"

"Do you think it was?" Savannah asked softly. "You lived with Jason; you probably knew him better than anyone. What do you think happened to him?"

Without warning, Thomas burst into tears. He covered his face with both hands and sobbed uncontrollably.

Savannah leaned over and placed her hand on his shoulder. She could feel his entire body trembling.

Neither she nor Dirk said anything as he continued to cry for what seemed like a very long time.

Finally, he began to speak—harsh, broken sentences between his sobs. "It was over . . . at least a year ago. But my mom . . . cancer last winter. Jason felt sorry for me. Put off telling me. In love with . . . someone else."

Savannah reached into her pocket and pulled out some clean tissues. She considered tissues a mandatory tool in her business. Almost as important as the Beretta strapped to her side.

She handed them to Thomas and said, "There, there. I know it must be just awful. But if you can collect yourself for a minute and tell us—was there anybody that Jason was on the outs with? Did he have enemies? To your knowledge, did anyone have anything against him?"

He lowered his hands from his face. His eyes were big with

alarm. "That's why you're here, isn't it? You think that because we just broke up, I might have done something to him."

"Now why would we think a thing like that?" Dirk said with a distinct tone of sarcasm in his voice. "To my knowledge, Jason didn't have a family. But did he have a will? Let's see now. . . ." He paused, pretending to be thinking hard. "If he prepared some sort of will during these past five years when you two were together, and he didn't have a family, I wonder who he would've left it all to."

Dirk leaned forward, his elbows on his knees, and locked eyes with Thomas. "Did you wonder if he'd leave it all to you? Or do you already know? Did he have time to change his will since the two of you broke up? He's been pretty busy with the movie and all. I bet he didn't get to it."

Thomas jumped to his feet and headed for the door. "I'm done talking to you," he said. "If you want to find out anything else about my life or Jason's, I suggest you pick up a magazine at the grocery store checkout line. Now get out of my home."

Dirk did as he was told, but Savannah lingered behind.

This was the time, after Dirk had grossly offended the interviewee, when Savannah's "good cop" act often worked best.

It was a routine they had perfected years ago, and most of the time it worked very well.

"Try not to let him get to you," she said. "Back in the police academy he skipped class the day they taught us how to deal with the public."

"No kidding. He's a real jerk."

"And you aren't the first to say so." She rested her hand on his shoulder. He didn't shrink away. In fact, he seemed to welcome the friendly touch.

As his tear-filled eyes looked into hers, Savannah tried to read what she could see there. Sadness, to be sure. Fear—definitely. And maybe a bit of guilt? She couldn't be certain.

"I don't know what to do," he said, his voice shaking. "They just called and told me that the funeral's tomorrow. His manager's setting the whole thing up. Just a private, little gathering for those closest to him."

He gulped. "Not that long ago, I would've been the chief mourner. Now I don't know if I'm even welcome at the service. Am I one of the closest to him?"

He began to cry again, and instinctively Savannah reached out her arms and hugged him. As he clung to her she could hear him say through his tears, "He was my life. My everything. And he's gone. Now I don't even know who I am."

Chapter 14

"One of these days," Savannah told Dirk as they drove over the stone bridge, leaving Owen's property, "you're gonna overdo that bad cop bit of yours and get us shot. Or maybe bludgeoned with a frozen leg of lamb or perforated with a fireplace poker."

He laughed. "Naw. That's what I've got you for, kiddo. I'm pretty sure that on our marriage certificate there's something about you hurling yourself between me and flying bullets."

"Really? Hmmm. I don't recall anything about bullets or hurling myself anywhere for any reason. Hurling you? Maybe."

"It was on the back. In the fine print."

"I'll have to borrow Tammy's Nancy Drew magnifying glass and read that itty-bitty print sometime and see what I agreed to."

"While you're at it, read the part about the experimental sex you agreed to try every Friday night."

She giggled. "Oh yeah. I can hardly wait to see you in a French maid's costume, finding creative new uses for a feather duster."

"That'll be the day."

"Yeah, the day I bleach my eyeballs and scour them with steel wool. If I were to see you in a short, black skirt and fishnet hose, I'd never recover."

"Don't fret. It ain't gonna happen. You'll be the one wearing the French maid's costume."

"And what are you gonna wear for me? I'm an enlightened woman, you know . . . comfortable with my own sexuality and all that liberated stuff. I think the man needs to perform, too."

He thought for a moment. "I could probably scare up a cowboy outfit and a Lone Ranger mask."

"Now you're talking."

As they neared the freeway, which would take them either north or south, he said, "What now? Whose tree needs shakin' next?"

"I think we should go back to the hotel. We didn't really talk much to the staff, except for when you got snippy with that one gal—the manager, I think it was—and plum near twisted her finger outta its socket."

"She shouldn't have stuck it in my face. Nobody gets to stick a body part in my mug without it gettin' broken or, at the very least, dislocated."

Savannah recalled the look of agony on the woman's face as Dirk had bent the pointing finger backward until everyone present heard an ominous crack. "Oh, well," she said. "Hopefully, she won't be on duty."

"She's on duty."

"Of course she is. Just my luck."

"And her finger's in a splint."

"It is?"

"Yeah."

"Oh, damn."

"Yeah."

They crossed the hotel's luxurious lobby, heading toward the reception desk. And there was the manager in question, still wearing her maroon blazer, white shirt, and baggy, black pencil skirt.

She was having a conversation with a pretty, young employee who was also wearing the standard uniform. The younger woman was far more attractive, but it had nothing to do with her youth or the fact that her skirt fit much better. It was because of the nasty scowl on the manager's face. And her grimace deepened the moment she spotted Dirk walking toward her.

"Uh-oh," Savannah said. "She remembers you. That's a problem you have with women; you're just so darned unforgettable."

He grumbled something under his breath, and Savannah was pretty sure she heard some rather distinctive curse words that her husband seldom used in her presence.

"What was that you were saying?" she asked.

"You don't wanna know. But I'll tell you one thing I do know—I didn't twist her finger backward bad enough for her to need that contraption she's got on it. That's for sure."

As they approached the reception desk, the manager grabbed a telephone and quickly punched in three numbers with her unbandaged hand.

Savannah whispered to Dirk, "Oh no. Dude, I think she's calling the cops on you. Should we run? Maybe take off for Mexico, hide in Tijuana for a few days?"

Dirk quickened his step and arrived at the desk just in time to hear her say, "Yes, dispatcher, I need you to send a patrol car to the Island View Hotel. My name is Linda Gerard and I'm the manager here." She paused, listening for a moment. Then she said, "The nature of my emergency? The rogue cop who attacked me the other night has just walked into my hotel again."

But Dirk had already pulled his own cell phone from his pocket and had called 911 himself. "Hi, Sally. Coulter here. The call you guys are getting on the other line—ignore it. The woman's a nut job. I'm here at the hotel and Savannah's with me. We'll take care of the situation." He listened, smiling. "What's that? Oh, thank you. I'll tell her. See you at the barbecue in a couple of weeks."

He hung up and turned to Savannah. "Sally says to tell you, 'Congratulations, and she hopes that we'll have a long, happy marriage and that you don't murder me.' "

Savannah chuckled. "That makes two of us."

Meanwhile, Manager Gerard stood, phone in hand, glaring at them with total loathing. But she seemed to realize she had lost round one of this match, so she hung up the phone.

She stuck her bandaged finger in Dirk's face, wagged it, and said, "You better be damned glad that I didn't sue the police department for what you did the other day. If the regional manager hadn't talked me out of it, I would've sued you for everything you've got."

"Oh?" Savannah turned to Dirk. "Everything you've got? Well, let's see . . . that's mostly an ancient Buick, a battered bomber jacket, and your collection of Harley Davidson memorabilia."

She turned back to the manager, who was still shaking her mummy-bound finger in Dirk's face. "How do you feel about shot glasses, ashtrays, and Christmas ornaments—all with the proud Harley Davidson logo on them? My guest room is full of his treasures. I'd consider it a personal favor if you'd sue him for all that junk and get it out of my house."

"And while you're at it," Dirk added, "you better get that finger out of my face, or you really might need that splint thing you've got on it."

"What do you two want anyway?" she asked, as she removed the offensive digit.

"We need a favor," Savannah said, batting her eyelashes.

Gerard gave them a nasty little smile. "Oh right, I'm going to do something nice for you—when hell freezes over."

Dirk gave her an equally ugly grin. "No problem. I'll go get a subpoena, and Satan will be wearing ice skates."

Gerard's eyes narrowed. "Get out of my hotel."

"Listen," Dirk said, "I'm in no mood for—"

"Get out! Now!"

Gathering their tattered dignity around them, Dirk and Savannah lifted their chins, straightened their backbones, turned on their heels, and walked across the lobby toward the door.

"We're just going to leave like this?" Savannah whispered.

"What else are we gonna do? You know I can't get a subpoena when, according to the coroner, no crime's even been committed."

Savannah glanced back at the manager, who looked obnoxiously pleased with herself. "We can still win this one, you know," she said.

"How?"

"Easy. We just hang around out front and wait."

"Wait for what?"

"Until she takes a break. Didn't you notice—that younger gal loved it when you were giving it to her boss. She doesn't like her."

"Can you blame her?"

"Exactly. That's why we just wait, bide our time for a little while. Sooner or later that grumpy old biddy's gonna have to go to the bathroom."

"And when she does—"

"Bada-bing bada-boom."

* * *

"How long do you figure the lovely Ms. Gerard's gonna be gone?" Savannah asked the young woman, whom they had learned was named Nancy.

"Forever. At least an hour and a half," Nancy told them. "She's supposed to only take a forty-five-minute break. But she's having an affair with one of the security guards, and they always hook up in room 327. Sometimes she takes two or three hours. He must be doing something right and for long enough."

For just a moment, it occurred to Savannah that she wouldn't want Nancy as an employee. She spilled the state secrets a bit too quickly and eagerly.

But at the moment, a degenerate gossiper was about the best friend she and Dirk could have.

Nancy leaned across the reception counter, her eyes aglow with curiosity. "What is it that you guys wanna know? I keep tabs on everything that goes on around here. I can probably help you."

"Were you on duty the night Jason Tyrone died?"

Instantly, Nancy's pretty face crumpled into a pout. "No. I got Jessica to take my shift for me, because I had a hot date. And I could just kick myself for it. I missed out on all the excitement!"

"Uh, yes, that is a crying shame," Savannah told her, feigning great sympathy. "But mostly, we were wondering if there's any security video of the lobby and hallways from that night."

Nancy brightened again. "Sure there is. And I know how to get it for you, too. I go into the office on my break sometimes and watch it. That's how I know about Ms. Gerard and Leonard, the security guy. You want me to show you?"

Dirk gave her one of his best smiles and a wink. "More than life itself, Nancy, my dear. Right now, it's all I'm living for."

Thirty minutes later, as Savannah, Dirk, and Nancy sat in the hotel office and stared at a grainy black-and-white security video,

Savannah was feeling far less celebratory than she had when they'd entered the room.

"That's it?" Dirk asked. "Jason and his chauffeur walked through the front door like regular people and went straight to his room?"

"Apparently so." Even the oh-so-helpful Nancy seemed a bit less perky than before.

Savannah sighed and turned away from the monitor and its boring images. "His chauffeur carries his bags upstairs for him, then leaves? And nobody else enters the room until Ryan and John arrive? Woo-hoo. We got this case wrapped up in a sparkly, silver package with a big, red bow."

Nancy stared at her for an awkwardly long time, then said, "You're kidding, right?"

"Yes, darlin'," Savannah replied, trying to keep any hint of condescension out of her voice. It wasn't easy. Usually she automatically defaulted to Condescending Tone whenever she found herself dealing with bimbos. "That was just a little sarcasm there—born of acute frustration. You know what I mean?"

Nancy nodded, but her eyes were frighteningly blank. "Yes, I think so. I get frustrated myself sometimes. I wouldn't really call it 'cute,' but . . ."

Savannah turned to Dirk. "Now that we've got our bunch of nothing, can we leave? Please? Pretty please with sugar on it?"

"Babe, we are go-o-one."

When Savannah and Dirk returned home, they were surprised to find Tammy alone in the house. She was sitting at the desk, glued to the computer—her usual, pre-Waycross pastime.

"What happened?" Savannah asked, as she peeled off her linen jacket and her weapon holster. "Did you two lovebirds have a fight?"

No sooner had the words left her mouth than Savannah reconsidered. It was ridiculous, almost unthinkable—the thought of her mellow brother, Waycross, and Miss California Sunlight herself actually having any kind of disagreement.

They were both the type of tender souls who went through life tripping over themselves in an attempt to harm neither man nor beast.

Unlike Savannah, who would never hurt a cat, a dog, a bunny rabbit, or even a seagull who was trying to snatch a hamburger out of her hand . . . but felt little or no guilt at all when she found it necessary to smack a human being half-silly. But only when she deemed it necessary, of course.

Tammy gazed at Savannah with open, guileless eyes. "What? Who? A fight? Us?"

"Never mind." Savannah sighed and rolled her eyes. "Whatever was I thinking?"

"Don't tell me you and Brother Waycross never have a tiff," Dirk said, as he walked in behind Savannah, dumped his bomber jacket on the sofa, and kicked off his sneakers.

Tammy shook her head. "Nope. Not one cross word. Not one difference of opinion. Not one misunderstanding. Never."

Savannah resisted the urge to gag on her own spit. As she watched Dirk meander into the kitchen, she lowered her voice and said, "You just wait until he leaves the toilet seat up or, worse yet, forgets to flush. You'll be ready to take him to the nearest dog pound and give him up for adoption."

It took only one second for Tammy to go from meek and mild to outraged and offended. "I would never do that. Not even to a real dog, let alone a wonderful person like Waycross."

Savannah walked over to the desk, placed her hands on Tammy's shoulders, and began a gentle massage. It was a gesture that usually remedied any unpleasant situation. "Of course you wouldn't, dear heart. It was a joke. A tasteless one, I admit. But please consider the source. I'm a newly married woman in that awkward period of adjustment. The time when—if it weren't for the fact that you're getting all the great sex you want for the first time in your life—you'd be running to the courthouse for divorce papers."

As Tammy melted beneath Savannah's expert hands, she glanced toward the kitchen.

They could both hear Dirk puttering around the kitchen—opening drawers, rattling silverware, and running the sink faucet.

"Is it really that bad?" Tammy asked.

"It's Dirk."

"Oh, right. Gotcha."

A moment later, he stuck his head into the living room and said, "Hey, Van, I'm making me a bologna sandwich. You want one?"

"I told you when I bought that junk and stuck it in the refrigerator that you'd be the only one eating it. Believe me, I had way more than my share of bologna when I was growing up."

"Then how about ham and cheese?" he asked, undeterred.

Their eyes met, and for a moment, she could see the love he had for her. This simple, unsophisticated man absolutely adored her. She wasn't sure why. But she had the sneaking suspicion that it had less to do with her own sterling character than with his deep capacity for unconditional love.

She didn't know what she had ever done to deserve his adoration. But at simple, everyday moments like this, she found she was infinitely grateful for it.

"I would love a ham and cheese sandwich," she told him. "With a smear or two of Dijon mustard, if you don't mind."

He smiled. "You got it. One ham and cheese with mustard for

my beautiful bride. And what can I get for you, kiddo?" he asked Tammy.

"Since you offered . . . that cut-up mango in the little glass jar," Tammy told him.

When he disappeared back into the kitchen, Tammy looked up at Savannah. Savannah shrugged and said, "Great sex, any time of the day or night, and room service. Pretty good, huh?"

"I'll say. Might even be worth having to lower the toilet seat yourself once in a while."

Savannah chuckled dryly. "Oh, the naïveté of youth. 'Once in a while,' she says, as though it were a rare occurrence."

Since Tammy appeared to be recovered from the whole dog pound conversation, Savannah ended the massage, pulled up a chair, and sat down beside her assistant.

"While he's slinging hash in the kitchen, maybe you and I can get some work done in here," she said.

Tammy smiled and lifted one eyebrow. "We? We are going to get some work done on the computer? That would be you, as well as me?"

"All right, all right. You're going to work, and I'm going to watch. Is that better?"

"No, but it's more accurate." She placed her hands on the keyboard and focused on the monitor. "Okay, let's have it. What do you need to know?"

"The name of the livery company that transported Jason to the premiere. And also the name of the chauffeur who drove the limo."

"No problem."

"No problem? Really?"

Tammy's fingers were already flying over the keyboard, and images were popping up on the screen.

"I just watched some really good footage of Jason arriving at the premiere," she said. "I think I can get the plate number of the limo."

A few seconds later, there it was—the video of the star's arrival. And just as Tammy had predicted, the image was sharp enough that they both could clearly see the letters and numbers on the license plate.

Tammy jotted them down on a bit of notepaper.

"And now," she said, "all we have to do is run them through the DMV records."

"California's DMV records? The official state records?"

But the question was moot, because Tammy had already hacked into the government files and was entering the license number.

"How did you do that?" Savannah asked, more than a little surprised and a bit indignant.

Tammy snickered. "I shouldn't reveal my sources."

"Spit it out, kid, or I'll slap you neckid and hide your clothes."

"Oh, you and your quaint Southern phrases. Okay, not because you threatened me, but since you're my boss, I'll tell you. At the last SCPD barbecue, Dirk introduced me to a nice lady who works in the records department at the station house. She slipped me her card and told me that if I ever wanted to know how to do it—hack the system, that is—she'd tell me how. And she did."

"Well now, wasn't that just mighty nice of her?"

"It was. And in exchange, I taught her how to make homemade bath soap and organic, lavender-scented shampoo."

Savannah nodded. "Okay, as long as you're reciprocating by sharing your wealth of knowledge—and don't get caught by any authorities—I reckon you're good to go."

"And see here, it's already paying off." She pointed to the screen. "The limousine is owned by a company called Diamond Transportation Services. It's located in the valley, the town of Rosado."

With only a few clicks, Tammy brought up an image of a simple, modest house, draped with bougainvillea, on a tree-lined street. "That's it," she said. "Right there. That house."

"But it's a . . . a house," Savannah said. "That's the whole business, right there?"

Tammy produced an overhead, bird's-eye view of the property. "They have an extralarge garage," she observed. "But even at that, it looks like there would be room for only one limousine, at most."

"Why would Jason Tyrone use a small, obscure company like that?"

"That might be something you need to check out," Tammy suggested. She did a bit more searching and found what she was looking for. "The company owner's name is Leland Porter."

At that moment Dirk stuck his head back into the living room. "Okay, girls. Your lunch awaits. Come to the table before it gets cold." His announcement done, he ducked back inside.

"Ham and cheese sandwiches get cold?" Tammy asked. "And my mango was in the refrigerator. How much colder can it get?"

"I don't know," Savannah replied. "But I've learned one thing about Dirk—never get between him and his food bowl. You just might get bit."

"You go ahead and have lunch with your husband," Tammy told her. "I'm curious about this owner of Diamond Transportation Services. While you're eating your ham and cheese sandwich I'm gonna find out how tall he is, if he's ever been convicted of a heinous crime, and if he likes Dijon mustard on his ham and cheese."

Savannah gave her friend a playful, loving smile. "What would I ever do without you, golden girl?"

Tammy laughed. "I don't know what you would do without me. Or what I would do without you. Let's don't ever find out."

Savannah stood, leaned over, and kissed her on the top of her glossy blonde hair. "I absolutely agree. Let's never find out."

Chapter 15

The San Fernando Valley was home to many charming, family-oriented towns with well-maintained houses, carefully groomed yards, and bevies of children frolicking in public playgrounds.

The town of Rosado wasn't one of those.

It wasn't uncommon, when watching the evening news, to see stories of drive-by shootings, multiple murders, and drug and prostitution sweeps done by the cops in the vain attempt to improve its troubled neighborhoods.

On the surface, it didn't look all that sinister. The tree-lined streets with their single-family houses seemed peaceful enough—in the daytime. And though the homes had been there a while, they had a certain Old World, Spanish charm. Much like Savannah's house.

With one exception.

Savannah's house didn't have wrought-iron bars across the windows and doors.

However decorative those bars might be, with their graceful, swirling scrollwork, they made a statement. The residents of Rosado lived in fear. Some with only minor and occasional anxieties. Others in constant terror. But the wrought iron said it all. No one fastened metal bars across their doors and windows just to enhance their décor.

"Our buddy, the limo dude, ain't exactly raking in the dough," Dirk said, "if he lives in a place like this."

"We're spoiled," Savannah told him, "living where we do, there on the ocean. San Carmelita is nice."

"That's true. It is. I forget how nice until I come here to the valley. All the smog and the heat and the traffic and the noise."

"I don't blame the folks who live here for piling into their cars and racing to the beach every weekend."

"I do," Dirk grumbled. "I wish they'd keep their asses at home, where they belong."

"That's what I love about you, darlin'—your love for humanity."

"I love humanity. But people . . . people suck."

Uplifted by that sage bit of enlightened philosophy, Savannah turned her attention back to the business at hand. She glanced at the piece of paper in her lap and the address that Tammy had scribbled on it.

"We're just about there," she told him. "It should be in the next block on the right-hand side."

And sure enough, there it was. The simple little cottage Tammy had shown her on the computer screen. She recognized the curtain of red bougainvillea nearly obscuring the right side of the house.

Savannah had two lovely bougainvillea plants herself, one on each side of her front door. And even though she was very proud of them—and had even given them names, Bogey and Ilsa—she had to admit these were much larger and more lush than hers.

Down the driveway of broken cement at the back of the property sat the oversized garage she had seen from the satellite image. One of the two doors was open, and she could see the rear end of a Cadillac limousine.

She was pretty sure it was the one that had transported Jason Tyrone to the movie premiere on the day of his death.

Dirk parked the Buick at the curb. They both got out and started to walk up to the front door. But at that moment, Savannah saw a figure coming out of the garage.

It was the same man who had chauffeured Jason on the night of the show—Leland Porter, the proud owner of Diamond Transportation Services.

He looked quite different without his formal livery. Instead of the elegant black uniform, he wore a dingy, formerly white tee-shirt and jeans with ripped knees. And although it hadn't been so obvious in his suit, his casual attire revealed a body that was nearly as muscular as the ones in the movie they had seen the other night.

In his hand he carried a portable vacuum cleaner and several attachments. When he spotted Savannah and Dirk, he set the vacuum on the driveway, brushed his palms off on the seat of his jeans, and walked over to them.

"Can I help you?" he asked with a friendly but curious tone.

They met him in the middle of the driveway.

Dirk extended his badge with his left hand and held out his right for a handshake. "I'm Detective Sergeant Dirk Coulter with the San Carmelita Police Department."

"And I'm Savannah Reid," she said, "also from San Carmelita."

Leland shook Savannah's hand vigorously, then Dirk's. "You two are a long way from home."

"A half-hour, give or take," Savannah added. "Three hours if there's a nasty accident and everybody on the road wants to stop and gawk at it."

"I hear ya," Leland said with a chuckle. "I can't tell you how many times I've been stuck in traffic for an hour, all because some blonde in a pair of short-shorts is changing a tire."

Savannah and Dirk laughed along with him. But not for long.

"We need to talk to you about Jason Tyrone," Dirk said abruptly. "I'm sure you heard what happened to him after you left him at the Island View Hotel."

Leland nodded. "I heard he died in the middle of the night. Something about a heart attack and some drugs he was taking? I think that's what they said on the eleven o'clock news last evening."

Dirk nodded. "We were just at the hotel, looking at their security video. And as it turns out, you were the last one to see him alive."

Leland looked surprised. "Really? Wow! That's creepy. After I escorted him to his room, he told me that some friends of his were going to drop by very soon. So I figured he had somebody with him when he, well, you know . . ."

"No," Savannah said. "From what we know now, we think he was alone when he passed. By the time his friends had arrived he was already gone."

Leland shook his head sadly. "Man, that's too bad. Nobody should be all alone when they check out."

There was a long moment of silence, as though they were honoring the dead. Then he added, "It's kind of ironic, when you think about it. Different magazines and newspapers had listed him as one of the sexiest men alive. There must've been ten million people—especially women—who would've been happy to hold his hand and comfort him until he was gone."

"Yes, it is sad," Savannah said. "But I reckon when it comes to the business of passing over to the other side, everybody's pretty much on their own."

The two men nodded in agreement, and all three stared down at the broken cement for a few seconds—again showing respect for the recently departed.

With her eyes averted, Savannah found herself looking at the front of Leland's tee-shirt. The old fabric was thin, almost threadbare in places, and she couldn't help but notice that he seemed to be wearing bandages on both of his nipples.

She did a quick mental scan of her memory banks, trying to think of any type of injury or medical condition that would warrant a man having to bandage his breasts.

She couldn't help being curious. But it wasn't the sort of thing you asked about. So she filed the information away for future consideration.

But not quite soon enough.

He had noticed her looking. She could see it in his eyes—the embarrassment, the humiliation. And she felt guilty for gawking.

After a few more moments of awkward silence, Leland said, "If you don't mind me asking, why are the cops investigating his passing? From what they said on the news last night, I gathered it was an accidental overdose or something like that. One of the reporters even said it might've had something to do with him taking steroids—like doping, so that he could bulk up."

"There's no proof of that," Savannah said. She could hear the indignation in her own voice. It was already beginning, the rumors, the sullying of Jason Tyrone's reputation.

So much for not speaking ill of the dead.

Leland seemed to realize that he had offended her. He quickly added, "Right. The reporter even said that it was just speculation on her part, that they don't know for sure."

Savannah was eager to change the subject from Jason's chosen medications. "How did he seem to you throughout the evening?" she asked. "Anything unusual about his mood, or anything he said or did?"

Leland thought it over for a moment. "Not really. He might've seemed a little nervous. Maybe a bit jumpy. But I figured it was just because of the premiere. Jason didn't like that sort of thing.

He was a big star and all that stuff, but he didn't really enjoy having the spotlight on him. He was always a little nervous at those sorts of events."

"Sounds like you knew him pretty well," Savannah observed.

"Had you driven him before?" Dirk wanted to know.

Leland smiled, and it was a sad, poignant smile. "Oh, I've known Jason for years. We were friends back when he first started bodybuilding. In fact, my claim to fame is that I was the one who first told him he should give it a whirl."

"Really?" Savannah was impressed.

"Yeah. He told everybody that if it hadn't been for me, he never would've even tried it. But he was a big kid with way too much energy. I was into it myself, and I thought it might do him good."

He paused and for a long, awkward moment, Savannah wondered if he was thinking the same thing she was. Maybe the thought had crossed his mind that if he hadn't suggested that particular path to Jason, his friend might still be alive.

"Now I feel guilty," Leland admitted, instantly confirming her suspicions. "It's almost like I killed him myself by even suggesting that he get into this mess."

"This mess?" Dirk asked.

Leland shrugged his massive shoulders. "I'm sure it's a positive thing for most builders. If you do it right, you wind up strong and healthy. Plus there's the psychological boost it gives you— being your own personal best."

A small, shy smile crossed his face. "And then you've got the competitions. Nothing's more fun than winning one of those big trophies with your name on it and sticking it on your mantel-piece."

"Have you won quite a few of those?" Savannah asked.

"A couple of the major ones. But that was a long time ago." He waved a hand in the direction of the garage and the limousine. "Now I mostly drive crazy teenagers to proms and stuff like that."

"You don't have a lot of celebrities on your client list?" Dirk asked.

"Naw. Just Jason. And that was only because he knew me from the old days, and he knew that I'm hurtin' for cash. With the economy in the tank, not as many people pay for limousine service." He paused, and a look of deep sadness crossed his face. "Jason was a really good friend to me. I'm sure going to miss him."

"I'm really sorry for your loss," Savannah said. "I hate to ask what might be a painful question but can you tell me—what was the last thing he said to you, when you left him there at the hotel?"

"I don't mind you asking, if you need to. I took him and his suitcases up to his suite. I set them down in his bedroom and asked him if he wanted me to stay for a while. Sometimes, when he had a suite like that, I'd hang out, maybe even spend the night on the sofa. A star like Jason has a lot of women after him. Guys, too, for that matter. The hotels do a pretty good job of keeping them away from the celebrity guests. But fans get pretty creative and insistent, too, pounding on the door at all hours. It helps to have somebody who can tell them to get lost."

Savannah considered his height and breadth. "And I'll bet you did that very well."

He shrugged. "It's not that hard. Most fans scare pretty easily."

"But you didn't stay that night, right?" Dirk asked.

"Right. He said a couple of his friends were going to be showing up any minute, and they were FBI agents. So he didn't need any extra security."

"And that's when you left?" Savannah said.

"Yes, I thought he'd be all right. He seemed fine." Leland's entire body seemed to sag with the sadness of the memory. "Believe me, you never, never would've looked at him and thought, 'He only has a matter of minutes to live.' "

"What do you think killed him?" Dirk asked.

Leland took a long time answering, and when he did, his voice was shaking. "I think that years ago a well-meaning friend turned Jason on to bodybuilding. And in the end, the sport killed him. That's what I believe happened. And I can tell you, thinking about that is going to keep me awake at night."

No sooner had Savannah and Dirk left Leland and gotten back into the Buick when Savannah's cell phone rang.

"It's Tammy," she said, looking at the caller ID. "Wonder what she's got."

"What makes you think she's got anything?"

"Tammy has her faults. But calling people to chat endlessly about nothing—that's not one of them."

"True. She waits until she's face-to-face with you to bore you to death."

"Be nice."

"I'm always nice."

"There's room for improvement."

Savannah answered the phone. "Hi, puddin' cat. What's shakin'?"

"Dr. Liu called," was the cheerful response.

"Oh, yeah? What did she want?"

"To tell you that the funeral's tomorrow at Forest Lawn."

"Which one?"

"The one in Glendale where so many celebrities are buried. Sorta fitting, huh? It's going to be at two in the afternoon. Are you going?"

"Absolutely. And so are you and Waycross."

"Really?"

Savannah could tell that Tammy was trying to stay calm, collected, and respectful. It simply wasn't couth to dance in your bloomers at the thought of going to someone's, anyone's, funeral.

"Yes," Savannah told her. "We need your young eyes there to scope out the crowd."

"To see who's taking it hard . . . who isn't taking it hard enough? To see who appears to be sincerely grieving and who's just putting on a show to draw attention to themselves?"

"Exactly. Just like at your average Southern funeral, I'm sure that each of those groups will be represented among the crowd."

"I have to go buy a black dress."

Savannah chuckled. "This is California. I'm pretty sure that anything even moderately somber will do just fine."

"Just no tropical or animal prints?"

"A quiet leopard would probably be okay."

"And there's something else I want to tell you about. Something I uncovered when I was researching."

"Tell me all about it, kiddie-o."

"Okay." Tammy drew a deep breath. Such a big one that Savannah knew she was in for a long-winded tale and a half. "Here goes . . ."

"I told you she was a bag of hot air," Dirk said when Savannah finally hung up the phone.

"You said she was an airhead."

"And the discernible difference would be . . . ?"

"Before you switch all the way into Bash the Bimbo Mode, you should hear about the article she found online about Jason."

He drove the Buick south, heading for the Ventura Freeway. "Okay, lay it on me. What did she find that was so interesting?"

"It was an article on one of the bodybuilding sites about Jason and a problem he and some others were having. It's what Ryan was telling us about in the hotel, where they obsess about getting bigger. Tammy says it's a real disorder, sort of like anorexia."

Dirk snorted. "You can say what you want about Jason Tyrone, but he sure didn't look like he starved himself to death."

"I didn't say it was exactly like anorexia, just similar because they're both body dysmorphic disorders."

"What's that?" he asked.

"Well, I'm no expert. But according to what Tammy just told me, the people who have these disorders don't see their bodies the way they really are."

"Oh, yeah, I saw one of those gals on TV one time. She was talking about how fat she was, and she was nothing but skin and bones. She was regular height, but she weighed something like eighty pounds."

Savannah nodded. "That's right. And apparently, if you have this bigorexia disorder, you worry that you're a wimp or whatever. No matter how big and muscular these guys are, they worry about being too small. They think their muscles are underdeveloped and obsess about working out to make them bigger."

"Even guys who look like Jason Tyrone?"

"Especially guys who look like Jason. The rest of the world thinks they're a hunk, but they think they're a shrimp."

"That's messed up."

"You have no idea. Apparently, it takes over their whole lives. They neglect their friends and families so that they can work out constantly. They obsess about their diet and eat way more protein than they should. And they take gobs of supplements—without any kind of doctors' advice. And then, of course, you've got the steroids, diuretics, the human growth hormone. They abuse stuff like that constantly and put their health at risk, just like Ryan said."

"Are you telling me that this is a serious problem?"

"Apparently it's a big deal now. Tammy said that even high school boys are developing this disorder. They think that a man can't be masculine unless he's all muscle-bound."

Dirk shook his head. "That's like all the girls who think they have to be stick thin to be pretty. It's a shame."

Ahead they could see the signs, indicating the entrances to the Ventura Freeway.

Dirk said, "Which is it going to be—north or south?"

Savannah knew what he meant. They could head north, go home, and get back to their normal lives. She could paint the downstairs half bath, launder her dusty curtains, and maybe even find the time to go shopping for some sort of futon for the guest room. And, of course, she could give Dirk his very first honey-do list. Enforcing it would, no doubt, prove to be a challenge. But it was never too early to begin training one's new husband.

Or they could take the freeway south to the 405, and then jog over to Beverly Hills. On a second piece of paper lying on her lap was Jason Tyrone's address.

"Are we really going to take this all the way?" Dirk asked her.

"With nothing but an 'accidental death' ruling from the coroner, it seems kind of silly. We don't have one shred of evidence that this was a murder."

"Very true," Dirk said. "Nobody would blame us if we just dropped the whole kit and caboodle right now."

"Exactly."

The entrance ramps were coming up. One with a big "S" for south, and the next with its "N" indicating north—home, home improvement, and impressing the new relatives.

"The smart thing would be to close the case and let them just bury old Jason in peace tomorrow."

Savannah held her breath, waiting to see which he would choose.

A moment later, the Buick was taking the tight ramp a bit too fast. So fast, in fact, that the tires squealed a bit.

And then they were headed south. Toward Beverly Hills. Toward Jason Tyrone's home.

Savannah smiled and said, "But then, we've been accused of many things over the years—and being smart ain't one of them."

Chapter 16

As Dirk watched Savannah pick the lock of Jason Tyrone's Greek revival mansion on a hilltop in Beverly Hills, he was speaking on his cell phone to Tammy. "I don't suppose an old place like this has an alarm system," he said. "But could you find out? The last thing we need is to alert the whole neighborhood the moment we get in the door."

"How are you getting in without a key?" Tammy asked.

He sniffed. "I have Savannah with me, and you would ask a question like that?"

"Oh, right. Duh."

"She's going to have it open in about five seconds, so if you could check on that alarm system for me . . ."

"Or if you could have given me more than a five-second warning, I might have been able to help you. You know, Dirko, I can perform the impossible on demand. But it's nice if I can have two minutes or so."

"Never mind," he said, as he followed Savannah through the newly opened door and into the foyer of the old plantation-style house. He looked around, searching the walls with their cabbage rose–print paper.

"There's no alarm box," Savannah told him. "I would've seen it through the beveled glass in the front door. And I wouldn't have picked the lock if there'd been one."

She walked over to him, took the phone out of his hand, and said into it, "We've got it, babycakes. Sorry to have bothered you."

"It was no trouble," came Tammy's polite reply. "But give Dirk a big, nasty raspberry for me, when you get a chance."

"You've got it, kid." Savannah turned off the phone, handed it back to Dirk, stuck her tongue out at him, and gave him a grotesque, wet, noisy raspberry—as requested.

"That's from Tammy," she said.

He grimaced. "I sorta figured. One of these days, if she becomes my sister-in-law, she's going to have to start showing me some respect."

"Why? I'm your wife and I don't show you respect."

"True."

The playful grin she gave him belied her words. That was one of the things she liked best about Dirk—it was almost impossible to really, deeply insult him. He knew she would die for him in an instant; it had been that way for years, even back when she was just his partner on the force. So a bit of mountain oyster breaking once in a while could be overlooked.

"What do you reckon we're going to find here?" she asked him.

"You know the drill. We never know what we're looking for until we find it."

As they walked across the black and white checked floor of the foyer, Savannah looked up at the gracefully curved staircase with its elegant wrought-iron and wooden railings, and she had to resist the urge to hum "Dixie."

"All that's missing," she said, "is a Southern belle in a hooped skirt floating down the stairs."

"I know what you mean," he replied. "The theme from *Gone with the Wind* keeps running through my head."

They walked into the parlor, which was decorated with ex-quisite, Victorian-era antiques. A matched pair of diamond-tucked fainting couches in claret velvet were drawn up to a massive fireplace with a carved mantel. And everywhere Savan-nah looked she saw luxurious fabrics that invited a touch. A fringed, brocaded scarf was spread over an old piano. Drapes of thick, lush velvet hung from the windows.

And on the walls hung mirrors, scenic paintings, and portraits, all in gilded frames.

"It might be a little bit gaudy in some ways," Savannah admit-ted, "but it's still an awesome place. It reminds me of that ante-bellum mansion just outside of my hometown. You were there. Remember Judge Patterson's old house?"

"How could I forget? That was the spookiest place I've ever been. This one isn't so dark or creepy, but then, nobody got mur-dered here."

"That we know of."

"Yes, that we know of," he said. "But does this look to you like a house that a guy like Jason would live in?"

"That wouldn't be my first guess," she replied. "But when it comes to people, you just never know. Maybe he was an Elvis fan, like you, and this place reminded him of Graceland."

Dirk nodded thoughtfully. "Yeah, that would work for me."

"Then if someday one of those lottery tickets you're always buying pays off big, are you gonna buy me a place like this?"

He slipped his arm around her waist and gave her a big squeeze. "If that's what you want, babe, that's what you'll get. We'll name it Graceland West."

"And Granny will come visit us, and we'll never be able to get rid of her."

"That's fine with me. I never get enough of your grandma." He paused for a moment and gave her a nervous smile. "I hope you feel the same way about my family, once you get to know them."

"If they're even the least bit like you, darlin', I'm gonna be crazy about 'em."

"Is that true?"

"Why, of course it is, babycakes. Leastwise, till I change my mind."

"That's reassuring. . . . I think."

As they meandered through the mansion, they grew increasingly frustrated, failing to find anything they would classify as significant.

The refrigerator was filled with all sorts of liquid concoctions. Most of the labels bore the words "super" and "energy" and the omnipresent "power."

Looking over the bottles and jars, Savannah shook her head and said, "You couldn't make a decent meal out of the ingredients in this icebox. Human beings weren't meant to live on liquefied lettuce."

"Except Tammy," Dirk added.

"Yes, except for our Tammy, who could run a marathon and light up a lighthouse with the energy she gets out of one measly carrot."

They found not one, but three separate workout rooms brimming with heavy steel contraptions that Savannah didn't recognize. They looked like medieval torture devices.

"Boy, I wish I had some of this stuff at home," Dirk said in a tone usually used by little boys who were coveting their best friend's train set. "I could put it in the garage and—"

"And I could hang the laundry on it, as soon as I took it out of the dryer," she interjected gleefully. "No more wrinkles!"

"That's almost blasphemous. You don't know what he's got here. This is about a zillion dollars worth of the highest-tech bodybuilding equipment in the world."

Savannah gave the world's best-equipped private gym a dismissive wave of her hand as she walked out of the room. "Any guy who spends more money on a stationary bike than a private limousine that can actually take him somewhere—well, that guy's two pups short of a litter."

"I didn't see you pooh-poohing the results when you were gawking at him up there on the screen."

"That's when I thought it was all natural. Now that I'm learning all he had to do to get it, I'm plum disillusioned."

They proceeded on to the master bedroom, where they found only one thing that was ever-so-slightly interesting.

"Look at this," Savannah said, pointing to a framed picture on the nightstand. It was a glamour head shot of Alanna Cleary. It had been signed in the lower right-hand corner, "Love always, 'Lanna."

Instinctively, Savannah pulled out the top drawer of the nightstand and looked inside. There it was—a similar photograph of Thomas Owen. And like Alanna's, it was signed, "Love always, Tom."

"Never believe what you read scribbled on a picture," Savannah told Dirk, showing him Thomas's photo. "One day you think your love's gonna last forever, and the next day you're facedown in a drawer, staring at a TV remote control and some empty condom wrappers."

"Life sucks."

"For some more than others."

Savannah closed the drawer. As she walked around the room, she couldn't help noticing how many mirrors there were. The front of the armoire, the wall over the dresser, the back of some bookcases, a standing cheval mirror, and several tabletops—all had mirrors. And on the underside of the canopy suspended over the bed were bronzed mirror tiles.

It occurred to her that, if you were making love in Jason's bed, you could not only watch and critique your own performance, but the bronzed mirrors would give your image a nice tan as well.

She said, "Tammy mentioned that part of this disorder is an obsession with constantly looking at yourself in mirrors."

"Hey, the jury's already come back with the verdict on Jason having that bigorexia thing. But that's not what we're trying to find here."

Savannah was standing in front of the closet, which held only the most mundane contents—the simple evidence of a man leading a surprisingly simple life.

Except for a deadly disorder.

"That's true," she said. "We're looking for evidence that might indicate he was murdered. And we aren't finding it."

She turned back to Dirk. She could see her own frustration reflected in his eyes. "This is just so weird," she told him. "Finding out that somebody died accidentally rather than as a result of foul play—that's good news, right?"

"Yeah. You'd think so anyway."

"So why does all this good news make me feel sick to my stomach?"

"Me too."

"Oh, crap! I forgot all about the futon!" Savannah said that night as she, Dirk, and the kitties cuddled in bed.

"The what?" he asked. He rolled away from her, as the romantic mood he had been trying to kindle dissipated.

"The futon. You know, the fold-out bed thing-a-ma-doodle for the guest room."

"What guest room? You mean my man cave?"

Her annoyance meter ticked up a few notches. She wasn't in the mood for any static tonight—especially when it had to do with making his parents comfortable during their weeklong stay.

"Just FYI," she said, "for the time that your folks are here, you don't have a man cave."

He rose up onto one elbow, and she could feel him staring at her in the darkness. "But that's my room, my sanctuary. That's where I get away from it all."

"And by 'all' you mean *me*."

It took him so long to answer that she knew she'd scored several points with that one.

But Dirk was as good at offense as defense. "You told me that you like it when I watch my boxing in my cave and let you watch your chick flicks in the living room."

He had her there. If she were truthful, she would admit that the man cave benefited her as much as it did him. If she had to be totally honest, she would admit that, as a person who had lived alone for years, she greatly enjoyed those precious moments of solitude.

But honesty was sometimes overrated in the middle of a marital spat.

"I know you enjoy watching your sports alone," she said, with just the right touch of whine in her voice. "And being an independent woman, I don't take it personally when my husband expresses a need to be alone once in a while."

He lay back down and cleared his throat.

She knew the old throat-clearing trick. He used it when he was trying to think of a good reply and needed to buy some time. Finally, he said, "I appreciate that, Van. I hear other guys complaining that their wives demand their attention all the time. I'm glad you're not like that."

She could hear a note of apology in his words, and she felt a little bit ashamed of herself. She reached over and trailed her hand down his arm. "Thank you, sugar. You're the best husband on God's green earth," she said. "And I gotta tell you, if I had a woman cave, we'd use that instead when your folks are here."

"It's okay. I understand. I just hope they don't mind sleeping in a room that's decorated with Harley stuff."

Savannah groaned inwardly, sensing that their momentary peace was about to be shattered all over again. "No, darlin'," she said. "It ain't the two of them who's gonna be sleeping in there. It's you and me."

"What?"

This time he sat straight up. The movement was so abrupt and violent that one of the cats bounded out of bed and ran from the room.

"You heard me, sweet cheeks," she said in her softest, least confrontational, good ol' girl voice. "You and I will sleep in there, and they'll be in here."

"But this is *our* bedroom! It's like, sacred or something."

Savannah resisted the urge to tell him that, until a few weeks ago, this had been *her* bedroom. And she certainly hadn't kicked up this much of a fuss when she needed to share it with him.

"Dirk, listen to me. . . . They'll be our guests. And the rules of Southern hospitality are clear on this point. You give guests—especially out-of-state guests who've driven the length of the West Coast to come see you—the best bed in the house. And that's this one."

"But my back! I just now got used to this bed change. If I have to adjust to another one this soon I'll . . . I'll . . ."

"You won't die, you little hothouse orchid you."

"What does that mean?"

"What does *what* mean?"

"That hothouse orchid thing you call me sometimes. What do you mean by that?"

Savannah felt like the frayed elastic in her favorite pair of panties was just about to snap.

"It means," she said, "stop acting like such a tender buttercup and show me some of that Navy Seal, manly man stuff you claim to have."

"I never claimed to be a Navy Seal."

"No, but you're always telling me that you're pretty sure you could pass their training regimen. And you make me watch those stupid videos of them running on the beach, carrying that big log over their heads, crawling through the mud, and—"

"Stupid?! The Navy Seals aren't stupid! Why, they're the greatest fighting machines in the whole wide—"

"I didn't say the Seals are stupid. They're amazing, absolutely wonderful! But after watching all those videos of them with you a hundred times, I've practically memorized them, and—"

"And now if I want to watch one of those great videos, maybe with my dad and do a little father-son bonding, we won't even have a proper man cave to do it in!"

Savannah lay there on her back, staring up at the ceiling, doing the arithmetic in her head. Her parents-in-law were going to leave the Seattle area early tomorrow morning. And according to the latest message that Dirk's dad, Richard, had left on their machine, they estimated they would arrive at their hotel in San Francisco tomorrow afternoon.

They intended to squeeze in a trip to Alcatraz before having a wonderful seafood dinner on Fisherman's Wharf. The next morning they would get up early and, taking the scenic Pacific Coast Highway, arrive in San Carmelita about eight hours later.

Did that give her enough time to commit husband-cide and thoroughly dispose of the body?

That last part was most important, because if Dirk ever turned up dead in their county, his body would be taken to Dr. Liu's morgue.

And since she had known him and Savannah so long and so

well, the coroner would instantly deduce—without even an autopsy or any investigation—that Savannah was the culprit.

Of course, Dr. Liu could be counted on to testify at her trial. She could probably convince the jury single-handedly that Savannah had been driven to utter insanity by Dirk's eccentricities and was in no way responsible for her actions.

But there was one fatal flaw in Savannah's master plan.

Dirk's dad was a retired cop.

And if he'd been half as good at his job as his son was at his, he'd nail her for sure.

Putting her evil plans aside—at least for the moment—Savannah rolled over toward her husband and slipped her arm around his waist. "It'll be okay, sugar," she whispered into the darkness. "We'll get the most comfortable futon we can find. And I promise, I'll do my best to keep you happy on it. Let's just say, we'll make sure it's firm." She giggled. "And I'm not even talking about the mattress."

She waited for his lusty response. Very early in their married life, she had learned that a simple reference to tomfoolery would lift his mood several notches instantly.

But when no response was forthcoming, she started to worry a little. Maybe he was madder than she'd thought.

"Dirk? Honey? Did you hear me?"

Finally, he responded. With a wall-shaking snore.

Chapter 17

As Savannah sat next to Dirk in one of the wooden pews of the Wee Kirk o' the Heather, with Ryan and John to her left and Tammy and Waycross in the row behind her, she couldn't help feeling a little guilty for several reasons.

First, she felt uneasy about the fact that she and her entourage had been allowed to attend the small, private funeral when thousands of others had been turned away.

The tiny chapel—one of three lovely churches located inside the famous cemetery Forest Lawn—held less than a hundred visitors at a time. So she had been surprised when Ryan had told her that Jason's manager had invited not only him and John, but the rest of Savannah's Moonlight Magnolia Detective Agency as well.

"He appreciates the work you've all done on Jason's behalf," Ryan had said. "And he wants you at the service, if you can make it."

If they could make it?

If they could attend an event in a venue as wonderful as this charming and famous little chapel? Of course they could. She would've been there with bells on, if bells were appropriate funeral attire.

Instead Savannah wore a somber black dress, and Dirk had dusted off his only suit, which was navy. And although they had discussed acceptable animal prints, Tammy had opted for an egg-plant sheath. Waycross had borrowed Dirk's old sports coat.

And now she sat here with her team, feeling guilty, because she couldn't keep her mind on what the minister up front was saying. Her mind was even straying from the deceased, who lay in the closed coffin at the front of the church.

She couldn't help thinking about this building and its luminous history.

Inside these stone walls, beneath the dark, wooden ceiling with its heavy, arched beams, so many beloved celebrities had gathered to memorialize and celebrate each other.

Ronald Reagan had married Jane Wyman here, and Regis Philbin had taken Joy to be his wife only a few feet away from where Savannah was sitting. She couldn't resist the thought that Clark Gable or Carol Lombard may have sat right here in this pew when they had attended Jean Harlow's funeral. And what a unique experience it must have been when Chico Marx's rabbi had delivered his eulogy here in this reproduction of a lovely, old Scottish church.

And outside the chapel, interred among a quarter of a million lesser-known people, were the earthly remains of such beloved celebrities as James Stewart, Elizabeth Taylor, Walt Disney, Errol Flynn, Michael Jackson, Sam Cooke, Red Skelton, Louis L'Amour, and L. Frank Baum, as well as George Burns and Gracie Allen.

It was nearly impossible for her to keep her mind trained on the business at hand when surrounded by so much history.

But she forced herself to do so. Anything less would have been disrespectful to Jason Tyrone.

And although she knew it was true, she couldn't imagine that the coffin in the front of the room contained that beautiful, vibrant human being. Once again, she was reminded of the often-used phrase "earthly remains."

Yes, those were merely the remains in that coffin. But Jason Tyrone deserved her respectful attention at his memorial service.

So she banished the ghosts of celebrities past from her mind and focused on the present.

Surprisingly, the chapel was less than half full. And she recognized most of the mourners in attendance.

In the front row sat a nondescript, middle-aged, bald fellow whom Ryan had introduced to the Magnolia team as Jason's manager, Sid Greene. They had thanked him profusely for the invitation and promised that they were still investigating Jason's passing. Sid had seemed grateful, expressing a mutual desire to keep Jason's reputation as clean and untarnished as possible under the circumstances.

In the same pew, sitting next to Sid, was Vladik Zlotnik, who had played the villain so convincingly in Jason's movie. But he was anything but ominous today, as he sat, head bowed and shoulders slumped, listening to all the accolades bestowed upon his costar.

On Sid's other side was Alanna Cleary.

Savannah was more than a little surprised to see that Alanna's beauty was as flawless at a funeral as at a movie premiere. Her beautiful hair glowed in the soft light of the chapel, like delicate spun copper spread across the black velvet of her dress.

She was crying softly into a white handkerchief. And when the minister began to list the many children's charities that Jason had supported with his time, money, and endorsements, she began to sob.

From the other side of the chapel, also sitting in the front pew, Thomas Owen shot her an angry, disgusted look. Savannah had noticed that the two appeared to be avoiding each other before the service. She suspected it was deliberate that they had stayed on opposite sides of the room, avoiding eye contact.

That wasn't so surprising, considering the fact that Thomas blamed her, at least in part, for the breakup of his and Jason's relationship.

Savannah couldn't help thinking that if she were sitting in a room with a woman who had ruined her marriage, she would probably be shooting more than dirty glances across the room. Why resort to nasty looks when you had a Beretta strapped to your ribs?

When the minister finished, the service ended with a soprano's beautiful rendition of "Time to Say Good-bye."

As her lovely voice filled the chapel, touching every heart with the song's haunting melody, Savannah glanced to her left and saw that tears were streaking down Ryan's cheeks. She reached over and slipped her hand into his. He gave her a slight nod and a sad smile.

One look at John told her that he was having an equally difficult time. She reminded herself to be especially kind to them in the coming days. Losing someone you loved took such a toll on the human spirit.

They would need some healthy doses of healing love.

Next came the closing prayer. Then everyone stood and watched reverently as six pallbearers—all robust, overly muscular men—carried the coffin from the front, down the center aisle, and out of the chapel.

As Savannah slowly turned, her eyes on the casket, an unexpected sight caught her eye. Among a few mourners who had opted to sit in the rear of the chapel was Leland Porter.

He wept openly as the coffin passed him, covering his face with his hands, and shaking his head—as though he could hardly stand to witness what he was seeing.

Savannah thought of all the kind things he had said about Jason. How he had described him as being a close friend for so many years. How a superstar, who could have afforded the luxury of any first-class limousine service in the world, had opted to help out an old friend in need of a dollar.

Jason Tyrone might have been loved by the world. But the world didn't know him the way these few people inside this tiny church knew him.

As Savannah's throat tightened and her own vision became clouded, she glanced around the room and saw not a single dry eye. From those who were consumed with wracking sobs to those who were merely dabbing their eyes and noses with tissues, all were grieving their loss in their own private ways.

When she and Dirk, Ryan and John, Tammy and Waycross exited the church, they stepped into the bright sunlight and the seemingly endless lawn, which was covered with a seemingly endless crowd.

Those gathered to pay their respects from afar appeared to be as grief-stricken as those who had been inside the chapel. They cried, holding flowers, candles, and handmade signs that proclaimed, in the simplest words, their devotion to their hero.

Savannah decided, then and there, that if tears shed by mourners at one's departure were any indication of a life well lived and a person well loved—then Jason Tyrone had lived the life he had been given well.

She vowed she wasn't going to stop until she made absolutely sure that no one had deliberately caused the pain she saw manifested here.

Jason deserved as much. And so did these people whose hearts were breaking because they had lost him.

Savannah was never happier than when her kitchen table was surrounded by the people she loved most. Feeding them, making them laugh, letting them know how much she loved them—those were her favorite pastimes.

When everyone within her immediate vicinity had eaten a bit too much and drunk a little more than they should have of beverages either intoxicating or simply delicious, she felt she had fulfilled her mission in life.

Usually. But not tonight.

Tonight the normally boisterous mood at her table was subdued, at best.

Oh, the food had been good—the fried chicken crispy and seasoned just so, the mashed potatoes fluffy and buttery, the green beans crisp from her garden and flavored with just a bit of bacon left over from breakfast.

And of course, the pineapple upside down cake had been a thing of beauty. Granny Reid, who had won blue ribbons at the county fair for her pineapple upside down cake, had taught Savannah well.

But even though she was sure that Ryan and John appreciated her hospitality, Savannah knew it was going to take more than a plate full of good vittles to lift their spirits.

"It was lovely of you, dear, to have us this evening," John told Savannah, as he took a sip of the vintage port they had contributed to the feast. "But I'm afraid we've been poor company, and I apologize."

"I don't want to hear you apologizing for anything," she replied. "I'm just glad you came over. I was afraid the two of you wouldn't be up to socializing tonight."

She handed Ryan a small wine glass, which he filled halfway with port.

"If it hadn't been you who extended the invitation, we probably wouldn't have come," Ryan said. "Today turned out to be even harder than we'd thought it would be."

"I understand," Savannah said, as she set a fresh bottle of herbal tea in front of Tammy and refilled Waycross's root beer. "Funerals are never fun, but when it's someone young like that . . ."

"And when it's unexpected," Dirk added, accepting the beer she was handing him, "that makes it even worse."

"It was a very nice service though," Tammy said to Ryan in her most comforting, sisterly voice. "A glowing eulogy and pretty music."

"I didn't realize that Jason had no family to speak of," Ryan said. "I remember a long time ago I asked if he had brothers or sisters living in the area. He said he'd been the only kid of a single mom. I guess even she's passed on."

At the mention of single moms, Savannah noticed that Dirk looked down, as though he was suddenly interested in the label on his beer bottle. "At least she kept him and raised him," he said softly. So softly that, at first, Savannah wasn't sure if any of the others had heard him.

But they had.

A heavy silence descended on the room. Savannah searched for the perfect thing to say and couldn't think of anything. Everything that crossed her mind had the potential to make the situation even worse.

As she tried to decide whether to reply or just let it pass, Ryan spoke up. "How're you doing with that, buddy?" he asked Dirk. "They're coming to visit pretty soon now, right?"

When Dirk didn't answer, Savannah said, "Day after tomorrow. The suitcases are all packed and ready to go, last we heard."

"Oh, that *is* soon," John said.

Again there was a long, awkward pause. And this time it was Dirk who spoke up. "How am I doing? Okay, I guess. Frankly, it's a bit nerve-racking. Most people don't meet their parents for the first time when they're in their forties."

Waycross nodded and gave him a compassionate look. "That must be mighty strange. Savannah and me—our daddy won't ever win the Father of the Year award. But at least we got to see his face a few times a year."

Tammy leaned across the table, closer to Dirk. Her big eyes were filled with concern as she said, "Are you sorry that I found them for you? Do you wish I'd just left well enough alone?"

Savannah held her breath, hoping Dirk would say the right thing. The last thing Tammy needed was to think she had hurt her friend or interfered in his life. She was a gentle person with a tender heart and was easily wounded by such things.

"Don't be ridiculous," Dirk said, giving her a warm, brotherly smile. "I'll be grateful to you till the day I die for hooking us up. When I think about how it was, not knowing who my parents were or why they'd given me away like that. . . . Let's just say this is way better. Even if they turn out to be superweird or somethin', it's better knowing than not knowing."

"Oh, good," Tammy said, sinking back into her chair. "You had me worried there for a minute."

"He's just a mite nervous about their visit," Savannah offered as she sat down next to Dirk, a cup of hot chocolate in her hand. "Nervous in a manly man, Navy Seal, Ponderosa cowboy sorta way."

Ryan snickered and nearly choked on his port.

John guffawed.

Dirk pouted. "I don't think it was all that damned funny."

Savannah slapped him on the back. "It was all in the delivery, darlin'. All in the delivery."

Later, when Ryan and John had left, Tammy and Waycross volunteered to do the dishes. So Savannah and Dirk retired to the living room.

Savannah sat in her comfy chair with Diamante on her lap. Dirk stretched out on the couch with Cleo draped across his chest.

These had been their favorite relaxation positions for years.

Even back when they were partners and friends, but never lovers.

For the first two weeks of their marriage they had done the lovely-dovey, newlywed thing and snuggled together on the sofa. But old habits die hard, and it hadn't been long before they had reverted to their previous arrangement.

And the cats were more than happy, each having a pets-providing, chin-scratching, treat-giving human at their disposal.

"That was nice of Ryan and John to ask me how I was doing," he said, "with all they've got going on right now."

"They care about you," Savannah told him.

"They care about *you*, and you care about me, so they care about me."

"What?"

"Never mind."

"I think they feel bad because we've been spending all this time on their friend's case. Time we really don't have, considering your parents' visit."

He sighed and sank deeper into the sofa. "They shouldn't feel guilty about something like that. Honestly, it's kinda taken my mind off the visit. If I didn't have this case to work on, something to keep my mind occupied, I'd probably be a screaming Mimi."

"That bad, huh?"

"Absolutely. Whenever I'm not thinking about the case, I start imagining these scary scenarios in my head. Stuff like my mom sitting me down for this big, heavy, serious talk."

"You think she's going to do that?"

"I guess she kinda has to, doesn't she? You don't just waltz into your kid's life after forty years and say, 'Hi, sonny boy. Anything new? So much has happened since the last time we saw each other—what with the dinosaurs going extinct and all.'"

"Yes, I see your point. That could be a little weird."

"A little? I gotta tell ya, I do not want to hear about how my parents went up to Makeout Point after the prom and spawned me in the backseat of his Chevy Impala. Call me old-fashioned, but that's an image I do not want in my head."

Just for a moment, Savannah's own mind was polluted with an image of her mother, Shirley, getting it on with her trucker daddy in the bed of his sleeper cab. She shuddered at the thought.

"Yes," she said, "if she even starts down that road, you'd better head her off quick."

"That's the worst part about stuff like that. Once you've heard it you can't unhear it. And, I swear, I think it'd scar me for life."

Savannah chuckled. "With all you've seen and heard on the job? Dude, you're a lot tougher than you think you are."

He perked up. "You really think so?"

"Naw, you're a marshmallow. I was just trying to perk up your spirits a bit."

"Gee. Thanks."

They both sat in silence for a while, petting their respective cats.

Then Dirk said, "What I need to perk my spirits up is to find out, once and for all, what happened to Jason Tyrone. I want to either find some solid evidence that there was foul play, or something to prove, once and for all, that it really was an accident."

"You and me both. I need to be getting ready for your parents. I could write the Declaration of Independence with my finger in the dust on top of the bedroom dresser. I've got leftovers in the icebox that need to be pitched. I need to stock up on groceries and run several loads of laundry. I can't have your mother thinking you married a slob."

"But *I'm* a slob."

"That doesn't matter. Mothers always cut their sons a lot of slack in that department. But daughter-in-laws, that's a different story. If the house is a mess, it's her fault. Plain and simple. Women's Liberation stopped short of correcting that little problem. Now we gals are expected to have jobs *and* run the house. Bum deal, if you ask me."

Dirk sat up, placed Cleo on the floor, and walked over to Savannah. He sat down on the ottoman at her feet. Reaching over and taking her hands in his, he said, "I am so, so proud that I managed to marry me a great gal like you. Hell, I married so far above myself that, from where I'm at up here, I'm looking at clouds."

He waved a big hand, indicating the furniture, the wall decorations, and the carefully chosen, carefully placed knickknacks. "You've made us a wonderful house, Van. It's warm, and cozy, and comfortable, and pretty . . . just like you. And my parents are gonna see that. And they're gonna see that I love you and you love me. And that's all that matters."

She gazed into his eyes and saw nothing but unconditional love and total acceptance. What was a little blue shaving cream on the bathroom mirror in comparison to gifts like those?

Placing her hands on either side of his face, she pulled him to her and gave him a long, passionate kiss.

When they finally came up for air, she laughed and said, "You just said all that mushy stuff so you could get in my bloomers. Right, boy?"

He laughed. "Busted. You got me." Slowly he trailed his finger tip from her lips down her throat and into her cleavage. "So tell me," he said, his voice husky, "is it working?"

She grabbed his hand, stood, and pulled him to his feet. "What do you think?" she asked, as she dragged him toward the stairs.

"I think I'm about to get lucky."

"Imagine that. Me too."

Chapter 18

Savannah woke from a restless sleep and sat straight up in bed, her heart pounding. She was trembling and short of breath, and although she was sweating, she felt cold. It was the kind of cold that came from something deep inside her—not from the temperature in the room.

"The patch!" she said.

"What?" Dirk stirred in his sleep and rolled toward her.

"It was the dadgum patch!"

He groaned and looked at the clock on the nightstand. "Babe, it's six forty-five in the morning. Could this wait another half an hour or so?"

"Huh? Oh, sure. Sorry, darlin'. I guess I was dreaming about it and . . . well, you know how I figure stuff out in my sleep?"

"I know how you *think* you figure stuff out in your sleep."

"Like the time I figured out that Gloria Houston was embez-zling from her boss there at that florist shop."

"Didn't that turn out to be the boss who was embezzling from his own company?"

"Um, maybe. But there was that other time when I woke up

just knowing that Old Man Cronin had been killed with a fire-place poker, there in his own house."

Dirk yawned. "It was a baseball bat. His nephew did him in for the insurance money."

She was starting to get annoyed. "Fireplace poker, baseball bat, what's the difference? They were both from inside his house. And I'm telling you, it was the patch."

"But those patches were checked. Dr. Liu or Eileen or some-body told us they checked them and all the rest of the medica-tions there in his room. There was nothing in them except what was supposed to be."

He punched his pillow a couple of times, fluffing it, then snuggled into it. "Seriously, Van, I'm startin' to think he really did die of an accident, and we just won't accept it because that means he died because of his own foolishness. Now, if you don't mind, I wanna catch a few more winks before I rise and shine. Go back to sleep."

"You go ahead," she said, crawling out of bed. "I'm gonna get up and make some coffee and think about this grand revelation of mine. I'm telling you, it's gonna turn this case around."

When he didn't reply, she knew he had already slipped back into Dreamland.

She shook her head as she pulled on her robe and slipped into her house shoes. How lovely it would be to be able to fall asleep so easily.

Dirk had two things down pat—eating and sleeping.

Then she flashed back on the previous night's activities. Okay, three things.

She plucked Diamante off the foot of the bed and tucked her under her arm. There was no point in reaching for Cleopatra. Cleo was snuggled against Dirk's ribs and would have fought tooth and nail if Savannah had tried to remove her.

Yes, Cleo had turned into a bona fide daddy's girl.

Savannah tiptoed out of the room and quietly closed the door behind her. And as she and Diamante passed the door to the much-disputed man cave, Savannah told the cat, "We'll just let those two sleep their lives away, while we solve the problems of the world. And while those two snooze, you and I are gonna have first dibs on the coffee and the Kitty Vittles."

As they descended the stairs, Savannah chuckled and added, "You know, if I remember right, the two of them slept right through the Northridge Earthquake. Dirk said he didn't even wake up. But I was screaming my head off, and you were running around the house like a chicken with your head cut off, while your sister . . ."

By the time Dirk and Cleopatra joined the land of the living downstairs, Savannah and Tammy had been on the computer for more than an hour, panning for the gold nuggets of knowledge to be found on the Internet.

"She's right!" Tammy announced, as he shuffled into the living room, wearing a pair of black pajama bottoms spangled with Harley-Davidson logos and a rumpled tee-shirt.

Originally, probably sometime back in the early seventies, the shirt had also been black. Then it had morphed into a strange, unappealing shade of brown. Now it was a weird, muddy green most commonly seen on Halloween costumes. And the sage quote that had been printed on the front was now illegible—its wisdom forever lost to the world. All that remained of the faded letters was "Mustache" and "50 cents."

"We've been researching those medicine patches that people wear," Tammy fairly shouted, "and it looks like they could be lethal if—"

He held up one hand in a gesture that was reminiscent of his traffic cop days. "No! I don't care if you've found Jimmy Hoffa and he was hanging out with Jack the Ripper. I need coffee."

As he passed by them and made his way to the kitchen, Savannah said to Tammy, "Boy, what a grump he can be first thing in the morning. Imagine somebody being that grouchy just because they haven't had their coffee yet."

Tammy turned in her chair and stared at Savannah. "Are you serious?" she asked, an incredulous look on her face. "I mean, really? Are you kidding me?"

"What?" Savannah asked, clueless.

Tammy shook her head and returned to the monitor. "Oh, to see ourselves as others see us," she mumbled under her breath.

"Huh?"

"Nothing. Oh, look what I found here . . ."

As Savannah tossed her kitchen curtains and her best bath towels into the washing machine with one hand, she called Ryan on her cell phone with the other.

He answered quickly. "Good morning, Savannah. This is a bit early for you."

"I know," she replied, as she chose the "warm" setting and added the detergent. "I've got a lot going on."

"I can only imagine."

"But I woke up this morning with one of those flashes of insight that I get during the night."

There was a long silence on the other end. Then, "You mean, like when you woke up after sleeping on the Stevenson case and thought she had put antifreeze in his sports drink?"

"Well, that wasn't one of my best ones, but—"

"And it turned out to be carbon monoxide poisoning?"

She closed the washing machine lid with a loud bang. "Do you want to hear what I've got to say or not, boy?"

She heard a soft chuckle, then he said, "Sure. Let's hear what you've got. Lay it on me."

She paused, her hand on the detergent bottle. There had been a time, not that long ago, when hearing Ryan Stone use the phrase "Lay it on me" would have set her fantasies and hormones racing.

But now she was a married woman, and she firmly believed that marital fidelity began in the mind.

So she set the hotsy-totsy fantasies she might have otherwise entertained on the top shelf over the washing machine, along with the detergent bottle.

"Okay," she said. "I need to ask you a couple more questions about the night of the premiere."

"Ask away."

As she left her garage–utility room combo and walked back to the house, she noticed that a batch of weeds had taken up residence in her daylily bed.

She didn't tolerate weeds among her lilies at any time. But with a mother-in-law on her way to visit, an untidy garden was unthinkable. She bent over and yanked out the offenders as she continued her conversation.

"You said he was messing with that patch on his chest there in the men's bathroom in the theater," she said.

"That's right."

"Now think hard, 'cause this is real important. From that time on, was he ever out of your sight?"

"Not until John and I and his chauffeur put him into the limousine."

"Are you absolutely sure? You had eyes on him that entire time?"

"I'm one hundred percent sure. Why do you ask?"

She felt the sweat trickling down her forehead and wiped it away with the back of her hand, before tackling the weeds again. "I'm asking because I woke up thinking about that patch."

"What about it?"

"Where did it go? He was wearing it when you guys left the bathroom, right?"

"Yes. Definitely."

"Yet when you found him on the floor of the hotel room, it was gone."

"That's true."

"Is there any chance it might have fallen off by itself?"

"No chance. Those things stick really well. I remember he gave me one a long time ago, when I pulled a muscle in my upper back. When I peeled it off twelve hours later, it felt like it was taking a chunk of my back along with it."

Savannah gathered up a handful of the pulled weeds, then stood and groaned as her knees popped. She didn't recall her knees popping when she'd been in her twenties or thirties. And she wasn't thrilled about this new development.

Creaky knees and crow's-feet. What other lovely gifts did her forty-plus body have in mind for her?

"Then he must've taken the patch off at some point."

"Okay. And your point is . . . ?"

"Where is it? It wasn't on his body or there in the hotel room. I didn't see any used, loose patches among the stuff that Eileen and her techs collected."

"Maybe he took it off in the limo."

"I already thought of that," Savannah said, as she walked to the garbage can and tossed the weeds inside. "I thought I'd ask you first. The chauffeur's next. I think he'd been cleaning out the limo when we went by to question him. He might've found a patch. And with any luck, he might still have it."

"You think there might've been some kind of poison or something on it. Like someone tampered with it?"

"Stranger things have happened."

"But mostly in your imagination and especially when you first wake up in the morning."

"Now listen, boy, you could've talked all day and not said that."

She hung up on him. She had a chauffeur to question, a futon to buy, and a husband who had drunk quite enough morning coffee and needed to be roused off the sofa. He had a honey-do list the length of his arm, and he'd put off tackling it for long enough.

"The bathroom floor? You want me to clean the bathroom floor?"

Dirk stood in front of the refrigerator, a cold, unopened beer in his hands, a look of astonishment and horror on his face.

Savannah's hands were refreshment-free and propped on her hips. And her expression was one of cold, hard determination. "Seems apropos, don't you think, considering your lousy aim?"

"But I don't know how."

She marched over to the kitchen sink, opened the cupboard beneath it, and pulled out a bottle of liquid floor polish. "Oh, please. Like I'm gonna buy that lame excuse. You were a bachelor for years. Don't tell me you never cleaned the floor in that trailer of yours."

"Of course I did. I'd wet a paper towel, get down on my hands and knees, and give it a once-over. But I'll just betcha that wouldn't be good enough for you. No way. I know you, Savannah. You've got some fancy-dandy process you want me to use. And then if I don't do it just right, I'll hear about it for the rest of my life."

She placed the bottle in his free hand and gave him an "atta boy" swat on the shoulder. "You'll figure it out," she said. "When all else fails, read the directions on the back."

"And where are you going?"

"I'm gonna go try to solve a murder."

"Without me?"

"You told me you're starting to think it didn't even happen. How much good would you be?"

"So you go off investigating while I stay home and do house-work? Is that what you're telling me?"

She gave him a benevolent smile. "It's your day off, darlin'. And that means, as a married man, you're supposed to devote your spare time to home improvement, yard maintenance, or automobile upkeep."

"I never agreed to that."

"Yes, you did. It's in the fine print on the back of the marriage certificate."

He sighed. "With the flying bullets and the experimental sex."

"Exactly."

She grabbed her purse off the counter and headed for the back door.

"I just want you to know, I think this is messed up," he grumbled.

"Objection noted."

"Listen up, girl," he called after her. "You and me—we're gonna have to renegotiate that fine print crap."

But she was already out the door.

"Just you alone? No Dirk?" Eileen asked when she answered the laboratory's door.

"Just me, myself, and I," Savannah responded. "So I didn't feel the need to bring cookies."

"Hmmm." Eileen lifted one eyebrow and ushered her inside. "I follow your logic there, but I think cookies should be a standing order. With or without Dirk."

"I'll keep that in mind."

Eileen smiled. And Savannah realized, for the first time, that she smiled a lot more when Dirk wasn't around.

That was too bad.

Dirk was such a good guy, but he was definitely an acquired taste. And too many people spit him out before taking the time to savor the flavor—a mixture of components that were somewhat bitter and more than a little salty, with a slight undertone of sweet.

"What brings you here today, if it isn't to bring me cookies?" Eileen said, as they made their way past the techs in their cubicles.

"Patches."

"Patches?"

"The pain patches you found at the scene."

"I thought you knew; we've already processed those. Nothing was out of the ordinary."

"Yes, but I was wondering if I could see them again. I'd like to look them over myself."

Eileen's mouth curled up on one side. Savannah knew that expression. It wasn't a particularly friendly one. "And you think you're going to find something that we didn't?"

"I doubt it," Savannah replied, in her finest ruffled-feather-smoothing tone. "But I'd sure like to try. Then maybe I could sleep a little better at night."

Eileen thought it over. "Okay. In the interest of your good health, you can have a look. But don't expect much."

Savannah smiled. "I always hope for the best and prepare for the worst, 'cause that's what you usually get."

"Words to live by."

Eileen led her to the back of the room, to the counter where Jason Tyrone's evidence box sat.

Savannah already had her surgical gloves on by the time Eileen had taken the box to a table and opened it.

As Eileen once again wrote her name, the date, and the time on the chain of custody label, Savannah dug in. She headed straight for the small, blue cardboard box with the prescription label on the side that identified it as "Lido-Morphone."

She carefully opened the box and saw the individual envelopes inside.

One by one, she took them out and looked them over. They were unopened and made of a thick, sturdy substance that looked like a combination of heavy paper and foil.

"Those envelopes are waterproof," Eileen told her, as though reading her mind. "It's to keep the gel on the patches from drying out."

Savannah noted that the label said the box contained ten patches. She counted as she took out six envelopes that were unopened—still completely intact.

But the remaining four were different; their ends had been cut off. And those ends that had been removed were also tucked into the box.

"Why would he put the empty wrappers back in the box?" she wondered aloud.

"They aren't empty. Look inside," Eileen told her.

Savannah opened one, reached in, and pulled out a patch. It was rumpled, as though it had been worn, and it had been folded in half with the sticky, gel side inward.

"Okay," Savannah said. "Then why would he keep a worn patch?"

"Apparently, he was a conscientious user. If you look on the label, that's how it tells you to dispose of them. Fold them in half, medicine to the inside, and put them back in their waterproof wrappers before throwing them into the garbage."

"Why?"

"Because they contain powerful, even deadly, medication.

And if a child, a pet, or even a wild animal were to put it in their mouth, it could kill them."

Savannah nodded thoughtfully. "Gotcha." She reached into the next wrapper and pulled out another used one. "That was very responsible of him."

"More than most people. You'd be horrified if you knew what people do with their leftover medicines. They flush them down the toilet and into the water system. Then you and I wind up drinking them in tap water and watering our plants with them."

Savannah had looked inside each of the open envelopes and found a patch, until she got to the last one. "Hey, this one's empty. Did you test the packets?"

"Not the packets. We tested all of the patches—the used ones, that is. We didn't bother with the sealed ones. That envelope you have in your hand, it was empty."

"This envelope must have held the last patch he used."

Eileen nodded. "That would make sense. And he never got a chance to put that one back into its envelope."

Savannah studied the envelope carefully. She wasn't sure what she was looking for. Any abnormality would do. But she didn't see one. It was just a simple packet with one end cut off.

It looked like it had been opened with a pair of sharp scissors. The cut was clean, not jagged, as it probably would have been if someone had sawed it open with a knife.

And yet the cut had not been made in one single snip. She could see where the scissors had stopped and then begun again three times.

"Were any scissors found among his belongings?" she asked. "Small ones. Larger than nail scissors, but smaller than regular office scissors."

"Yes," Eileen said, "among his toiletries."

She began to rifle among the items inside the box. In a moment she had found what she was looking for. She handed Savannah a pair of scissors that were about the size used by young children. But the ends were sharp, not blunted, like school scissors.

"My granny has a pair like this," Savannah said. "She uses them when she does her needlepoint and embroidery—to cut the threads. But I've seen guys use these, too, to trim their beards and mustaches."

"Jason Tyrone was clean-shaven."

"Yes, but he might've kept these around just for those envelopes. You can't exactly rip them open with your teeth."

Savannah looked around the room. "Do you happen to have one of those big, lighted magnifying lamps? Gran uses one of those, too, for her needlework, now that her eyesight isn't what it used to be."

"As a matter of fact, we do. Follow me."

Eileen led her to the other side of the room, where she opened a cupboard and pulled out a version of what Savannah had described. She set the lamp on the counter, plugged it in, and flipped the switch.

The illumination was far brighter than what Savannah had even hoped for. And when she examined the empty envelope through the lens, she found the magnification much greater than she'd expected.

Gran needed one of these gadgets.

She held the small scissors up to the severed edge and found that the blades were the exact length of the first cut. So was the second. The third was a bit shorter.

"Look at that," she told Eileen. "He used the scissors. I'll bet that if you were to swipe a swab across those blades, you'd pick up a bit of that gel and medication."

Eileen nodded and took the scissors from her. "I'll have that done, right away. Though I'm not sure where you're going with this."

Savannah continued to examine the empty packet, comparing it to the other ones and finding no differences. Her excitement began to wane a bit. So what if they had discovered how Jason Tyrone opened his medication there in the hotel room? That proved nothing, one way or the other.

Finally, she laid the envelope aside, more than a little discouraged. She was about to abandon the whole exercise when she remembered the tops of the packets that had been cut off and put into the box.

She walked over to the table, retrieved them, and brought them back to the magnifying lamp.

One by one, she patiently held the ends up to her empty envelope. The cuts hadn't been made exactly straight. Each one varied slightly; the lines were a bit crooked, every one unique in its own way.

At last, she found the one discarded end that lined up perfectly with the empty envelope.

Sticking her face so close to the magnifying glass that her nose was nearly against it, she examined the cut-off end as closely as she had the envelope. Again, just looking for something, anything extraordinary.

And she saw it.

A tiny, tiny hole near the edge. It was so small that at first she thought she was seeing things. But the closer she looked, the clearer it became.

She could feel her pulse rate quicken even as a surge of optimism, mixed with dread, flooded her system.

"Hey, girl, look at this!" she said to Eileen. "If I'm right, we've got us a puncture, right there, plain as the nose on your face."

"What do you mean a 'puncture'?"

"A nice, even, little hole. So little, in fact, that I have to say it was made by a needle. Nothing else is that tiny."

"Let me have a look at that." Eileen practically snatched it out of her hand and pushed her out of the way, so that she could use the magnifying lamp.

It didn't take her long for her to agree with Savannah. "That's exactly what it looks like," she said. "Let's get it over here underneath the microscope, so that we can tell for sure."

A few moments later, they were bending over the microscope. Eileen was looking through it, and Savannah was practically dancing with impatience as she stood next to her, waiting her turn.

"Well?" Savannah said. "What have we got?"

Eileen moved aside so that Savannah could take a look. And when Savannah bent over and looked through the lens, there was her evidence staring her right in the eye. The evidence she had been looking for that proved what she had known all along.

Finally, she pushed away from the microscope and looked at Eileen. In the laboratory director's eyes was the same gleam of triumph and exhilaration that she was feeling.

"You know what that is, don't you?" Eileen said. "That's product tampering."

"Oh, it's way more than that, darlin'," Savannah told her. "That there is murder."

Chapter 19

The moment Savannah left the laboratory, she took her phone out of her purse and called Dirk.

He sounded slightly out of breath and definitely out of sorts. "Yeah?" was his curt greeting.

"I'm on my way to the morgue to see Dr. Liu," she told him, as she hurried across the parking lot toward the Mustang. "Meet me in the parking lot there ASAP."

"I'm kind of in the middle of something here—"

"Then drop it. Seriously, get over there as quick as you can."

"If you must know, I'm working on this stupid bathroom floor like you asked me to. And it ain't going well at all."

She unlocked the Mustang's door and slid inside. "Dirk, forget the floor. Forget everything else and haul ass over to the morgue, pronto."

She clicked the phone off, stuck her key in the ignition, fired up the Pony, and took off like a horsefly from a swatter.

Savannah was waiting for Dirk in the parking lot, as promised, when he pulled the Buick into the space beside hers. She jumped out of the Mustang, the small, brown paper bag clutched tightly against her chest.

The Buick had barely stopped rolling when she jumped into the passenger seat.

Taking one look at her face, Dirk dropped all signs of pissyness and said, "Wow, this is the most excited I've seen you since our honeymoon night. What's up?"

She shoved the paper bag into his hand.

He looked at it and said, "An evidence bag? Ol' Eileen let you leave the laboratory with evidence? What about the chain of custody?"

"Yeah, yeah, yeah. I know, I'm a civilian now. So as far as you and Eileen and I are concerned, she handed this directly to you. Right?"

He smirked as he opened the bag and looked into it. "Craft and corruption, right here in little San Carmelita. Go figure."

"I think that's 'graft' not 'craft.' And illiterate or not, your terminology's a bit harsh. I prefer to think of it as creative, harmless sneakiness that doesn't amount to a hill of beans in the overall scheme of things."

"Okay, okay. So this bag went directly from Eileen's hands to mine. What's inside here? It looks like one of those envelopes the patches came in."

"That's exactly what it is," she said, with a grim smile. "And the end that Jason cut off with scissors right before he applied it to his chest."

"And you're so excited about this because—?"

"Because somebody poked a needle through it."

Savannah could tell by the look in Dirk's eye the instant that the significance of her news registered on him.

"No kidding?"

"Sugar, I might pull your leg about a lotta things. But cold-blooded, premeditated murder ain't one of them."

* * * *

"We ain't signing your damned clipboard now, Bates," Dirk told Officer Kenny, as he and Savannah strode through the reception area, past the check-in counter.

"But you can't do that! Everybody's gotta sign in or else I'm gonna call the chief on you, Coulter. I'm going to tell him that you're letting civilians in here right and left and—"

Savannah paused just for a moment, long enough to blast him with her infamous blue lasers. "You go right ahead, you peckerhead. While you're at it, you remind the chief that since this department fired me, I've solved more homicide cases for him than anybody on the job in this town. Except for Dirk here."

Dirk piped up, "Yes, and most of those I solved because she helped me out. So call the chief right now if you wanna. Hell, I'll even dial it for you."

Bates just stood there fidgeting, staring down at the floor, clearing his throat.

"That's what I thought," Dirk said. "Go back to lookin' at your dirty pictures on the Internet and leave us alone. You're interfering with a police officer in the lawful discharge of his duties."

After searching for Dr. Liu in the autopsy suite and not finding her, Savannah and Dirk finally located her in her office. It was rare to see the energetic coroner sitting behind a desk, doing paperwork. They were more accustomed to seeing her standing beside her autopsy table, wrist deep in gore.

Savannah was always surprised at how feminine and demure Dr. Jen looked when seated at a desk—unless you looked down and saw her fishnet stockings.

Deep in thought as she studied one of the folders spread out in front of her, the doctor didn't notice them until Dirk rapped on the half-opened door.

"Oh, hi," she said. "Come on in."

As Savannah took the seat closest to the desk, Dr. Liu gave her an intense, searching look, and said, "Do we have good news or bad news?"

Savannah glanced over at Dirk, who shrugged and said nothing.

"Well, now," Savannah said slowly, "I reckon that just depends on how you look at it."

Dr. Liu's autopsy suite contained many of the same pieces of equipment that Eileen and her CSI lab used. So when the coroner took Savannah and Dirk into the suite, Savannah headed straight for a magnifying lamp on the counter.

It took only a couple of minutes for her to show the doctor the puncture hole in the cut-off end.

Dirk leaned over the doctor's shoulder, peering at the evidence through the lens as best he could without giving away the fact that this was his first time seeing it.

Savannah couldn't tell if the coroner was pleased or upset by this new development. The expression on her face as she stared down through the lens was both interested and grim.

"Eileen ran a test, just now, on the inside of that envelope," Savannah told her, after she had explained Jason's habitual method for disposing of his patches.

Dr. Liu looked up from the lamp. "And? Well, speak up. What did she find?"

"Lido-Morphone," Savannah replied.

Liu looked disappointed. "Oh. That was to be expected. That's what she found on the patches. Just like the rest of the medications, they were exactly what they were supposed to be."

"Lido-Morphone at twelve times the standard dosage," Savannah said. "Twelve times the levels found in the other envelopes."

Dirk let out a whistle. "And the patch he was wearing that

night came from that envelope. Or at least it's a safe bet, considering that it was the only one without a used patch in it."

Dr. Liu shot him a quick, questioning look, and Savannah held her breath. He had to be careful to hide any surprise about this evidence which he supposedly had received directly from Eileen's hand.

"So, Doc, what do you think?" Savannah asked, creating a diversion. "Would twelve times the standard dosage of that stuff kill a person?"

"Absolutely," was the reply. "In fact, two or three times the standard dosage could have been fatal. Lido-Morphone is an extremely potent drug, a powerful opiate. When the pharmaceutical company first started distributing the patches, there was a slight flaw in the manufacturing. And it cost several people their lives before they figured it out."

"But you said all of the drug levels in his blood work came back within the normal range," Dirk said. "Did the lab blow the test?"

"No, I don't believe they did," Dr. Liu replied. "But the test was done on blood levels. With those falling within normal, nonlethal ranges, I had no reason to order a tissue test."

"Do you think a tissue test would've shown the elevated level?" Savannah asked.

The doctor nodded thoughtfully. "It's very possible. Especially a tissue specimen taken from the area where he placed the patch."

"Can you, um," Savannah gulped, finding it difficult to even make the suggestion. "Can you do those tests, um, now?"

"To get a tissue sample, the body would have to be exhumed."

"That's an ugly thought," Dirk added.

Dr. Liu looked like she was going to be sick. "It certainly is— very painful for the loved ones. I never do it unless absolutely necessary. Where did Ryan and John say he was wearing the patch?"

"Right over his breastbone," Savannah said. "He had a condition called costo . . . costro . . ."

"Costochondritis?"

"That's it."

"Okay. Then I'd need to excise the tissue in that area and have it tested."

The three of them stood, silently, as each considered the dark possibility of removing Jason Tyrone from his so-called eternal resting place.

Finally, Dirk said, "There's just no gettin' around it. It's gotta be done."

Savannah nodded. "There's no logical, innocent reason why that envelope would have a perfect little hole in it."

"And twelve times the dosage as the other packets," Dr. Liu added. She reached over and flipped off the lamp. "Yes," she said. "It has to be done. Nobody's going to murder a young man like that and get away with it. Not on my watch."

As Dirk drove the Buick down the tree-lined street that led to Leland Porter's house, he told Savannah, "We really could've just made a phone call and asked him, instead of driving all the way out here. You know I don't like the valley."

"I also know, just as you do, that there's nothing like questioning somebody face-to-face. You catch all sorts of things you can't see on the phone."

He grunted.

"And besides, if he has that patch or some other bit of juicy evidence, do you really want him putting his ungloved mitts on it?"

"Back in the old days, we all used our ungloved mitts when handling evidence. I remember when we didn't have to put on a pair of hot, sweaty, sticky gloves just to blow our nose."

She chuckled. "Oh, right. The good old days—when we'd search for a subject for weeks or even months, trying to track down the DNA left on a murder weapon, only to find out it was the sweat from some rookie patrolman who'd played around with the bloody tire iron before the lab techs got there."

They pulled up to the front of Leland's house, which now had a FOR SALE sign posted in the front yard.

Glancing quickly up and down the street, Savannah said, "That's the fourth house for sale on this block alone. Looks like the neighborhood's going downhill."

"I thought it was already at the bottom of the hill, facedown in a ditch," he said. "Pretty hard to go deeper than that."

They got out of the car, and not seeing Leland in the yard or garage, they walked up to the house.

As they neared the front door, they could hear the distinct sound that cops know all too well—a man and woman arguing inside.

Dirk elbowed Savannah. "Hey, been a time since you and me's responded to a ten-sixteen. Years, I think."

"And I could've gone a few more years without one," she replied, thinking back on nights when, as partners on the SCPD, they had responded to one domestic disturbance after another.

"I don't hear any furniture breaking."

"No crashing glass or screams."

"Just your average feud, I'd say."

"Not unlike the one we had today," she said.

"We had one today?"

She gave him a flirty grin and a wink. "If we didn't, we will . . . a couple of feisty old farts like us. It's inevitable."

"Naw. You're the feisty one. I'm the farter."

"Sadly, that is so, so true."

They had stepped up onto the porch, and Dirk had raised his fist to knock when the door flew open and a woman emerged.

Her face was red, and so were her eyes. She was carrying a duffle bag in one hand and a small suitcase in the other. As she stomped past them, she didn't even acknowledge their presence, but she shouted back at the house, "Do not call me, Lee! I mean it! And if you set foot on my mom's property, I swear, I'll call the cops on you!"

She marched across the yard to a run-down sedan, got into it, and laid rubber peeling out of the driveway.

As the car made its squealing retreat down the street, Savannah saw Leland Porter through the screen door. He was standing there, shirtless, wearing boxer shorts and a forlorn expression on his face.

When he saw them, the depressed look disappeared, replaced with one of embarrassment.

He grabbed a pair of jeans, slipped them on, then slid a tee-shirt over his head.

When he opened the screen door, he gave them a sheepish nod and said, "Hi, guys. So-o-o, what's happenin'?"

In unison, Savannah and Dirk turned and looked over their shoulder at the now deserted street.

"Oh, nothin' much," Dirk said in his best pseudo-jolly tone. "You?"

Leland shrugged. "Oh, same ol', same ol'. You know."

They all three chuckled. A little.

"You wanna come inside?" he asked.

"If you don't mind," Savannah said.

"I don't mind if you don't mind the mess."

"We've seen messes," Dirk replied, as Leland held the door open for them.

Once they were inside and Savannah had looked around, she could see that it was, indeed, a disaster. But not in an untidy, dirty house way.

Leland and his wife were moving.

Stacked against the wall, cardboard boxes with their lids fastened with packing tape were labeled "living room" and "bathroom cupboard," as well as "pots and pans."

Savannah didn't envy them. It had been years since she had moved from one house to another. But she would never forget the aching muscles, the frazzled nerves, or the terrible mental anguish of not being able to find your salt shaker or your underwear.

No, when you were moving, life was hardly worth living.

"Moving, huh?" Dirk asked, stating the obvious.

"Yeah. The bank foreclosed on us. My wife lost her job, and the limo business is in the toilet right now."

He glanced toward the door where his wife had just made her ignominious departure. "Financial stress—it's hell on a marriage."

"That's a tough break, man," Dirk said. "I'm sorry."

"Are you married?" Leland asked.

Dirk smiled from ear to ear. "I sure am. To her." He pointed to Savannah.

Leland seemed surprised. "Oh. I didn't realize that. I thought you were partners, like cop partners."

"I'm a cop. She used to be," Dirk explained. "And when she was, we were partners. Now we really are."

"But your last names are different."

Savannah gulped. That was one little issue that, so far, she and Dirk had managed to not quite discuss. She had decided to keep her maiden name. And although Dirk must have noticed that she was still using it, he hadn't complained.

"Um . . . we don't want to keep you if you're busy packing and all that awful stuff," she said, "but we have a couple of questions, if you have time. It won't take long."

"Sure. I'd like to get my mind off my moving—and my pissed-off wife—for a while. Fire away."

"We have a couple of questions about your garbage," Dirk said.

"My garbage?"

"The garbage you took out of the limo when you cleaned it, after you took Jason to the premiere. Do you still have it?"

"There wasn't any."

Savannah wasn't expecting that. "Any? None at all?"

"Not a bit. Jason didn't drink, even though I provide liquor in the bar. He didn't eat anything or make a mess of any kind. He never did. He'd just get in, take his ride, and get out. I vacuumed the carpet; that was all."

Dirk gave Savannah an "I told you we could've phoned" look, which she skillfully ignored.

"Why?" Leland asked. "Were you looking for something in particular?"

"Yes. A white patch about this big." Savannah showed him, making a square with her fingers. "He wore it for pain relief."

Leland thought long and hard. "No. I'm sure I'd remember if I saw something weird like that."

"There's no chance you might have vacuumed it up?" Dirk asked.

"No way. The carpet's black. If something that big and white had been lying there, I would've noticed it for sure."

"Damn," Dirk whispered under his breath.

"Yeah," Savannah replied.

"You say Jason had to wear pain patches?" Leland asked. "That's a shame. He never complained. But then, Jason was like that. Really easy to be around, you know?"

Later, as Savannah and Dirk were walking back to the car, Dirk surprised her with a philosophical observation. "That's nice, what Leland said about Jason. That Jason was easy to be around because he never complained. It'd be nice, after you died, to have people say that about you."

Savannah thought about Dirk and how he had to be the grumpiest fellow that most people ever met. She didn't want to tell him that if he didn't amend his ways, his reputation as a non-complainer was in great jeopardy.

"I've heard," she said, "that it's a good exercise to try to go a whole day—twenty-four hours—without complaining about a single thing. They say that if you can do that, your whole life will change almost immediately."

"Naw, I've tried that crap, and it never works for me. It works for everybody else, but not for me." He took his sunglasses off and wiped the sweat off his forehead with the back of his hand. "Man, it's just too stinkin' hot today. I hate hot weather. When it's hot, it drains all the energy outta me, and I just feel like I'm gonna puke sometimes, because I just can't stand . . ."

As soon as Savannah and Dirk returned home, Savannah raced up the stairs to the bathroom. Between the visit to the morgue and then the lengthy ride to Rosado, it had been a long time between pit stops.

Even as she scurried down the hallway, her mind was running over the long list of domestic chores she still had to perform before the arrival of the in-laws tomorrow evening.

She wasn't worried about the prospect of cooking for them. If there was one thing Savannah had down pat, it was spreading the table with delicious food for her guests.

And as Dirk had said, her home was pretty, cozy and charming—quintessential Southern décor. So she felt pretty secure in that department, too.

But housecleaning?

That was another story.

She wasn't filthy. Not by a long shot. She was the daughter of Granny Reid of McGill, Georgia, and had been taught that cleanliness was next to godliness.

She couldn't count the times she had heard her grandmother say, "A bar of soap only costs a nickel. So it don't matter how poor you are, there's no excuse for dirtiness."

And though the price of detergent had risen quite a bit since Gran had coined those phrases, the truth and wisdom of her words remained in the heart and mind of her granddaughter.

Throughout history, Savannah's housekeeping standards had been higher than those of most hospital operating rooms. But a lot had happened in Savannah's world during the past year or so. She had survived a nearly fatal attack, and it had taken her months to recuperate. And in some ways, she knew her body would never be the same.

Then there was the whole wedding fiasco.

Although most brides have their share of challenges and traumas, she and Dirk had endured far more than fate should have allowed.

And the honeymoon . . . they hadn't nicknamed the whole adventure the "Killer Honeymoon" for no reason.

Then, if all that hadn't been enough, there was Dirk.

With his shaving cream and toothpaste on the mirrors, underwear and cut fingernails on the kitchen counter, and his propensity for leaving things in strange places—sunglasses in the freezer and ice cubes in the microwave—she had nearly given up on keeping the house tidy as long as her husband was living in it.

She had considered fixing up the garage, transforming it into a nice little bachelor's apartment for him. After all, this was California, where alternate lifestyles were considered avant-garde.

But her in-laws would probably frown upon her banishing their son to the garage—even if she had been strong enough to bind and transport Dirk to the proposed new living quarters.

So her house was a mess, and they were arriving in less than twenty-four hours, and there wasn't anything she could do about it at this point.

Maybe if she fed them often and well enough, they wouldn't notice the fact that her kitchen curtains were in her washing machine and not hanging from her windows.

At least, thanks to Dirk, her bathroom floor was clean. Maybe this having a husband around could be a beneficial thing once in a while. At least you—

She halted in mid-thought and mid-stride the moment she set foot in the bathroom. Her shoe stuck to the floor as if she were walking through a movie theater after a visit by a kindergarten class on a field trip. And it couldn't have been any stickier than if every kid in that class had spilled a soda and dropped a melted ice cream cone and a handful of half-chewed Jujubes on it.

"What the hell?" she yelled, trying to unstick her foot and back her way out of the nightmare. "Dirk! What in tarnation did you do to this floor!?"

She heard his heavy, plodding steps coming up the stairs. "What are you yelling about, woman?" he shouted back. "Criminy, girl! I could hear you all the way from the kitchen!"

She managed to get her shoe loose and herself back into the hallway just as he joined her. "What on earth did you put on this floor, boy? Horsehide glue?"

"Of course not. How stupid do you think I am?"

"Right now is probably not the best time to ask that question." She took a deep breath and counted to ten. "Now just tell me truthfully, what did you use on this floor."

"The stuff you gave me. The junk with the picture of the ditzy woman in a dress on the front who was grinning while she was mopping the floor." He gave a sniff. "And I've gotta tell you, I think my testosterone level went down several notches just looking at that damned picture."

"Did you read the directions on the back?"

"What? Well, no. But I've used stuff like that when I was in the service. I had to clean a few latrines, and it wasn't all that complicated."

Savannah thought over the directions she had, herself, followed for years when using her favorite "clean and shine" product.

(1) Squirt small amount onto floor. (2) Spread evenly with damp cloth. (3) Rinse cloth in warm water and wipe floor. Repeat (3) as needed until floor is clean.

Yes, they were simple directions. So what was the problem?

He sighed as though weighed down by the cares of the world. "All right. Here's what I did—I got that bucket out from under your kitchen sink, squirted about half of the bottle in the pail, filled it up with water, and mopped it."

Ah, if all mysteries were so easily solved, she thought.

"Again I ask you, 'What did I do wrong?' " he said, his hands and arms waving about as though he were conducting the San Carmelita Philharmonic Orchestra.

"Just take a little stroll in there, darlin', and I'm sure you'll get a sense of it."

"I know it was a little sticky after I first did it," he said, "but I figured after it dried, it'd be . . ."

She left him and walked back down the hall toward the stairs. A second later, she heard him curse quite colorfully.

"Yeap, Daddy just discovered the problem," she whispered to one of the cats who had come upstairs to see what all the hullabaloo was about. "I'd stay clear if I were you."

She was walking through the kitchen on her way to the enclosed back porch and the half bath—where she could take care of her much overdue visit to "see that man about that horse," as Granny used to call it—when the phone rang.

"Dadgummit. I don't have time for this," she said. "My eyeballs are a-floatin' as it is."

But she hurried into the kitchen and scooped up the phone from the counter.

"Hello," she said breathlessly.

"Hello, daughter," said a sweet, deep male voice. A voice that sounded a lot like Dirk's. On a good Dirk day.

Not today.

"Oh, howdy, Richard." She glanced at her watch. "Did y'all get to San Francisco yet?"

"We got here in record time. We already took our tour of Alcatraz."

"Did you like it?"

"Loved it. Next time I'm in the doghouse with Dora, I think I'll head down this way and see if I can get a room there."

Savannah smiled. She liked this man already. Anybody with a deep, Dirk voice and a corny, down-home sense of humor was pretty much all right in her book.

"We're looking forward to your visit so much," Savannah said, knowing that her nose might grow a half an inch for that little half-fib. "Dirk's real excited."

"Us, too, dear," he replied. "Believe me, this is a dream come true for both of us."

"We'll do all we can to make you comfortable once you get here."

"Ah, don't worry about that. I was a cop, remember? Did a lot of stakeouts. I can get comfortable anywhere."

Savannah knew exactly what he was talking about. Spending fourteen-hour stretches in Dirk's Buick, waiting for a bail jumper to sneak into his old lady's house to score some love, afforded many life lessons—including how to find comfy positions under challenging conditions.

"Don't you worry about anything, honey," he said. "This is going to be a nice visit. The first of many, I'm sure."

Instantly, she felt better about everything: the curtains in the washer, the sparsely furnished refrigerator and cupboards, the bathroom floor that felt like flypaper.

"I'm sure you're right," she said, basking in the warm glow. "When do you reckon you'll be arriving? In time for supper, I hope."

"Oh, we're early risers. Up before the sun. We'll be on the road by four at the latest. We'll be there by noon!"

Dirk found her in the kitchen—the phone in her hand, a brain-dead look on her face, as though all her circuits had been blown.

"They'll be here for lunch," she told him in a flat monotone, her eyes staring straight ahead.

"Noon? Lunch? Tomorrow?"

She nodded woodenly. "They're early risers, up before the sun."

"Damn."

"No kidding."

Chapter 20

The next day, Savannah and Dirk sat in the living room, each in their favorite spots, as they petted cats and resisted the urge to jump up and run to the window every time they heard a vehicle drive by.

In spite of the fact that her stomach was tied in knots and her hands were trembling from all the adrenaline and caffeine surging through her system, Savannah yawned.

She glanced at the clock on her mantelpiece. "It's only a quarter to noon, and I already feel like I need a nap."

"It's a good thing you found out that Freddie's Food Mart was open twenty-four hours a day, huh?"

"Oh yeah, grocery shopping at five in the morning! How fun! Reckon I can scratch that great adventure off my bucket list."

"And the bathroom floor looks pretty good, don't you think?" he said sheepishly.

"The house stinks like ammonia, and the floor's still streaky as hell, but at least you can walk in and out of the room without getting stuck like a poor pitiful mouse on one of those awful glue traps."

She happened to glance his way, and one look at his face told her that while she might be feeling nervous, he was positively terrified.

Feeling like a total jerk, she moved Diamante off her lap, stood, and hurried over to the sofa. She sat down next to him and reached for his hand.

"I'm sorry, darlin'," she said. "This is a tough situation for you, and I'm not making it any better by bellyachin'."

"That's okay," he said, more graciously than she felt she deserved. "I'm sorry you have to go through this with me."

She flashed back momentarily to the months of rehabilitation after she had been attacked. She remembered the ten thousand kindnesses, small and great, that he had so lovingly shown her during that time.

And he had never once complained.

She lifted his hand and kissed the back of it, then laid his palm against her cheek. "Sugar, don't you give it a second thought. Like the preacher man said, you and I are one now. If you're going through something tough, then so am I."

Suddenly, he grabbed her and hugged her against his chest, so tightly that she could barely even breathe.

"Thank you, Van. You don't know what that means. This is really hard for me. It's about the toughest thing I've ever had to do, meeting them. I was mad at them for so many years. I had it in my head that they'd just thrown me out like yesterday's garbage."

She pulled back from him, just enough to be able to look into his face. "But that isn't true, honey. You know that now. Tammy told you they've been trying to find you for years. Your mom had posted messages all over the Internet, hoping to connect with you."

She was shocked to see tears well up in his eyes and spill down his face. Dirk did a lot of complaining, but in all the years she had known him, she had seen him get misty-eyed just a handful of times. And usually that occurred only when the national anthem was being played or they saw a particularly sad animal story on TV.

Gently, she wiped his tears away with her fingertips. "I'll betcha that before this visit is over, they'll say some things that'll make you feel a lot better about what happened."

"Maybe. But what if what they tell me makes it worse? Van, you don't know how bad it was, growing up in that orphanage. Seeing the other kids get adopted. Wondering why nobody wanted you—not even your own mother or father."

She felt a shudder run through his body, and he closed his eyes, as though trying to shut out the painful memories.

Running her fingers through his hair, she said softly, "No, sweetheart, I don't know how bad that was. My folks had their problems, but at least I had Granny. I can't even imagine what you went through."

"And I'd done a pretty good job of putting it behind me," he said. "I'm not one of those people who sits around and complains about their lousy childhood. I never blamed any of my problems or who I was on them."

"I know you didn't, honey. Look how many years it took you to even tell me about it. You're a strong man. A self-made man. You should be proud. As we say down South, 'You rose above your raisin.' "

His eyes met hers with an intensity that frightened her. She'd never seen him like this and wasn't sure what to do or say to help him.

"I don't feel like a strong, self-made man, Savannah. I wouldn't tell anybody else on earth this—but right now, I don't feel like a man at all. I feel like that little boy back in the orphanage, and it sucks."

She grasped him by the shoulders and gave him a little shake.

"Stop it," she said. "You just stop it right now, Dirk Coulter. I don't care how you're feeling. Feelings ain't facts. And the fact is: Your parents are gonna be here in a minute, and we're gonna do everything we can to make them feel comfortable and welcome. And when I say, 'We,' I mean it. We're in this together, you and me. Got it?"

He nodded and offered her a half-smile.

She gave him a playful thump on the end of his nose. "Now stop with the gloom and doom. We're gonna have a nice visit. It'll be fun . . . you know, like rummaging through a dumpster looking for rotten body parts."

He laughed, and she could tell he was beginning to relax at least a bit.

"I just wish I could drop twenty pounds in the next two minutes," he said, "and maybe sprout some more hair up there on the top."

At that moment, they both heard it—the distinctive sound of a vehicle pulling into the driveway.

His eyes widened as he grabbed for her hand. "My blood pressure just went up fifty points, at least," he said.

"And I'll betcha dollars to donuts that theirs is even higher," she replied, jumping to her feet and pulling him off the sofa. "Let's go put 'em outta their misery."

The first thing Savannah saw, when she and Dirk ran out of the house to greet his parents, was a giant black box in her driveway, and a blur of red, white, and blue.

Then she realized it was an old, black, Jeep Cherokee with an enormous American flag painted across the hood.

The driver's door opened, and something gray and shaggy streaked across the lawn toward her.

Her instincts—and her overactive imagination—told her that it was an enormous rat. But fortunately, before she made a complete fool of herself and ran, screaming, for higher ground atop her antique lamppost . . . she realized it was a dog. A miniature schnauzer.

It raced up to her and began dancing at her feet, hopping up and down on her shoe, and scratching wildly at her kneecap with its forepaws.

In an effort to save her best linen slacks—and because it was so darned cute that she couldn't resist—she reached down and scooped it up.

Wriggling like a worm on a hot sidewalk, the dog began to lick her cheeks and chin with a violence that she, as a cat owner, had never experienced.

"Well, well. And a fine how-do-you-do to you, too," she said, trying her best to avoid being French-kissed by a canine who hadn't even bought her dinner and whose name she didn't know.

Returning her attention to the Jeep, she saw a tall, handsome man getting out. He looked remarkably like Dirk, only with glistening white hair and paler skin. He appeared to be in his early sixties. He was wearing a blue plaid flannel shirt and well-worn jeans.

So this is Richard Jones, my father-in-law, Savannah thought. And more important, it was Dirk's biological father.

She couldn't imagine the enormity of the moment for both of them.

Richard's eyes sought out Dirk, and when he saw him, his face glowed with one of the happiest smiles Savannah had ever seen on anyone.

He rushed across the lawn, his arms open, grabbed Dirk, and enfolded him in an embrace that looked like a cross between a bear hug and an NFL tackle.

Savannah watched on the sidelines, as the two men clung to each other, laughing from the sheer joy of the experience.

She glanced toward the Jeep, but the sun was glaring on the windows and she couldn't see the passenger still inside.

Finally, Richard held his son at arm's length so he could check him out. "Just look at you!" he said. "Boy, you're a chip off the old block."

"Then I guess that makes you the old block," Dirk said, still laughing. "How was your trip?" he asked, casting a quick look at the still-closed passenger door.

"Fine, just fine. It's a beautiful drive." Richard looked at the Jeep, too, a slightly worried look on his face. "It might've not been a good idea to take the Pacific Coast Highway, though. Turns out, it's quite a thrill ride. I think I scared the hell outta your mother when I was wringing out those curves, and she was looking over those cliffs. She was white-knuckling it all the way."

Both men and Savannah were quiet for a long moment as they waited, watching the closed door.

At last, Dirk said, "Is she all right?"

Richard shook his head. "To be honest, son—no, not really. She's scared, you know . . ."

Dirk cleared his throat. "Yeah. I know."

He looked over at Savannah. She had no idea what to say or do.

Finally, the Southern hostess in her came to the fore, and she started toward the Jeep. But Dirk met her halfway and said softly, "That's okay. I got it."

She paused, still holding the wiggly schnauzer, as Dirk walked up to the Jeep door and slowly opened it.

A woman with clouds of lovely salt and pepper hair sat there in the passenger seat. Like her husband, she was wearing jeans and a plaid flannel shirt. But other than that, it was impossible to see what she looked like, because her hands were spread over her face.

She was leaning forward, nearly against the dash. Her shoulders were hunched and shaking with sobs.

For only a second, Dirk hesitated. Then he reached inside and awkwardly put his arms around her. "Hey there," he said softly. "What's the matter, huh?" Ever so gently, he pulled her out of the Jeep and steadied her as she leaned against him, still weeping.

He stroked her hair and kissed the top of her head. "There, there," he said, "you're okay." She looked up at him, her pretty face wet with tears—as his had been only moments before in the house with Savannah.

"What's all this?" he said with a smile. "You haven't even met me, and you're cryin' already? Most people don't start bawling till they've known me at least five or ten minutes."

She gazed up at him with a mixture of awe, adoration, and heartbreak in her eyes. "It's just that . . . you don't know how long I've waited to . . ."

Again she dissolved into tears.

"I know. Me too," he told her. Then he put his arm around her shoulders and led her toward Savannah, Richard, and the house. "Come on. We've got a lot of catchin' up to do. And first of all, I want you to meet my beautiful, new wife."

Dirk looked at his beaming father and gave him a grin and a wink. Then he added, " 'Cause from what I can tell, the men in this family have a history of marrying women way better than they deserve."

For a woman who couldn't squeeze out a single word because she was crying too hard, she's sure making up for lost time now, Savannah thought, as she sat across the lunch table from her mother-in-law and listened to her seemingly endless stream of chatter.

I do declare, I don't think she ever stops to take a breath, Savannah told herself. *Maybe she just sucks the air in through her ears and lets it flow outta her mouth.*

She looked to her left to see if Dirk had noticed. And judging from the glazed look in his eye, the mechanical nods of his head, and the obligatory grunts of "Uh-huh," and "Huh-uh," he was finding it as difficult to follow Dora's verbal stream of consciousness as she was.

"I'm telling you," Dora was saying, as she helped herself to a third helping of Savannah's famous crab macaroni and cheese, "I felt like slapping Richard for driving so fast on that crazy road. But of course if I'd slapped him, we would've gone right over the side of one of those giant cliffs and splatted down there on those jagged rocks. I'm telling you, it was absolutely terrifying! Some of those cliffs had to be a hundred feet high!"

Savannah didn't have the heart to tell her that in some places the cliffs between the Pacific Coast Highway and the ocean below were actually *several* hundreds of feet tall. And the thought of slapping anyone who was driving that gorgeous but treacherous road was ludicrous.

Personally, Savannah had driven it once. She was absolutely delighted that she had and believed that everyone should do so. Once.

"And Richard kept wanting to pull off to the side of the road to look at the views. I was scared to death that somebody was going to run us over. If even one person decided that they were going to stop and look at the view in the exact same place that you are busy looking at the view they could run into the back of you, push you and your car off one of those cliffs, and it would be just like in the movies, when the car goes sailing through the air in slow motion—except that if it was for real it wouldn't be in slow motion—and then *splat*! The car and you in it would look like one of those cars that got mashed in a junkyard. You've seen those cars that get mashed in the junkyard, haven't you, Dirk? Savannah, you've seen them, right?"

Savannah's and Dirk's heads bobbed in unison like a couple of dolls in the back of a '59 Chevy.

Savannah turned to Richard, hoping that perhaps he had a solution to the problem at hand—the desperate need to rest one's ears with a second or two of blissful silence every once in a while.

But Richard was enjoying the crab macaroni and cheese as much as his wife. He munched away peacefully, not even attempting to interject himself into Dora's one-woman conversation. Nor did he look upset by the situation.

In fact, he didn't even seem to notice.

Savannah reminded herself that they had been married for more than forty years. No doubt, he had adapted to the situation long ago—or else he would've gone crazy or deaf or both.

"This macaroni and cheese is the best I've ever had," Dora was saying. "I've made a lot of macaroni and cheese myself in my life. No matter how tight the grocery budget is, you can almost always afford macaroni and cheese."

Savannah was infinitely relieved that they were finally off the subject of the terrors of the Pacific Coast Highway. She herself was starting to feel nauseous, just hearing about those winding curves and dizzying heights.

Cooking was a good topic of conversation. She was happy to be back on familiar ground.

"Yes," Dirk began, elbowing his way in, "Savannah's a great cook. And this is one of her best dishes. I asked her if she'd cook it for you because you—"

"But this isn't real crab meat you've got in here, is it, Savannah?"

Dora gave Savannah an intense, probing look. And for a moment, Savannah thought what it must feel like to be a perp in an interrogation room with Dirk.

"Well, I . . ."

"Because that would just be like throwing money away, using real crab meat when the fake stuff is so good and so much cheaper. You do use the fake stuff, right?"

"I . . . um . . . it's a special occasion, so I—"

"Oh, no. You might as well have put a match to that money and burned it up. We'll have to put a stop to that. Waste not, want not, you know. My parents were children during the Great Depression, and if they taught us kids one thing, it was 'Waste not, want not.' And you young people these days would do well to remember that because you never know when you're going to need something and you won't have it because you . . ."

Savannah laid her fork down on her plate and slowly, discreetly put her right hand up to her ear. Just for a moment she entertained a small, harmless fantasy. She imagined that there, near her earlobe, was a tiny button. And if she pushed it, just like that, one itty-bitty push, she was turning the volume on Dora's chatter from a ten down to a two.

Ah yes, she thought, *much better.*

It was a nice little fantasy. Far, far nicer than the other one that kept running through her mind, no matter how many times she willed it away. The other dark, evil fantasy, where she stuffed her mother-in-law's mouth full of crab meat—fake of course, so as not to burn up all that good money—then covered her mouth with a big ol' piece of duct tape, and then tossed her out the back door.

Lord knows, Dirk's put up with your crazy relatives all these years, Savannah, she told herself. Between her sister Marietta acting like a brazen hussy around him to her youngest sister, Atlanta, throwing juvenile hissy fits to sister Vidalia and her two sets of completely undisciplined twins—Savannah had an enormous debt to pay. And the currency was tolerance.

Suddenly, from the living room erupted a cacophony of indignant cat snarls, followed by the rapid-fire staccato of canine toenails racing across her hardwood floor. Wild hissing. Schnauzer barking. Two black streaks followed by a gray one—into the kitchen, around the table twice, then back into the living room.

"If you don't mind," Dora prattled on, "when we're done with our lunch, I'd like to bring our dishes in from the truck and wash them up there in your sink."

"Oh?" Savannah couldn't help being impressed by this unexpected show of gentility. "You brought along your china on your road trip?"

"Of course we brought dishes. We weren't gonna stop at restaurants along the way. They charge you an arm and a leg for a hamburger and fries these days. On the other hand, a can of pork and beans and a package of saltines—half the price, at least."

"Of course you can wash your dishes," Savannah assured her. "I just hope none of them got broken there in the car, on that rough, winding road."

"They didn't get broken," Dora said around her mouthful of mac and cheese. "They're plastic. You know, the kind that you throw away after you use them."

Savannah knew she shouldn't do it. Stating the obvious was a habit that frequently landed her in a heap of trouble.

But that had never stopped her before.

"Then why don't you just throw them away instead of washing them?"

There, she'd said it. There was no going back now.

She glanced at Dirk, who rolled his eyes and shook his head. She looked at Richard, who was busy buttering a corn muffin and paying no attention at all to the melodrama playing out around him.

Dora, for once, seemed to have nothing to say. She just sat there, staring at Savannah, her mouth open.

But it was a short reprieve. She quickly regained her composure and her gift of speech.

"Well, we certainly haven't used those plates and utensils enough times to warrant just throwing them away," she said with great indignation.

She turned to Dirk and shook her head sadly. "Son, you've got yourself a very pretty girl here, and obviously she's an excellent cook. But you're going to have to keep a tight rein on those purse strings of hers, or she'll run you right into the poor house."

Dirk gasped and shot Savannah a terrified look.

Savannah felt every drop of blood she possessed rush to her face.

Even Richard glanced up from his muffin and temporarily suspended his buttering.

A hundred hot, sarcastic words fought each other to be the first to spill out of Savannah's mouth as she struggled to keep them all inside.

But it was finally Dirk who came to the rescue. He chuckled, gave his mother a playful wink, and said, "Naw, I don't control Savannah's purse strings. In fact, I don't dare touch her purse. That's where she keeps her Beretta."

From the living room came another series of cat hisses and dog barks, followed by the sound of something crashing and breaking.

Yep, she thought. *Marietta, Vidalia, Atlanta, and all the rest of the crazy Reids notwithstanding—payback's a bitch.*

Then there was another sound, even more disturbing.

It was Savannah's cell phone, and the cheerless little tune it was playing was "Funeral March of a Marionette," the theme song of the old Alfred Hitchcock television show.

Dr. Liu was calling.

Instinctively, Savannah knew that she had way bigger problems to deal with than a cheap, chatty mother-in-law.

Chapter 21

Savannah felt terribly guilty for leaving Dirk alone with his parents while she worked a case. It was a bit like throwing Daniel into the lions' den with a string of pork chops tied around his neck.

Okay, it's only one lioness, she told herself as she drove the Mustang down the Ventura Freeway, heading south toward Malibu. And Dirk seemed to be holding his own with her—far better, in fact, than Savannah had been.

The telephone call she had received at the table had, indeed, been Dr. Liu.

"Savannah," she'd said, "you were absolutely right. The tissue sample taken from the skin above his breastbone showed extremely high concentrations of Lido-Morphone. Undoubtedly a lethal dose. I'm changing my ruling to homicide."

When Savannah had informed Dirk, she'd seen the struggle of conscience on his face. He had spent less than an hour with his parents, yet duty was calling.

Now that Dr. Liu had changed her ruling to homicide, the SCPD would no doubt initiate a formal investigation. And as their senior detective, Dirk would probably catch the case. Then he wouldn't have time to breathe, let alone visit at length with his guests.

Surprisingly, both Dora and Richard had tried to assure Dirk that they wouldn't be offended if he had to leave them alone to do his job. But during a quick, private conference with Savannah on the back porch, Dirk had agreed to accept her offer to drive to Malibu and interview Alanna Cleary alone.

Of course, not being a complete fool, she'd allowed him to believe that her offer was based entirely on selfless generosity. Had she been completely honest, she would have admitted to him and herself that self-preservation had a lot more to do with it.

Because if she didn't get a break from Dora, Dora might get a break from her—an arm break, a leg break. Or at the very least, a broken nose.

She still couldn't help seething when she thought about that snarky purse strings comment.

Keep a tight rein on her purse strings, my ass, she thought. She had been earning and managing her own money since she was fourteen years old, and she'd be damned if some gal she'd just met was gonna start telling her how to spend it. While she was chowing down on her 100 percent genuine crab macaroni and cheese!

As Savannah left the Ventura Freeway and jogged her way over to the Pacific Coast Highway, she passed some of the most fertile farmland in the country. At the moment it was covered with acres and acres of strawberries, glistening in the sunshine, as far as the eye could see.

She drove by numerous fruit stands, advertising flats of the colorful berries for deliciously low prices.

Dora would, no doubt, approve.

Unless frozen ones were cheaper. Maybe somewhere there

were artificial strawberries for free. Perhaps someone would even pay you to take them!

We could have them for dinner tonight, she thought, *with pork and beans and crackers and eat them off recycled disposable plates with broken forks that only have one or two tines left.*

Stop it, girl! You've plum lost your marbles! she told herself with a mental slap to bring her back to sanity.

Well, you haven't lost them all entirely, but there's definitely a hole in the bottom of your bag. It's a good thing you're getting away for a while, even if it's to investigate a murder.

"Call me just as soon as you're finished talking to Alanna," Dirk had told her as he'd kissed her good-bye at the door. "Right now, she's the only fresh lead we've got."

And he's right, of course, she thought as she drove the beautiful stretch of the PCH just north of Malibu. To her left stood the gently rolling mountains, and to her right was the sparkling ocean.

Surfers in their black wetsuits took advantage of the early-afternoon high tides, riding the glistening waves while trying to avoid the barnacle-encrusted shoals.

In designated areas, giant RVs had parked in their reserved spots, while families enjoyed the beach, the ocean, and each other on their quintessential Southern California vacations.

Savannah made a mental note to be sure her in-laws got a chance to visit the beach several times during their stay. She would dig the kites out of the garage, pack up a nice picnic lunch, complete with one-time-use paper plates, and a Frisbee for the mini-schnauzer named Mickey.

Dora should approve. California beaches were free.

Savannah had no trouble finding Arroyo Verde Canyon, where Alanna Cleary lived. Unfortunately, that region of Malibu had received quite a lot of attention only a few months before when brush fires had ravaged the area.

Thanks to the valiant efforts of courageous firefighters, the blazes had been extinguished before any structures were lost.

But Savannah recognized the canyon immediately when she saw the charred hills.

She had lived in this area long enough to know that wildfires were simply nature's way of cleaning house. The overgrown brush would burn, the ashes would fertilize the ground, and new growth would spring up in its place.

But nature could be cruel, clearing the land of both vegetation, man, and beast with no conscience and no regret.

Savannah turned left onto the secondary road, with its cracks and potholes, that led away from the major highway and deep into the hills.

She passed numerous fine homes and even a few mansions— all of which the flames had narrowly missed—as she noted the address numbers on mailboxes and gates. Finally, she saw the number 660.

As she had been instructed to do when she had called to make the appointment, Savannah stopped at the security gate and pushed the red button on the entry panel.

A moment later, a soft, feminine voice, which Savannah recognized as Alanna's, spoke through the speaker mounted above the panel. "Hello?"

"It's me, Ms. Cleary, Savannah Reid," she said.

"Yes, Savannah, come on in," was the reply.

A buzzer sounded, and the tall, broad iron gates swung open.

Savannah wasted no time going through. She never entered a set of security gates without entertaining at least a fleeting fantasy of them snapping closed too quickly and scrunching the Red Pony flat with her trapped inside it.

And she never entertained that fantasy without cursing herself for having an overly vivid, more-than-a-little-bit paranoid imagination.

She drove down a somewhat long driveway until she saw, nestled among some orange and lemon trees, a surprisingly modest home.

It was a simple, Cape Cod–style place. Its one beauty was the large porch that appeared to wrap all the way around the house. And on the porch, sitting in an oversized wicker rocking chair was the beautiful red-haired actress herself.

As Savannah parked the Mustang and got out of the car, Alanna left the porch and walked down the cobblestone sidewalk to greet her.

She was wearing a simple white camisole and a long, gauzy, aqua skirt that swept her bare feet when she moved. Her famous auburn locks hung loosely around her shoulders, and her only adornment was the pair of oversized gold hoops in her ears.

Although her clothing could be considered beach attire, she looked so elegant that Savannah felt dowdy and underdressed in her simple linen blazer, slacks, and cotton shirt.

But Alanna's warm smile quickly put her at ease, as she extended her hand and said, "Savannah, how nice to see you again."

Her handshake was pleasantly firm—the sign of an open and confident woman. And Savannah decided she liked her already.

"I'm surprised you remember me," Savannah said. "You had so much going on, so many people around you, at the premiere the other night."

She didn't mention the funeral. She'd have to bring up painful topics too soon anyway.

Alanna turned toward the porch and waved a hand in the direction of the rocking chair she had just been sitting in and a matching one beside it. "Come have a seat. I'll get you something to drink, and you can tell me why you came to visit me today. I have a feeling it's important, or you wouldn't have driven all the way down here."

"Yes, I'm afraid it is. And don't worry about the beverage. I've got out-of-state company at home, so I don't really have time to visit very long. I just have a couple of quick questions."

Savannah sat in one of the rockers, and just for a moment, she allowed herself to enjoy the setting. The landscaping around Alanna's home was lush and tropical, with many different types of palm trees, hibiscus, and even a few purple and blue hydrangeas, which made Savannah feel quite at home.

"My granny would go crazy over your yard," Savannah told Alanna, who settled into the other chair and tucked her bare feet under her. "She just loves her hydrangeas. She calls her white ones 'snowballs.' "

"Where are you from, Savannah? Alabama? Mississippi?"

"A little town called McGill in Georgia."

Alanna chuckled. "Savannah. Georgia. Of course. I didn't think that one through. But I knew it was somewhere in the South. I love your accent. I had to do a Southern Gothic movie one time, and no matter how much coaching I had, I couldn't quite nail it."

"Reckon you have to be born to it. Are you a California girl, as the Beach Boys say?"

"Born and bred in Oxnard."

Savannah ran her fingertips over the woven wicker on the chair's armrest, took a deep breath, and said, "Alanna, we have a serious situation on our hands."

"Yes, I gathered as much. How can I help?"

"I have to ask you a couple of really personal questions. You can help by being completely honest with me. Believe me, I'm not trying to pry into your life. I'm sure you get enough of that already, being a celebrity and all."

"Yes, I do. But I understand that you're just doing your job. And I trust you. Ask whatever you need to."

"Okay, thank you." Savannah turned in her chair so that she could look directly into those world-famous green eyes. "I've heard rumors that you and Jason were romantically involved. In fact, if you believe the tabloids—and I don't—you were the reason he and Thomas ended their relationship. Is there any truth to those stories?"

Alanna toyed with a lock of her long, red hair a moment before replying. "I'd have to say that's a bit of a 'yes' and a 'no.' "

"I'm sorry, but you'll have to clarify what you mean by that."

"Did Jason and I have a sexual relationship? No. The only time we kissed or touched each other was what you saw right there on the screen." She hesitated. "But did we have a romantic relationship? That's a bit harder to answer."

She looked down and ran her finger along some of the tiny beads on her skirt. "It's hard to explain to someone who isn't an actor, but working on a film is an intense experience. The stress of it all heightens one's emotions. I find that I have very strong feelings about the individuals I work with on a set. I either loathe them or draw very close to them. There's not a lot of middle ground."

Savannah nodded, thinking it was very similar for police officers. When she had been on the job, she had bonded with some of her fellow cops, and the rest she avoided like roadkill skunks.

"That makes sense," she said. "Did you love or loathe Jason?"

"Oh, I loved him. I adored him. He was one of the dearest people I've ever met in my life. And I'll miss him until the day I die. But I knew he had no interest in me, at least not as a lover. And it's a real shame that those closest to us couldn't see that."

"Those closest to you? And who was that?"

"Jason's partner, Thomas. And my boyfriend, Mick. They both thought that something was going on between me and Jason. And that's a shame, because it ruined two relationships."

Instantly, Savannah's antennae rose. "So the tabloids were right? That was the reason Jason and Thomas called it quits?"

A flash of anger crossed Alanna's face, and it occurred to Savannah that Alanna Cleary could go from "gentle" to "riled" in a heartbeat—mellow, California girl or not.

"Before we go any further," the actress said, "I just want to make something perfectly clear. *I* did not cause Jason and Thomas to break up. Thomas's insane jealousy is the reason Jason had to end their relationship. Thomas has some major trust issues, and he made Jason miserable by spying on him constantly, accusing him of being sexual with everyone around him—male and female."

"To your knowledge, did Thomas abuse Jason?"

"I don't know if he was ever violent with Jason, but he most certainly abused him verbally. I witnessed it myself several times, and I have to tell you, it broke my heart. I don't blame Jason for dumping him. I would have, too, in a heartbeat. No one should have to put up with that crap."

"Amen to that, sister." Savannah thought she sensed an anger in Alanna that seemed to be coming from a more personal source. "Did you ever find yourself in that position, Alanna?"

"Yes, I certainly did. And that's why my ex-boyfriend, Mick, is now touring Europe by himself. One night when we were in the middle of filming Thomas called here looking for Jason. Mick answered the phone, and that stupid, drunken Thomas told him that Jason and I were having a wild, passionate love affair. Mick believed him, not me. And while I might have forgiven Mick for that, under the circumstances, I'll never forgive him for the way he spoke to me when he confronted me about it. I don't put up with that kind of disrespect."

Savannah gave her a grim smile. "Good for you, girl. I wish more women felt that way. There'd be a lot less sorrow in the world—for them and for their kids."

"Thank you. Something tells me you don't put up with a lot of crap yourself, Savannah from McGill, Georgia."

"I don't have to. I've got a good guy at home. And if he wasn't a good one, he'd be out the door."

"Maybe I'll find myself one of those good guys someday."

"You will. They're everywhere. You just have to toss all the jackasses aside to get to 'em. And speaking of jackasses, tell me a little more about Mick. You say he's in Europe now. How long has he been there?"

"Six weeks."

Savannah did some quick math in her head and realized that not only was Mick out of the country the night Jason died, but he had left the continent two weeks before the prescription on that box of patches had been filled.

Like many of the roads she had traveled in this case, Mick was a dead end. And apparently so was this interview.

"Alanna, this has been lovely—our little chat and getting to know you better. But I've got to get going." She stood and tucked her purse under her arm.

Alanna Cleary unfolded her long legs and rose from her chair. She reached over and laid her hand on Savannah's shoulder and looked intently into Savannah's eyes. "I was honest with you," she said. "Now I want you to return the favor. Okay?"

"Fair enough. What do you want to know?"

"Did somebody kill Jason? Is that why you're here questioning me?"

Savannah met her gaze, straight on. "Jason was murdered. And, yes, that's why I'm here."

Tears filled the actress's eyes. "I knew it. I felt it in my heart." Her voice caught in her throat, and she choked. When she recovered herself, she whispered, "Oh, God, that makes losing him so much worse."

Savannah reached for her hand and gently squeezed it. "Alanna, think hard. . . . Do you have any idea who might've done it?"

"No. I can't stand Thomas, and I think he's a creep. But I can't picture him or anybody else killing someone as special and wonderful as Jason. It's just unimaginable."

Savannah left Alanna standing, brokenhearted, on her walkway and got back into her car.

And as she drove through the charred hills on her way back to the Pacific Coast Highway and the sparkling beaches of Malibu, she had to admit that she, too, found the thought of anyone murdering Jason unthinkable.

She also had to admit that she knew no more now than she had before she had made this trek.

And she certainly wasn't looking forward to telling Dirk.

Dirk took the news better than Savannah had expected. In fact, he'd been so blasé about the whole thing that she had to resist the urge to put her hand on his forehead and see if he had a fever.

She and Dirk and his parents were sitting in her backyard, beneath the wisteria arbor, sipping cold lemonade, when she had delivered her depressing news. But during her entire Alanna Cleary debriefing, Dirk had hardly seemed to hear half of what she was saying.

"Where do you think we should go from here?" she asked him.

When he didn't respond, Richard piped up, "Sounds to me like you need to have another talk with that ex-boyfriend. When it comes to murder, you know it's almost always the significant other."

Savannah chuckled dryly. "In Seattle too, huh?"

Richard gave her a nice smile and a wink that reminded her so much of Dirk. "In Seattle, in San Carmelita, and in Timbuktu, I'm afraid."

"We had a girl get killed by her boyfriend right on our block," Dora began. "She'd called the cops on him a hundred times or more." She turned to Richard. "Hadn't she, honey? You answered some of those calls yourself. Don't you remember? I think it was back about ten years ago, or was it twelve? I think it was twelve. No, it was ten, because that was when you were working out of . . ."

Savannah glanced over at Dirk and saw that, yes, his fuses were fried. No doubt about it. Any minute now he was just going to keel over dead from acute boredom, and what would she say to Dr. Liu? "You can't understand, doc, unless you'd actually spent ten minutes with the woman. She's lethal. Really."

This was a Code 3 emergency call. Savannah had to rescue her husband. It might already be too late.

She noticed that both Richard and Dora were sweating profusely, even in the shade of the arbor. Long-sleeved, flannel shirts might be the perfect attire for the cool, damp clime of Seattle. But they were highly inappropriate for a summer day in sunny California.

"Is that there all the clothes y'all brought?" she asked, abruptly interrupting Dora.

Dora prattled on about her abused neighbor and assorted tangent topics, but Richard replied, "Yes, I'm afraid so. What you've heard about Seattleites is pretty much true. Our favorite color is plaid and we love our flannel."

"I love flannel, too. But not here and not in the summer." Savannah forced a bright smile onto her face—the sort of saintly countenance she imagined the martyrs had worn as they'd been tied to the stake. "Tell you what," she heard herself saying, "why don't you boys go interview Thomas again, while us girls go shopping for some California-style outfits?"

Dirk's mouth dropped open, and he stared at her—at first with amazement, then with utter love and gratitude shining in his eyes. "Really?" he said. "Really, Van? You'd do that?"

"Sure," she replied, before he said something he might regret. "It'd give us girls some bonding time, and who knows, Papa Richard here might put the fear of God in Thomas, and y'all might wrestle a confession outta him, right there on the spot."

Dirk gave her a smile that made her melt and mouthed the words "I love you."

She winked and held up two fingers—their unspoken gesture for "I love you, too."

But this time, what she was thinking was . . . *Boy, oh, boy, you owe me a five-pound box of Godiva truffles.*

As Savannah drove the Mustang down Lester Street, heading toward the mall, it occurred to her that if she were going to actually follow any of her mother-in-law's stories, she would need a flow chart.

Between all the subplots, the backtracking, the overlapping, and the frequent retractions, it was impossible for a mere mortal to truly keep track of a Dora story, no matter how hard they tried.

"And that's how we met, Dick and me, there at the junior high prom," she jabbered along happily. "Did I tell you that everybody used to call him Dick back when he was a kid? It was only after we got married that he started going by Richard. Or was it before we got married? Hmmm. I'm not sure. I know it was when LBJ was president because—Hey!"

She shouted so loudly that Savannah jumped and nearly lost control of the car as she was pulling into the mall parking lot. "What?" Savannah shouted back. "What's wrong?"

"Where are you taking me?"

Savannah glanced up and down the long line of stores, flanked on the ends by a Sears and a Macy's, then up at the enormous sign hanging practically over their heads, that said SAN CARMELITA MALL.

"Um . . . the mall? We're going shopping, right?"

"Yes, but who goes shopping at a mall?"

Savannah looked around at the hundreds of cars parked in the lot and the hordes of shoppers going in and out, carrying bags and boxes filled with their purchases.

At least a dozen smart-aleck replies rushed to her lips, but she swallowed them all.

"I'm sorry, Dora. Where would you like to shop? We have a Kmart and a Target, but if you'd prefer to go to Walmart, we could drive to Oxnard."

Dora lifted her chin a couple of notches and gave Savannah a haughty, disapproving look. "Don't tell me that you throw my son's money away shopping in those stores."

Savannah brought the Mustang to a screeching stop in the middle of the parking lot, turned to her mother-in-law, and said through gritted teeth, "No, I spend *my own* money in stores when I need to buy something. But if you would rather go somewhere other than this mall, I'd be more than happy to take you there."

"Good. Because if there's one thing I've learned over the years, it's how to survive on a cop's salary. And you'd better learn to, or you'll be living in the poor house."

Savannah reached over, grabbed her mother-in-law by the throat, and strangled her until she was absolutely certain she was dead. Then she drove to the swamps and fed her body to the gators.

But, of course, that was only in her fantasies.

In reality, she bit her tongue bloody and said in a voice that was so patient and kind, she was certain she deserved the Nobel Peace Prize, "Dora, where would you like me to take you? Please just tell me. Now."

Dora thought it over. "Well, it's too late to take in any garage sales. All the good stuff will be long gone by now. You have any good flea markets?"

"We have markets, and we have sand fleas galore. But no flea markets. Sorry. Your next choice?"

"Do you have thrift stores?"

"I reckon we do. Somewhere."

"Somewhere? You mean you don't even know where your thrift stores are?"

Savannah took off, squealing the Mustang's tires so badly that, if she had still been a cop, she would've given herself a ticket.

"You know that kind of driving eats up a lot of gas," Dora told her as she reached out and clutched the dash for dear life. "And you shouldn't have a car like this anyway. These muscle cars cost a fortune to run. Why, my cousin had one of these back in '69 or was it '68? I think it was '69 because that's the year that my sister got in trouble for—"

Savannah lay in bed, staring up at a ceiling that was much farther away than it usually was.

That was because she and Dirk were sleeping on the blow-up camping mattresses they had borrowed from Tammy. She could tell that hers had a leak. It was almost flat already, and her fanny was dragging on the floor.

She listened to her husband's breathing and tried to decide if he was awake or asleep.

They hadn't said much when they'd first gone to bed, and she had attributed that to exhaustion—and the fact that Dirk hated the new sleeping arrangements.

But judging from the lack of snoring, she was pretty sure he was awake. And if Dirk was conscious and had nothing to say— not even to complain about—something was wrong.

"You asleep?" she whispered, just loud enough for him to hear, but not enough to wake him.

"Yeah. Out like a log."

"You okay?"

He took much too long to answer, then said, "I guess."

She rolled toward him and onto her side, having to rearrange two cats in the process. "What's the matter?"

"Nothin'. It was just sorta a tough day."

"You were wonderful with your parents. Especially your mom, when they first got here. I was so proud of you."

"No big deal. That was the easy part."

She wondered whether to venture into those waters. She knew she probably shouldn't. But then, she had always been a dive-off-the-high-board-into-the-icy-water sorta gal.

"Your mom . . . she kinda talks a lot, huh?"

He groaned. "I always thought you talked a lot, but her . . . ? She could talk the dogs off a meat truck."

"And then there's the cheapness thing," Savannah ventured.

"What? What do you mean?"

"You know, the thing about washing the plastic dishes and only shopping at thrift stores."

"Oh, yeah. Those were great ideas. I should start getting my socks and underwear from there. Did you see those shirts she picked up for them? Said they were only a buck each."

Savannah cringed. Yes, how could she not notice? Most of Southern California would notice those shirts. Dora had found several eyeball-searing, Hawaiian-print monstrosities and snapped them up. And though Richard had blushed bright red when modeling his that evening before dinner, Dora had strutted around in hers like a runway model at Paris Fashion Week.

"Your dad's a peach, and I really think your mom has a heart of gold," she said, "but how are we gonna stand a whole week of that constant chattering?"

"I don't mind it. We've got a lot of catching up to do," he snapped back in a tone that told her she'd crossed the line.

Granny Reid had often told her granddaughters, "Don't you ever say a bad word to a man about his beloved momma. No matter what he says about her hisself, it don't give you the right to chime in. If you know what's good for ya, you'll bite your lip and keep it to yourself. Nothin' good ever came from criticizing a man's mother to his face. Just hold it in and wait till you can gossip about her behind his back."

And apparently, Granny Reid's rule applied even when that man had known his mother for less than twelve hours.

"It'll be fine," she said. "It's gonna be a nice visit, and maybe we'll get some leads on this case. Do you want to fill me in on your visit to Thomas? And I'll tell you the finer points of my talk with Alanna."

"Van," he said, sounding as weary as she had ever heard him, "I gotta go leak the lizard. And when I get back, do you mind if we don't talk anymore tonight. I don't think I can stand to hear another word outta anybody's mouth. I just want to enjoy the silence because, come tomorrow, we're gonna have to do that al-l-l over again."

"Gotcha," she said. "Just be quiet and don't wake them up. And don't you pee on that floor or I swear I'll talk to you for the rest of the night."

He grunted and left the room. She rolled onto her back once again and stared up at the ceiling.

He didn't take long. In less than three minutes he'd returned to bed, and true to her word, she said nothing, giving his ears, and hers, a much needed rest.

Thirty seconds later, he was snoring.

Oh well, so much for blissful silence.

Vaguely aware that her bladder was bursting and in desperate need of a potty visit, Savannah opened one eye and looked at the clock. 3:04 AM.

The night was only half over, and already nature was calling.

It was her own fault. She had drunk way too much sweet tea at the supper table. After all, what else was there to do but eat and drink, when you couldn't get a word in edgewise?

She rolled out of bed and shuffled out of the guest bedroom, down the hall, past her bedroom, which was now occupied by her in-laws, and into the bathroom.

She tried to be as quiet as possible. There was no point in waking up the whole house just because she'd had trouble pushing away from the tea.

Her bare feet stuck to the floor only once or twice on her trip to the toilet, for which she was infinitely grateful. Most nights when she had to make an unscheduled bathroom visit, she managed to get up, do her business, and go back to bed while maintaining a half-asleep, dreamlike state.

With any luck, tonight would be the same.

She lowered her pajama bottoms, took the position, and—

"Ah-wa-a-what the-ah-gh!" she screamed as her warm, still half-asleep butt hit water as frigid as a Yukon mountain stream and the cold, slimy hardness of the porcelain rim—the tiny, skinny edge of the toilet bowl itself, not the warm, wide comfort of the new wooden seat she had recently installed.

She struggled, trying to pull herself out of the cold, slick, God-only-knows-what's-in-there mess, only to sink all the way to the bottom. Her boobs were squashed against her thighs, her knees mashed against her chin, and her feet completely off the floor.

"Aw, shit!" she screamed, forgetting all about her sleeping in-laws in the next room. "Damn it, Dirk, I am gonna kill . . . you . . . de-e-a-ad!"

She flailed about, trying to push herself up, but she succeeded in doing nothing but splash the freezing water all over herself and the surrounding floor.

"Dirk!" she yelled, forgetting her former threat. "Get in here and help me! You lop-eared, flea-bitten numb-nut, I'm swear I am gonna—"

The bathroom door flew open, and even in the semi-darkness, she could see the look of alarm on Dirk's face.

"Savannah? What the hell?" he asked, hurrying to her.

"You left the damned toilet seat up again! And I—" She struggled some more, her arms outflung, twisting back and forth like an agitator in a washing machine. "Damn you! Get me outta here."

She could see him hesitate, as though weighing the wisdom of giving her her freedom at a time like this.

"Now!" she screamed.

"Okay, okay. Calm down, sugar."

He reached down, slid his hands beneath her armpits, and lifted her out.

"You're gonna be okay, darlin'," he said, trying to pull her now-soaked pajama bottoms back up. "It's just water."

She slapped his hands away. "Just water? Just water? It's stinkin' toilet water! Did you even flush?"

"Of course I did." He thought for a minute. "I think."

"Ugghh! Get outta here!" She kicked off the wet bottoms, then realized she couldn't go back into her now-occupied bedroom to get clean ones. "No, wait a minute. Give me your tee-shirt. I'm gonna have to take a shower."

As he peeled off his shirt, she turned on the tub faucet, then flipped the lever to turn on the shower. She mopped the floor with her pajama bottoms, then shoved them at him. "Take those out to the garage and throw them in the washer."

He gave her a sheepish grin and he took them. "Sorry, babe."

"Gr-r-r. If you weren't so cute, I'd murder ya."

"I know. Thank God I'm cute."

"Go."

"I'm gone."

He turned toward the door, and that's when he and she saw them—his parents, standing there in the doorway, staring, their mouths wide open.

Savannah squealed and pulled the shower curtain in front of her.

Dirk waved the wet pajamas at them. "Move along, move along," he told them. "Nothing to see here."

Dora and Richard looked at each other, then scooted back into the bedroom.

It was several seconds before Savannah heard Dora's titters, then Richard's guffaws.

She unwrapped herself from the shower curtain, telling herself that it was good to be able to laugh at yourself once in a while. A healthy dose of humility was character building.

She tossed a towel over the shower rod and got ready to step inside.

Yes, someday, they would all laugh about this. Ha ha, remember the night when Savannah—

"Awww-h-h-u-u-ugh!" she screamed again, even louder than before, as the frigid water hit every inch of her already traumatized skin. "What the hell?"

She jumped out and checked the faucet. Had she forgotten to adjust it to "warm"?

No, it was halfway between "cold" and "hot," just as it always was.

She dialed it closer to "hot" and tested it with her hand.

Cold. It was ice cold.

Then she turned it all the way to the left. But what should have been boiling water was still chilly enough for a polar bear.

"I can't believe this!" she shouted, not caring anymore who heard her. "Now there's no hot water!? What's going on around here? I—"

There was a knocking at the door. Then it opened. She turned to see Dirk.

"What's the matter now?" he said, standing there in the doorway, concerned and confused, her wet laundry still in his hands. "I got halfway down the stairs and heard you yell again."

"There's no hot water! The water heater must've blown. Of all the damned luck, having it go out just when I need to—"

The master bedroom door opened. Just a couple of inches. And Richard stuck his head out.

"Uh," he said, "just so you know. Your water heater didn't blow up."

"What?" Savannah and Dirk asked in unison.

"I thought I should tell you, before you start trying to fix it . . .

there's nothing wrong with your hot water heater. It's just that, well, Dora turns hot water heaters off at night."

Savannah and Dirk stared at him, speechless for the longest time.

Finally, Dirk asked, "Why?"

Richard looked over his shoulder back into the room. Then down at the floor. Then at them. "You know," he whispered, "to save electricity."

Chapter 22

If it hadn't been for coffee, Savannah would have never come downstairs again. She would've been perfectly content to remain in Dirk's man cave until she died of dehydration and starvation—dehydration being the more likely of the two, since she was pretty sure that she could live for six months or so off the Godiva truffles she had stored on her buttocks.

In a year or two, she would be pretty much mummified, and then they could place her in some sort of museum on display with a sign at her feet that read, "The Woman Who Died of Dehydration and Mortification."

And with any luck, every time Dirk went to the bathroom to choke the chicken or drain the dragon or dangle the snake, he could feel pretty dadgum awful about what he had done to her.

Yes, when Savannah had awakened the next morning and realized that she was wearing Dirk's tee-shirt instead of her Minnie Mouse jammies, it had all come rushing back to her. Her humiliation. Her fury. Her in-laws laughing their Seattle asses off in the next room. *Her* bedroom!

Many times, Granny Reid had told her to never, ever wish ill upon another human being.

But Gran had never sunk her bed-warmed butt into an ice-cold toilet at three in the morning, and then not even had a warm shower available to wash it off. If she had, Savannah was pretty sure that her righteous but fiery grandmother would understand.

At first, she considered witchcraft. Perhaps she could paint her naked body blue and bury a picture of a black cat—heaven knows, she had plenty of those—at a crossroads under a full moon, the whole time cursing Dora Jones.

But Savannah had been raised a Baptist, and that sort of thing was a bit of a stretch. So she decided to follow her upbringing and say a little prayer instead.

"Dear Lord, if it wouldn't be too much to ask, and if You aren't too busy working on world hunger and universal peace, I would really appreciate it if You would curse Dora Jones, for me, and work it out somehow so that she never gets to take another warm shower or hot bath for as long as she lives."

Feeling a bit better and smelling the aroma of the fresh coffee that was waiting for her in the kitchen below, she decided to abandon the whole mummy plan and join the land of the living.

They were the ones who should be ashamed of themselves, not her.

And if she could just remember that, she might be able to face them again without falling down dead on the spot from embarrassment.

When Savannah came downstairs and plodded across the living room, she saw Tammy sitting at the desk computer. Waycross was parked on a chair beside her.

They don't know, Savannah told herself. *They weren't here. They do not know.*

As she walked by them, she mumbled her customary precoffee greeting, "Um, hey. Yeah, mornin'."

They both shot back a simple "Good morning" and stared straight ahead at the computer. Tammy began to cough furiously, and Waycross covered his face with both hands, his shoulders shaking as if he were having some sort of seizure.

Okay, they know.

She raised her chin three notches, stiffened her backbone, and marched into the kitchen. At least, she marched as well as any woman could, wearing enormous, fluffy, red house slippers. As well as any woman could who had been fished out of a toilet bowl in the middle of the night.

Before she entered the room, she heard soft, hushed voices and the rattle of dishes, glasses, and cutlery. But the instant she walked into the dining area, the threesome sitting at the table fell silent. And they froze in mid-chew, as though someone had hit some sort of celestial "pause" button.

"Yeah," Savannah said, as she walked past the table and its occupants and over to the dish cupboard. "That's right. She's up now, so watch whatcha say."

Springing back to life, Dirk jumped up from his chair and rushed over to her. It was the first time she had seen him since "the incident"—since he had been banished to the living room to sleep on the couch.

He reached past her into the cupboard and pulled out her favorite Beauty and the Beast mug. "Here, baby, let me get that for you. You go sit down at the table, and I'll bring it to you. A nice, hot cup of coffee, that's what you need."

Although it was the last thing in the world she wanted to do, it had to be done. So she schlepped her way back to the table and sat in Dirk's chair—simply because it was the farthest away from Dora's.

The Joneses looked far more festive today in their tropical print shirts. Savannah needed a pair of dark sunglasses to look their way, which, eventually, she did. She ventured a glance at Richard first. And the affectionate, amused twinkle she saw in his eyes set her at ease faster than anything any of them could have said.

"Good morning, Savannah," he said.

She gave him a half-nod and a crooked smile. That was the best she could muster.

Finally, she forced herself to look Dora's way. She was surprised to see the embarrassment she was feeling herself registered on the older woman's face, plus a bit more as she stared down into her coffee cup.

For just a moment, Savannah allowed herself to consider that maybe, just maybe, Dora Jones wasn't the most evil mother-in-law on the planet and hadn't deliberately set out to humiliate her daughter-in-law beyond belief.

Maybe, just maybe, Dora's fiddling with the water heater temperature might have come out of a good place in her heart. Perhaps she was just trying to save them a dollar or two and didn't deserve to be executed at sunrise.

"I'm sorry," came a squeaky little sound from the other end of the table.

At first, Savannah wasn't even sure she had heard it. But then she forced herself to take another look at Dora. And sure enough, her mother-in-law had set down her coffee and was looking at her with eyes that were positively brimming with tears and sincerity.

Savannah gulped and squeezed out a simple, "That's okay."

"Really?" came the shaky reply. "Does that mean you actually forgive me?"

Savannah looked beyond Dora to her new husband, who was standing in the kitchen, her Beauty and the Beast mug in one hand, the coffeepot in the other, a hopeful, pleading look on his face.

She turned back to Dora and donned her sweetest, Southern-lady, butter-wouldn't-melt-in-my mouth smile. "Of course I forgive you, Dora," she said. "It was all just a sad, unfortunate misunderstanding." Then, as quickly as it arrived, the smile disappeared and her blue eyes turned icy. "But I'm warning you—if you ever so much as touch the temperature knob on my hot water heater again, I will get my gun, and I will shoot you dead where you stand. Got it?"

Dora nodded. "Got it."

"Good. Then I believe that this here's gonna be the start of a long and lovely, mother-daughter relationship."

Half an hour later, Savannah looked up from her breakfast plate and saw Tammy sticking her head around the corner, peeking into the kitchen. She had a tense, questioning look on her face.

"Yes, it's safe. You can come in now," Savannah said, as she shoveled in her last bite of grits.

Dirk snickered and added, "The dust's all settled. No casualties."

"You should have some of this ham," Dora said, helping herself to another large slice. "I've never eaten anything like this before. And Savannah made us something called red eye gravy. Have you ever had that?"

Tammy wrinkled her nose. "No, thank you."

"Tamitha doesn't poison her body with my cooking," Savannah informed her guests. "And that's probably why she can run to work and back every day, not to mention the frequent 10Ks and the occasional marathon."

Dirk grunted. "Yeah, but every time the Santa Ana winds start to howl, we have to stake her to the ground or she'll blow away."

Waycross stuck his curly red head around the corner, next to Tammy's. "If the fur's done flyin', and y'all are about done with stuffin' your faces, you might wanna hear some of the good gossip we dug up."

Richard stood, picked up his plate and Dora's, and headed for the kitchen sink. "Come right in," he said. "Juicy case gossip trumps food any day—even when it's as good as our Savannah's."

Three minutes later, the table had been cleared of all edibles and dishes, and only the coffee mugs remained. Tammy sat at the end of the table, her electronic tablet in her hand. But knowing her boss's propensity for living in the Dark Ages, she had printed everything out on paper and had passed the sheets around to everyone present.

"Your Honor," Tammy said, with an exaggerated head nod to Savannah, "I would like to present Exhibit Number One. These are the printouts of Thomas Owen's mean and nasty texts to Jason, referencing all the men and women that Jason was supposedly—" She glanced quickly at Dora and Richard, then to Savannah.

Without looking up from the paper in her hands, Savannah quickly supplied, "With whom he was supposedly dancing the Grizzly Bear Hump?"

Richard snickered. "You don't have to be so delicate. We're from the Great Pacific Northwest. Between November and March, Dancing the Griz is pretty much our only pastime."

Tammy tittered, then returned to the business at hand. "As you can see, Thomas didn't spare any words, even when he should have. I can't imagine having somebody I love talk to me like that."

Dora had sat still and quiet as long as she could. "I can imagine it. In fact, we had a neighbor that lived two doors down from us whose husband used to yell at her, night and day. I was so glad when they moved out two years ago. Or was it three years ago, Richard? It might have been three, because I think it was around the time that Gertrude next door had her gallbladder taken out. Or was it Gertrude's husband who—"

"Let's get on to Exhibit Number Two, please, Tammy," Savannah interjected quite loudly. So loudly, in fact, that Dora actually stopped to take a breath and a sip of coffee.

"Ah, yes," Tammy said, scanning her tablet's screen. "Next we have some information about an entirely different part of Jason's life. We go from his romantic escapades—"

"Objection." Savannah held up one hand. "*Alleged* escapades. Having some abusive s.o.b. accuse you of fooling around doesn't make it so."

"Duly noted." Tammy pointed to the next printed page in their stack of papers. "I'd like to draw your attention, ladies and gentlemen, to this information gleaned from Mr. Tyrone's bank statements."

Savannah scanned the page but didn't see anything too alarming. There were no checks written to bookies or drug pushers. No payments to arms dealers or blackmailers. At least none that were obvious.

"What are we supposed to be looking at here?" Richard asked.

"The payments to a particular health club where Jason had worked out for years. See those entries I highlighted in yellow? Those are all payments to that gym and his personal trainers there. He laid out thousands and thousands of dollars over the years to that place."

"So what?" Dirk shrugged. "Working out was his hobby and his livelihood rolled into one. Of course he would spend a fortune on it. What's the big deal about that?"

Tammy gave him a knowing little grin and said, "He stopped."

"What do you mean, he stopped?" Savannah asked.

Waycross leaned over and pointed to a particular area on Savannah's paper. "See there. Two months ago he just plum stopped going. And if you look right here, at the same time he bought a ton of fancy workout equipment for his house."

Suddenly, both Dirk and Savannah were highly interested.

Intently studying the papers in her hand, Savannah said, "That's right. We saw a whole personal gym right there in his house. And the stuff looked shiny and new."

"Apparently, that's because it was," Dirk said.

Richard laid the paper he was looking at on the table in front of them and poked it with his forefinger. "That's important, guys," he said. "For a bodybuilder like Tyrone, his gym of choice and his personal trainers are everything. He wouldn't leave them and start working out at home for no good reason."

Tammy gave them a self-satisfied smile that bordered on annoyingly self-righteous. "That's what we thought. We figured there must have been a big falling out of some sort."

Waycross draped his arm across Tammy's shoulders and gave her an affectionate little shake. "And that's when my girl here started checking them out."

Savannah couldn't help registering the "my girl" and feeling good about it. Apparently this Waycross-Tammy connection was official now, and that made Savannah very happy, indeed.

"That's good, you checking them out," Dora said. "People need to check everybody out these days. And you never know what you'll find. One of our neighbor's cousin's friends needed a babysitter for her kids—she had two of them, a girl and a boy, ages seven and five—and she got this teenager who seemed okay at first, but—"

"What did you find, Tams?" Savannah asked, trying to keep the frantic tone in her voice down to a minimum. "Tell us, quick."

"The owner of that gym, where Jason used to go, his name is Fabio Garzone. And he's got quite a reputation in Hollywood. He's known as the guy who can transform a Clark Kent, nerdy dude into Superman in a matter of weeks. Apparently, a lot of the major stars go to him before they start filming an action flick, or even a romance, where they're going to be showing off their killer abs and biceps. He and his trainers make sure that they've got some to show."

Savannah nodded thoughtfully. "I've noticed myself lately that nearly every actor in a starring role is all beefed-up for the screen."

Waycross nudged her with his elbow. "Yeah, I'll just bet you've noticed. Your eyeballs are probably sore from gawking at all that beefcake."

"I'm not saying they aren't pretty to look at. But I'm a little worried where it's all headed."

"What do you mean?" Richard asked. "What could be wrong with guys getting as strong and healthy as they can?"

"If they're truly strong and healthy, more power to them. But after watching women get more and more paranoid about their weight, feeling terrible about themselves because they're not super-skinny like the women on screen, I hope our men aren't headed down the same road."

Tammy nodded solemnly. "I heard that young guys are getting eating disorders now, like girls. And this bodybuilding and taking steroids is even popular with the high school kids now."

"That's what I mean. I hope you men don't fall into the same trap we women are in, risking our health to make ourselves look like society says we should."

Dirk looked down at his spare tire. It wasn't exactly a tractor tire, but it hadn't been there ten years before. "No danger of that happening around here," he said. Then he turned back to Tammy. "What else about this Fabio Garzone guy?"

"He's just as well known to law enforcement as he is to the rich and famous. Only for different reasons."

"Do tell," Savannah said.

"He's got a rap sheet going back to when he was fourteen and helped some other kids rob a pizza delivery guy. You'll find the long, sad list there on the next page."

Savannah scanned the paper, reading aloud, "Aggravated assault, second degree robbery, arson, distribution of Class A drugs, conspiracy to commit murder. And he's been to prison twice. Why is this guy walking the streets?"

"Other than the two he served time for, the rest of those charges didn't stick," Tammy said. "Apparently, the star witnesses at his trials tend to develop memory problems right before they testify."

"Oh, I don't like him one bit," Savannah said. "And it looks like Jason decided that he didn't either."

Dirk nodded. "When you go from paying somebody tens of thousands of dollars a month for years to zero, I'd say that constitutes a breakup of sorts."

He looked across the table at Savannah. "I think we need to go visit Fabio and see if he was as upset about Jason breaking up with him as our old friend Thomas was."

He turned to his father. "Wanna come along? Tangle with some musclemen?"

Richard beamed. "Sure."

"And how about you?" Savannah asked Dora. "It's Hollywood. While we're in the gym you could stroll up and down Sunset Boulevard and look at all the weirdoes. Maybe see a celebrity or two."

Dora thought it over. "Are there any thrift shops in Hollywood?"

Savannah resisted the urge to roll her eyes and sigh. "It's a pretty fair-sized town. I reckon we can find you one."

Chapter 23

The first thing Savannah always noticed when she walked into a health club was the smell.

No matter how much room deodorizer was sprayed into the air or how much disinfectant was squirted on the equipment, it smelled like a high school locker room. It stunk of sweat.

Although, as she looked around at the magnificent bodies that were producing that sweat, she decided maybe a whiff of BO was a small enough price to pay for the results. Because most of Fabio's clients were gorgeous.

But to Savannah, they were more like objets d'art than a objets de lust.

When it came to cuddling up with a male body in bed, she actually preferred her regular guy, who was masculine and muscular but not bulging to extremes. She wanted to cuddle up to a man she loved and snuggle with him, not feel like she was lying against a pile of rocks.

However, as she, Dirk, and Richard strolled into Garzone's Extreme Fitness Center, Savannah could certainly understand the appeal of a place like this.

The not-so-subtle message was: Walk through our doors, work your ass off, and you can look like the superheroes and super-heroines in the pictures that line the walls.

The bass from the hard-driving rock music that was piped into the center set the tempo for dozens of hard bodies who were working machines of steel, cables, and springs, running on tread-mills, and racing on bikes that went nowhere.

Others wore headphones and stared at their tablets, opting to live in worlds of their own choosing.

To their right was a merchandise center, selling tee-shirts, hats, hoodies, and multitudinous other fitness accessories, all with Gar-zone's logo—a muscle-bound, fire-breathing dragon. The giant Z in the middle of the name gave the dragon something that looked sus-piciously like an oversized phallus.

No point in being subtle, Savannah thought. *Go big or go home.*

To their left was a refreshment bar that, according to the sign on the wall, offered a plethora of protein-enriched delectables.

The food and drink here also followed the logo's theme, with names like Fire Eater, Dragon Slayer, and Blood of the Beast.

Sitting at the snack bar, drinking a perfectly normal, nonflam-ing bottle of beer, was a highly tattooed, swarthy fellow with thick black hair, whom Savannah recognized instantly from the mug shot Tammy had shown them.

"There he is, guys," Savannah told Dirk and Richard. "It's our friend, Fabio, in the buffed-up, tattooed-out flesh."

Fabio was having a conversation with an even larger fellow who stood behind the counter, mixing some sort of drink. From the looks on their faces, it was obvious that the conversation they were having wasn't an especially friendly one. It also looked like the big guy was losing the argument and wasn't particularly happy about it.

Dirk walked up to the owner, with Savannah and Richard fol-lowing close behind. When Fabio noticed their approach, his eyes quickly scanned Dirk from head to toe in a look that Savannah recognized all too well.

It was the same look that snooty women gave other females upon meeting them. For those who had perfected The Scan, it was a most efficient tool. In less than two seconds you could evaluate your competition, steal some new ideas about nail polish and accessorizing, and make the other woman feel like a country bumpkin wearing a burlap sack—even if they were in Dior.

Fabio's head-to-toe appraisal conveyed the male version, which said: You're a flabby wimp, unlike me, who's a major stud/tough guy. I can take you in ten seconds, and by the way, I could take your woman, too.

Dirk got the message and gave him his best You-Wanna-Piece-of-Me? glare. Dirk had perfected that look over the years, practicing it in front of Savannah's hallway mirror, storefront windows, and occasionally at the breakfast table, where he could see his image in the stainless steel toaster. With all that rehearsal, he was pretty good at it and enjoyed a reputation for striking terror in the hearts of lesser males.

And, apparently, Fabio Garzone must have been one of those lesser dudes, because he quickly glanced away and returned his attention to his hapless employee. "I mean it, Nico," he told the guy, who looked like a mob enforcer who ate steroids for breakfast, lunch, and dinner. "You put that blender away dirty one more time, and you'll be polishing every piece of steel in this place."

His position as alpha male reestablished, he turned back to Dirk. "Yeah?" he barked. "You need somethin'—like maybe a workout regimen?" He grinned widely, showing less than a full set of yellowed teeth.

Dirk walked up to him, put one elbow on the bar, and leaned far into his personal space. Pulling out his badge, Dirk shoved it under his nose. "Naw, I don't need no workout regimen. I get all the exercise I need bustin' morons who can't figure out how to stay out of the system."

Dirk gave him a grim smile as he stuck his badge back into his pocket. "And speaking of . . . Have you and I ever met? Your face looks familiar. Oh yeah, I recently saw it on a mug shot."

Fabio had his poker face firmly in place. But Savannah saw the guy he had called Nico wince and move a couple of steps away, farther down the bar.

Something told her that Nico's craggy features might have graced a mug shot or two during his career as a protein shake barista. And he had probably been arrested for a more serious transgression then just putting away a dirty blender.

"What are you cops doing here?" Fabio said, as he leaned back on his stool, trying to put as much distance as he could between himself and Dirk. "I finished my parole with no violations. You got no reason to be harassing me."

"Who's harassing you?" Richard said. "We're just here to check out your facility."

Not wanting the boys to have all the fun, Savannah figuratively stepped into the ring, too. "Yeah, we hear that you're the trainer to the stars, and I've got an audition to play Red Sonja coming up in a week. You got some iron I can pump, some machines I can work?" She narrowed her eyes. "Some illegal steroid cocktails I could take?"

She nodded toward the big guy behind the counter. "I betcha Nico back there could blend me up a nice concoction of human growth hormone, a diuretic, a laxative, and a big ol' scoop of that stuff that they feed to race horses to make 'em run fast. I hear that crap's real popular now, here in y'all's neck o' the woods."

Fabio gave Savannah one of the up-and-down looks that she loved so much and said, "It'd take way more than a week to get you in Red Sonja shape," he told her. "It'd take a couple of years, and by then you'd be way too old for the part."

Dirk threw back his head and roared with laughter. "Oh, man," he said, "you are taking your life in your hands saying something like that to her. You have no idea who you're dealing with."

Savannah took a step closer and locked eyes with Fabio. "That's okay," she said with deadly calm. "We're gonna let that one pass—for now. At the moment we've got bigger fish to fry, like that formal complaint that Jason Tyrone was about to file against this place."

It was a stab in the dark, of course. They had no solid proof that Jason even had a complaint against Garzone's Extreme Fitness Center, let alone that he was getting ready to file anything with anyone anywhere.

But she'd had a hunch, and she was glad she had played it. Because the look on Fabio's and Nico's faces said it all. Oh, yes, there had been a feud of some sort between Jason Tyrone and his gym. No doubt about it.

Fabio's otherwise swarthy complexion had just faded at least two shades, and Nico looked like he might swoon at any moment, like a Southern belle at a cotillion whose corset was too tight.

Yes, Savannah was quite sure of one thing.

That fight of theirs, whatever it had been about—it must have been a doozy.

Considering how badly the day had begun, Savannah was quickly deciding that it had ended well. Of course, it hadn't hurt one bit that the whole crew—she and Dirk, Tammy and Way-cross, and Dora and Richard—had been wined and dined by Ryan and John at Antoine's, Savannah's favorite French restaurant.

From the first time she had eaten there, Savannah had decided that if she was ever on death row and had to choose a last meal, she would just ask for three courses of Antoine's Chocolate Soufflé. She was pretty sure that she could then just float straight up and into heaven.

Yes. Friends, newfound family, and amazing food—life didn't get much better than that.

Even Dora had been on her best behavior. She seemed to be putting out an effort to listen, as well as talk. And she'd looked very pretty in the simple black dress she had scored at a Hollywood thrift store that specialized in vintage fashion. It was so nice, in fact, that Savannah was reexamining her stand on mall shopping.

And now, after their amazing and glamorous night out, they were all on their way home.

Savannah and Dirk had insisted that Dora and Richard ride in the Bentley with John and Ryan, while the other four piled into Dirk's Buick.

Sitting in the front passenger seat, Savannah was being careful to look only ahead, just in case her brother might be trying to make a move on Tammy in the backseat.

But romance seemed to be the farthest thing from Tammy the Super Sleuth's mind.

"Tell us again," she said, "about how mad that old Fabio guy got when you told him you knew all about the fight he and Jason had."

Savannah giggled. "At first he went sorta white, then red, then purple. His face was kinda like one of those mood rings we used to wear, constantly changing color."

"We figured Jason and the gym were on the outs," Waycross said, "with Jason quittin' them like that, but how'd you know their fight was about Fabio selling dangerous drugs?"

"We didn't," Dirk told him. "Savannah's bluff was so good that Fabio thought we already knew all about it. He spilled the beans on himself when he was arguing with us."

"Awesome," Tammy said. "So are you going to bust him for selling that stuff?"

"Maybe, after we close this case," Dirk replied. "But I told him I was definitely gonna. When we left he was one highly disgruntled gym owner."

"Yeap, we ruined his day," Savannah said, "and that was enough for me. That and finding out that he had a major motive to kill Jason. If Jason was about to blow the whistle on him, old Fabio's reputation as the trainer to the stars would have been out the window."

"We've got our work cut out for us tomorrow," Dirk said. "That's for sure. We'll have to ask Thomas and Alanna if they know anything more about the Jason-Fabio squabble."

"That's tomorrow," Savannah told him, placing her hand on his thigh. "For the rest of tonight, let's forget about the case and just savor the moment."

He put his hand over hers, squeezed, and said, "You got it, babe."

They had reached the foothill road that provided a nice, scenic shortcut from downtown San Carmelita and Antoine's to Savannah's house in midtown. Rounding one curve after another, they could see over the roofs of the houses and through the black silhouettes of the palms, down to the ocean below. The waters sparkled in the light of a full moon, like deep indigo velvet sprinkled with flakes of silver.

As they passed some orange groves, Savannah rolled down her window to let the smell of the dew-damp blossoms into the car.

And with that intoxicating perfume came another lovely scent that she seldom got to enjoy in Southern California—the smell of rain on its way. She breathed in the sweet fragrance and let it take her back to her childhood and walking to and from school on dusty Georgia roads.

Yes, it was a beautiful night, and all was well with the world.

Except for those glaring headlights behind them that were lighting up the interior of the car and ruining the whole moonlight-ambiance thing for Savannah.

She turned around to look and was nearly blinded by the searing, white beams.

"Is that Ryan and John back there?" she asked.

Dirk grunted. "No. This jerk cut them off a ways back and got between us and the Bentley. Now he's riding my tail."

Waycross turned to look. "Boy, howdy! Any minute now, he's gonna hitch onto your bumper and take a free ride."

"Tailgating is so dangerous," Tammy said. "Why do people—"

Slam!

Everyone in the car gasped as the vehicle behind them rammed into the rear of the Buick. The collision wasn't enough to run them off the road, but it gave them all a hard jolt and set their pulses racing.

"What the hell?" Dirk yelled, looking into his rearview mirror. "I think he did that deliber—"

Another slam! Then a third, much harder one!

Savannah's brain whirled, trying to make sense of what was happening. An accident was bad enough. But the driver of the giant SUV behind them was trying to run them off the road.

And with trees, telephone poles, and deep ditches on either side, this wasn't a road where anybody wanted to lose control.

"Hang on," Dirk yelled. "Everybody hang on."

He didn't need to tell them. Savannah was sure that her fingernails were buried deep into his upholstery.

They could hear the big engine revving behind them. Dirk sped up. They braced.

Again, it slammed them. Even harder than before.

The Buick swerved. Dirk fought the wheel, trying to keep the car straight.

"A dirt road!" he shouted. "Up ahead! I'm gonna try!"

Savannah could see it, the "Y" veering off about a hundred yards ahead. She told herself, *If he hits that dirt going this speed—*

But she didn't have time to finish her dark thought.

For just an instant she saw the shiny pavement. A wet spot.

Rain.

They passed over it, and the rear of the Buick swung to the right. The car turned. Turned, turned. Spinning around the road, as metal slammed into metal with a sickening, crunching sound.

Savannah looked behind her and saw the flash of the SUV's chrome bumper as it came up, up, and over the Buick's trunk.

Glass shattered. Passengers screamed.

Then, as quickly as it had started, it stopped. And there was nothing. Except . . .

Deadly silence.

Darkness.

And the sweet, sweet smell of orange blossoms kissed by a soft, summer rain.

Chapter 24

Savannah lay on her side, her hair covering her face, her ribs on her left side jammed against something terribly hard.

Her face was wet, and she didn't know why.

She was shivering as though she were standing naked in a snowstorm. Her teeth were chattering.

She couldn't move her legs, and she wasn't sure what that was all about either.

She heard someone groan. It was a man. Dirk.

Instantly, it all came back to her, and she knew exactly what had happened. The vague haziness vanished, and a desperate urgency took its place.

She struggled trying to get loose, all the while knowing something was badly amiss. Something kept pulling her to the left side of the car where, in the dark, she could see another figure, struggling as she was.

"Dirk?"

"Van? Honey, are you all right?"

"I'm not sure. You?"

"I think so."

She managed to get her seat belt loose, but the instant she did, she fell, hard, onto Dirk. Then she realized—the Buick was lying on its side.

But she could move her legs now. She was no longer pinned.

She tried to twist her body around so that she could see into the backseat. "Waycross?" she cried. "Tammy? You two okay back there?"

Savannah heard the blessed sound of her little brother's voice, though it wasn't much more than a mumbled "I reckon."

There was some rustling around in the backseat, and she heard him say, "I'm sorry, sugar, I'm mashin' you. Here, I'll put my leg over here. Try to move over that way, darlin'."

Savannah felt Dirk's arms, warm and strong, wrap around her. He was trembling, too.

"Sorry, babe." He hugged her close. "I'm so sorry. I tried to—"

"Sh-h-h." She buried her face against his chest and felt sharp little shards of glass scrape her cheeks. "It wasn't your fault. The pavement was wet and that jackass was—"

As though in unison, they both remembered the nightmare that had preceded their predicament.

"I'm gonna kill him," Dirk said in a voice that she had never heard him use before. Harsh, guttural, determined. "When I get my hands on him, he's dead."

As though from far away, Savannah heard the sound of running feet, pounding on the asphalt, racing toward them.

Excited, frightened voices cried out their names. A moment later, someone was climbing on top of the overturned car.

The Buick wobbled as someone jerked the passenger-side door open.

Thinking of the SUV driver who had nearly killed them, Savannah didn't know whether to pull away or take the hand of the person who was reaching down for her.

"Oh, my God, Savannah," said a deep, familiar, beloved voice. In the moonlight she could see Ryan's face, his horrified expression. "Are you all right? Is everybody okay?"

"We think so," she replied.

"Then we've got to get you out of there, right away."

That was when Savannah smelled it—the strong, distinctive odor of gasoline.

She twisted around to Dirk and said, "Gas."

"I smell it," he said. "Get out."

She reached up and grabbed Ryan's hands. Simultaneously she felt Dirk pushing her upward from below, and Ryan pulling from above. In a moment, she was out and clinging to the side of the car just behind the door.

She saw John scrambling to get up there with them. He stood to the front of the door and held it open as she and Ryan reached inside and grabbed Dirk by the arms.

In a few seconds they had pulled him out, as well.

"Waycross, Tammy," Savannah shouted. "You're next. Come on! Quick!"

"You first, darlin'," she heard Waycross say. "I'll help you."

Then there was a long, awful silence.

The smell of gas was so strong that Savannah gagged—and it reminded her of the urgency of the situation.

She shouted down into the dark interior, "Waycross, y'all gotta get out of there, now! Tammy, crawl over that seat and take our hands! Move!"

Suddenly, there was a light. Savannah turned and saw Dora shining the beam of a strong, LED flashlight through the empty space where the rear window had been.

Looking down into the backseat area, Savannah saw Tammy lying white-faced and still, amid the tangle of wreckage that had once been the side of Dirk's car.

Her eyes were closed. Her beautiful blonde hair was covered with blood and broken glass.

Savannah wouldn't realize until much later that she had screamed. Or that Dirk had leaped back into the car. Or that Waycross had begun to sob uncontrollably.

And whatever Ryan or John did . . . that was all just part of the awful blur that the memory would forever be for her.

But she would always, vividly remember Dora Jones, in her new-old dress, climbing through that narrow space where the rear window had been, getting into the car and pushing Waycross and Dirk aside so that she could examine the still, pale girl crumpled in an unspeakably tight crunch of metal, upholstery, and glass.

She yelled, "Be quiet!" and everyone fell silent. Instantly.

She put her face down to Tammy's. She listened and said, "She's breathing."

Placing her fingers against the side of the girl's neck, she announced, "She has a pulse."

Savannah wanted to utter a prayer of thanksgiving, but she didn't dare breathe.

With the light, confident touch of an expert, Dora checked Tammy's skull and the back of her neck. Then she ran her hands up and down her arms, around her ribs, her abdomen, pelvis, and each leg.

"No obvious fractures," she said.

Dirk leaned close to Dora and said gently, but firmly, "We have to get her out of here. Now."

"No. You can't move her. She could have spinal injuries and—"

"We have no choice. The gas. Smell it?"

The nurse stared at the cop for what seemed like forever, but it was truly only a couple of seconds. Then she nodded curtly. "You," she said to the weeping Waycross. "Take off that tee-shirt and rip off some strips for me." She turned to Savannah, John, and Ryan, who were watching in horror from outside. "I need a board. Something flat to bind her to."

"We've got a boogie board in the trunk of the Bentley."

"Get it."

Ryan jumped off the Buick, disappeared for a moment, then came running back with the board under his arm.

He passed it to Dora through the back window space.

"I'm going to hold her head and stabilize her spine," Dora told Waycross and Dirk, "while you two slip this down behind her head and back. Fast, but easy. Got it?"

They worked as best they could within the tight confines, while Savannah held the flashlight.

Once the board was in place, Dora strapped Tammy's head to it, using the strips torn from Waycross's shirt. Finally, she wrapped the rest of the shirt around Tammy's neck.

"Okay, now all you guys—as gently as you possibly can—lift her out. Smooth moves! No jerking or yanking."

Savannah held the light, and Dora supported Tammy's head as the four men pulled Tammy and her attached boogie board out of the tiny space where she was wedged. They moved her around and over the front seats, then straight up and out the passenger door.

The moment they had her out, Dirk shouted, "Everybody away from the car!"

"Nice and gentle!" Dora told them as Savannah helped her climb out as well. "Slow and easy!"

The men carried Tammy's short, makeshift stretcher a safe distance down the road, then carefully laid her down on the grassy shoulder.

Then Waycross sat on the side of the road nearby and covered his face with his hands. Ryan and John sat beside him and tried to offer the distraught young man some comfort.

Savannah knelt at Tammy's side, lifted her hand, and kissed it. "You're going to be all right, sugar," she told her. "You will be. The boys got you out, and Dora here's taking good care of you."

For a moment Tammy's eyelids fluttered, and Savannah thought she was going to open them, but she didn't.

Dora squatted on Tammy's other side and looked at the bleeding wound on her scalp. "I need another piece of cloth for this cut," she said.

Savannah glanced down and saw the silk scarf she had twisted around her neck right before they had left for the restaurant—a million years ago. She'd thought her outfit needed a bit of color.

She unwrapped it and handed it to Dora, who folded it several times and then pressed it to the wound.

"Could . . ." Savannah started to speak but was unable to. Then she tried again. "Could I please do that for her?" Savannah choked on the sobs that were gathering like hard rocks in her throat and strangling her. "I really, really need to do something for her. Anything. I love her."

Dora gave her a sweet, infinitely understanding look. "Of course you can. Here." She handed Savannah back her scarf and said, "The EMTs will be here soon. We called 911 as soon as we saw you'd crashed."

"Thank you, Dora. For everything." Savannah placed the scarf against the awful gash and pressed.

Then she felt someone's presence, standing beside her. She looked up and saw Dirk. He was watching her, looking at Tammy—a terrible expression of rage and pain on his face. "I'm so sorry," he said.

"Hush. She'll be fine. Just fine," Dora told him.

Chapter 25

Savannah stood beside the hospital bed where Tammy lay, still unconscious. And even though she had held that position for more than five hours and had her own aches and pains from the crash, it never occurred to her to desert her post.

What bothered her most was seeing that sweet, pretty face so still, so blank. Of all the people Savannah had known over the years, Tammy was the most lively, animated person she had ever met. She was never still. Her face was never blank.

This person with the frozen nonexpression, the bandaged arm, and the neck brace who was lying motionless on the bed—that wasn't Savannah's Tammy.

Just behind Savannah was Waycross, standing his own post. When they had first arrived at the hospital Waycross had refused to be examined or have his own wounds tended, because he wouldn't leave Tammy and Savannah.

Finally, when Tammy was taken in for X-rays, Savannah insisted that he allow them to stitch a particularly bad cut on his arm. But the moment Tammy had been placed in ICU, he was there, right with Savannah, and neither of them had left Tammy's side, not even to go to the restroom.

Dora stood to the left of the bed, where she busied herself, checking the IV, reading Tammy's chart, adjusting her oxygen mask, and mostly just keeping a close eye on her latest patient.

A few steps away, near the window, Ryan and John sat in a couple of uncomfortable, plastic chairs. They had tried to get Savannah and Waycross to sit down, but they had refused. So Ryan and John were performing their vigil, watching and waiting for the moment when they could be helpful, and yet staying out of the way.

Ryan leaned over and whispered something in John's ear, and John nodded.

"May I fetch us all some coffee?" John asked, as he stood and walked over to the bed. "Perhaps a bite to eat, as well?"

Savannah started to refuse, then thought better of it. "I don't want anything to eat," she said. "But coffee would probably help."

"Yes, sir," Waycross said, "I'd be much obliged. Black please, if you don't mind."

John nodded graciously, then silently slipped from the room.

As though for the first time, Savannah became aware of Waycross standing behind her. She forced herself to release Tammy's hand, turned around, and pulled her brother into the spot where she had been standing. "I'm sorry, sweetie," she said. "You stand here for a while."

He wasted no time at all stepping up to the bed and taking his girl's hand. Leaning over, he placed a kiss on her forehead.

Tears welled in Savannah's eyes. And rather than let her brother see them, she walked over to the window near Ryan and stood quietly, looking out.

The sun had risen, and San Carmelita was coming to life.

Her fellow townspeople were driving by in their vehicles, rushing to their various destinations. Others walked the sidewalks, crossed streets, bopped in and out of the diner and drugstore nearby.

A surge of anger swept through Savannah. *What the hell's wrong with them?* she thought. *They're going about their business like it's a normal day. As if one of the best people in the world isn't lying there un- conscious on that bed.*

The unshed tears of exhaustion, fury, and fear burned her eye- lids, and she knew she had to push down all of these terrible feel- ings or she would explode then and there.

And she didn't have that luxury. Her family needed her strength, even as she needed theirs.

She thought of Dirk and the distraught, conflicted look on his face when he had left her a few hours ago to take Nico to the po- lice station for booking.

"Are you sure, Van?" he'd asked her. "I can stay here if you want me to. I'll call a radio car to take him in."

"No, you need to question him. Put him in the box and sweat him. Find out what this is all about."

He had hugged her to him, long and hard. Then, as he re- leased her, he said, "If you need me, you call. I mean it. I can get over here in five minutes."

If I need you? she thought as she looked out the window toward the direction of the station house. *Of course I need you. You're my husband now. I'll always need you.*

She felt a hand on her shoulder and turned to see Ryan look- ing down at her, his green eyes full of concern.

"She's going to be okay," he told her. "I know she is."

Savannah didn't reply. She couldn't. How many times had she uttered those exact words to people in the same type of situa- tion? She, of all people, knew how meaningless they were. The only purpose they served was to get people through horrible, stressful times as they clutched at any form of hope they could find.

Ryan had no idea whether Tammy was going to be okay or not.

At this point, even the physicians who had examined and treated her didn't know.

"She's not out of the woods yet," they had said. "We'll know more in twenty-four hours."

They didn't know. Ryan didn't know. Nobody knew whether their Tammy would ever return to them, would ever be her sweet, bubbly self again.

"Thank you," she told Ryan, trying hard to sound like she meant it, whether she did or not.

"You should go home," he said, "and get some rest. You were in a bad car wreck. And now all the stress about her. You need to take care of yourself, too."

"I'm not going home," she replied. Her voice sounded bitter and angry, even to herself. "If I were going anywhere, I'd go to the police station and pick up where Dirk left off—beating the shit outta that yayhoo that did this to her."

No one said anything. Ryan, Dora, and Waycross just stood there with mixtures of surprise, sadness, and agreement on their faces.

Finally, Dora left Tammy and walked over to Savannah. She placed her hands on Savannah's shoulders and looked directly into her eyes.

The older woman radiated strength, wisdom, and confidence. She wasn't the chattering, bossy, annoying nitwit she had appeared to be when Savannah had first met her. Now she was a nurse, a woman who had saved lives, who had healed sick and injured people more than half of her adult life.

"Leave. Go to the police station," she said. "You won't beat anybody up—though I'm sure you'll want to. You'll help Dirk, like you have for years. You guys are a team, and he needs you."

"But Tammy," she protested.

"I'll take care of your friend, Savannah. It's what I do best."

She placed her hand on Savannah's cheek and gave it an affectionate pat. "Go do what *you* do best."

"How goz it?" Savannah texted to Dirk's phone as soon as she pulled into the parking lot of the police station.

"Sux. He 8nt talkn," came the almost instant, Dirk-code reply.

Her thumbs flew over her phone pad. "Comin in. Don't believe NE thing I say."

"OK."

She hurried into the station, by way of the back door. The chief of police, whom she loathed, along with the rest of the brass who had been instrumental in her firing, usually came and went through the front or side doors.

There was no point in announcing her presence.

Once inside the building, she headed down a narrow, depressing, dark hallway that led to the Box—or so she and Dirk liked to call Interrogation Room #1.

Dirk would be in there with Nico. No doubt about it. When Dirk was questioning a suspect, he was like a camel in the desert. He didn't even need to drink or pee. It was as though his entire digestive system just shut down. She'd never seen anything like it.

If only he'd been able to do that on stakeouts.

Sure enough, there was a sign hanging on the door of the Box: INTERVIEW IN PROGRESS.

She knocked lightly, then pushed the door open and stepped inside.

When she saw only Dirk and Nico sitting at the table, she was greatly relieved. No attorney.

Good.

Nico had been too stupid to lawyer up.

But he did seem to have enough sense to be scared when she

walked through the door. In spite of the fact that he had a body like a bull, Nico radiated the confidence and courage of a barnyard chicken.

Like most of the criminals Savannah had met, Nico hadn't committed his crimes because he had the fortitude to pay for his misdeeds if he were ever brought to justice. No, Nico wasn't brave or tough. He was stupid, thinking that he would never have to pay.

She walked to the table and stood beside Dirk, her hands on her hips. "I thought I should let you know, Detective, that your suspect here is now facing a first-degree murder rap. The girl in the hospital—she just died."

The moment the words left her mouth, Savannah felt a deep stab of conscience. In her line of work, she lied all the time. But she was just superstitious enough to be uncomfortable even uttering something like that.

Dirk glared at Nico across the table. "That's bad news for you, my man. First-degree murder. That's a tough one, even for a life-long career criminal like you."

"First degree?" Nico asked, looking like he was about to burst into tears or wet his pants or both. "How can it be first-degree murder when it was just a car accident? I never meant to kill that girl. I never meant to hurt any of you."

"That's not what your boss, Fabio, just told me," Savannah said. "He confessed to it all. Said he paid you to run us off the road and kill us."

She walked over and stood behind Nico's chair. She leaned over, literally breathing down his neck, and added, "Murder for hire. That's one of those special circumstances. Buddy, I wouldn't wanna be you for anything. The way I see it, you killing a pretty young girl like that, there's a needle somewhere with your name on it."

"Can't we make some kind of a deal?" Nico pleaded, his chin quivering like a kindergartner begging for dessert.

"Nope," Savannah told him. "Your boss is in the next room right now writing out a formal confession. He made his deal already while you were fartin' around in here. And now, he's the lucky one. He'll be outta jail in five to ten years—about the same time as you'll spend on death row, before they put you down like an old hound dog."

"No! It wasn't no murder for hire. He didn't even give me money. He let me have some old weights that he was gonna throw out anyway. And I was just supposed to bang into the back of your car a little bit. You know, shake you up some. My boss just wanted you to know that he wasn't somebody you should mess with."

Savannah looked over at Dirk, whose mouth was slightly open. But his eyes glowed with a grim satisfaction.

They had their confession.

Dirk stood, walked over to a small cabinet, and took out a yellow legal pad and pen. He returned to the table and said to Savannah, "Didn't you just tell us that Garzone's in there writing out his confession right now?"

"Yep, he's just about finished."

Dirk slapped the pad and pen down onto the table in front of Nico. "Then I hope you can write fast, boy," he told him. "First guy to hand in his confession gets the best deal. Maybe there's still time for you to get yours in before he does."

As Nico scribbled frantically, his tongue sticking out the right side of his mouth like a kid who was concentrating on his coloring, Savannah ventured a glance at Dirk and saw that he was looking at her with an expression of humor and adoration on his face.

Dora had been right; they were a team, and they always worked best together.

Savannah gave him a wink, pursed her lips, and sent him a silent air kiss.

Sometimes, it was especially nice to be needed.

When Savannah pulled the Mustang into the alley behind Garzone's gym, Richard was in the passenger seat, talking on the phone to Dora.

Dirk leaned forward from the backseat and whispered, "Tammy? Any change?"

Richard held the phone away from his mouth for a moment and said, "A few minutes ago, she looked like she was trying to open her eyes."

"Excellent," Savannah said. "Well, maybe not excellent, but encouraging."

Dirk sighed and fell back onto the seat. "I just want her to wake up and say something to somebody. I'm gonna feel horrible till I hear she's talking again. It's unnatural, the blabbermouth kid not talking."

Richard gave his wife a whispered "I love you, too" and hung up.

They saw a radio car with a couple of uniformed cops pull into the lot near them.

"Okay. There's our backup," Dirk said, checking his weapon. "Let's rock and roll."

For all of his muscles and in spite of his criminal history and lousy attitude, Fabio Garzone wasn't such a tough guy, after all.

When he saw Dirk and Savannah and their entourage entering his gym, he folded like an old map that'd been left in somebody's glove box for twenty-five years.

It was only a matter of minutes until Dirk was leading him out to the squad car and shoving him into the backseat.

Fabio had offered no resistance with his muscles, but that didn't stop him from running his mouth—much to Savannah's annoyance.

"What exactly am I being arrested for?" he asked, practically spitting the words at Dirk, who was fastening a seat belt around him.

"For ordering the killings of me and my family," Dirk replied, keeping his temper in check, but barely.

"I never told anybody to kill you or anybody you know—and not Jason Tyrone either."

"I'm not arresting you for Jason Tyrone's murder. Not yet," Dirk said. "But give me time. I'm not gonna rest until you get absolutely everything that's comin' to ya."

He slammed the door and turned to Savannah and Richard. "Let's get back to the hospital and check on our girl, then I'll run over to the courthouse and get the subpoena to search this guy's house."

Savannah nodded solemnly, glaring through the car window at the monster who had put Tammy in that hospital bed. "Can't think of anything I'd rather do. Well, actually, I can. But there're too many witnesses, and you'd have to arrest me, too."

Chapter 26

Savannah was holding a bouquet of daisies and Dirk a handful of balloons when they approached the door of Tammy's hospital room. Richard brought up the rear with a red, heart-shaped box of chocolates.

All were filled with dread over what they might find. And none of them really believed Tammy would benefit from their gifts.

It was going to have to be a case of "It's the thought that counts."

Already, Savannah had steeled herself against the probability that nothing had changed in her brief absence. And she had tried to convince herself that, in Tammy's case, status quo was a good thing.

But it wasn't working.

She didn't have to be a physician to know that unconsciousness was a terribly serious condition, and the longer it lasted, the worse the prognosis. She also knew that once someone had been out for six hours, they could be classified as comatose.

She didn't think she could stand it if she had to use the words "coma" and "Tammy" in the same sentence.

Dirk reached over with his free hand and grasped hers. She was almost grateful that he didn't give her the "She'll be fine" line. She'd heard enough lies for one day—even well-meaning ones.

The three of them crept into the room.

The first thing Savannah noticed were the voices. Fairly loud voices having a normal-sounding conversation, rather than hushed whispers filled with fear.

"That's what I'm seeing, too," she heard Ryan say. "She's got an R.O. against him. Wow! Wait till we tell Savannah."

"Tell me what?" Savannah said, as she was the first to step around the blue curtain that cordoned off Tammy's half of the room.

And there on the other side of that magical divide was the most beautiful sight Savannah had ever seen in her life.

Tammy, sitting up in bed, fully awake, her face bruised, her eyes swollen nearly closed, her arm in a sling, and the brace still around her neck.

Savannah had never seen her looking more gorgeous.

Instantly, Savannah burst into tears. Everything she had been holding back since the collision came pouring out of her heart and her eyes as she rushed across the room to her friend's bed.

"Oh, oh, honey!" she shouted. "You're awake! You're sitting up!" She glanced down at the electronic tablet that was propped on pillows on Tammy's lap. "You're working?"

Tammy snickered then winced. "Stop it! Nobody's allowed to say anything funny. My ribs hurt when I laugh."

Savannah tossed the flowers onto the foot of the bed and reached for her friend, to hug her. Then she thought better of it and said, "Where can I touch you that it won't hurt?"

Tammy took a lengthy inventory of her battered, bruised, and bandaged body. "I think you'd better just blow me a kiss," she said.

Standing on the other side of her bed, Waycross smiled and said, "I found a spot right here that's okay." He pointed to Tammy's left cheek.

Savannah wasted no time in planting one there.

Dirk did the same. Then he gave her a second one for good measure. "I'm really glad you're okay, kiddo," he said. "You had us all worried sick."

"Are those balloons for me?" she asked.

He grinned. "Naw. I brought 'em for Ryan and John. But I guess you can have 'em."

He glanced over toward the window, where John and Ryan sat, each holding their own electronic tablets.

Dora occupied a chair next to theirs and was sipping from a disposable coffee cup. She looked exhausted and, for once, uninterested in adding to the conversation. Richard quietly laid the box of chocolates on the bed next to Savannah's flowers and went to stand by his wife's chair.

Lovingly, he massaged her shoulders.

"What's going on here?" Dirk asked Ryan and John, pointing to their tablets. "You guys sitting around with your thumbs in your ears, playing video games?"

Ryan smiled. "Not at all. In fact, Tammy's giving us lessons on Internet snooping and cyber-stalking."

"Good," Savannah said, as she carefully sat on the edge of Tammy's bed, "because we need to nail this Fabio Garzone for everything we can. We've got him for setting up the attack on us, but we also wanna nail him for Jason's murder."

"Hell," Dirk said, "I wanna prove he's D. B. Cooper and the Zodiac before I'm done with him. Hurt my family and wreck my car . . . He's lucky I didn't lock those cuffs around his neck instead of his wrists."

John cleared his throat. "Those are lofty ambitions there, lad.

You might identify him as the Cooper chap, but you're going to find it harder to blame him for Jason's passing."

"Why?" Savannah said, somehow dreading the answer.

"He was in New York City before, while, and after Jason died," Tammy said with one hand against her left ribs.

"He was conducting workshops at the weeklong Sons of Zeus Bodybuilding Competition that's held there every year," John said, holding up his tablet so Savannah and Dirk could see the cavalcade of burgeoning bodies flipping by in a slideshow.

"And all of his club lackies were there, too," Ryan told them. "So he didn't get one of them to do it."

"This is documented?" Savannah asked, hoping against hope.

Tammy nodded, then groaned at the pain it cost her. "Unfortunately, yes. We were just watching the footage of him and his boys on top of the Empire State Building, pounding their chests like a bunch of idiotic, wannabe King Kongs."

Savannah felt like one of those giant, inflated balloons in the Macy's Thanksgiving Day Parade when it had just had its plug pulled.

She was sinking fast.

"We're back at square one, then, with Jason's case," she said. "And I was just so sure it was that jackass Fabio."

"You're not exactly at square one," Dora said, toying with her disposable cup. "Wait till you hear what your Moonlight Magnolia team here found out on those expensive phone-computer things of theirs."

Both Savannah and Dirk brightened. "Oh?" he asked.

"That's right," Savannah said. "When we walked in, I heard you say something about a restraining order."

"First things first," Ryan told her. "And here's number one on the list of things we've uncovered—Alanna wasn't the only woman Thomas was jealous of. According to some e-mails we dug up, Thomas accused Jason of breaking up a marriage. Apparently, an old girlfriend of Jason's was getting a divorce, and Thomas thought it was because she'd been unfaithful to her husband with Jason."

Dirk shrugged. "As juicy as that may be, it doesn't prove anything. Thomas thought Jason was messing around with everybody."

"True," John said, "but this couple is getting a divorce, and as recently as yesterday, the wife obtained an order of protection against him. Apparently the husband's been threatening her."

"That's unfortunate," Savannah replied, "but it's hardly evidence in our case."

Tammy piped up. "You know them."

Savannah raised one eyebrow. "We do?"

"Mr. and Mrs. Leland Porter."

Savannah's breath caught in her throat. "Really?" she asked, as the first puzzle piece clicked into place. "Jason had an affair with his old friend's wife?"

"Thomas and Leland thought so," Ryan said. "And Porter's wife and Jason were old friends, too. He'd known them both for years."

"Okay," Dirk said, "that gives Leland a motive. But how would he get his hands on that Lido-Morphone stuff to spike the patches. It's a Class A drug. You can't just pick that up at the neighborhood pharmacy. And he's not in the medical field."

Tammy turned to Dora. "Nurse Jones, do you have any theories about that?"

Dora thought it over, then said, "Other than as a pain reliever in a gel-patch form, Lido-Morphone is mostly used in outpatient surgeries. It's a good sedative. Keeps the patient calm and still during the procedure. Plastic surgeons like it."

"Plastic surgeons, huh?" Richard asked. "Does Porter have any connections to doctors or surgeons?"

Savannah flashed back on the bandages she had seen under

Leland's tee-shirt. She turned to Dora. "What kind of surgery would a man have on his nipples?"

Everyone looked at Savannah as if she were crazy.

"His nipples?" Richard asked.

"Yes. Leland had bandages over both of his nipples. In the same place, so I doubt it was from an accident."

"Gynecomastia," Dora said.

"What?" the others asked.

"More commonly known as 'man boobs.' It's an embarrassing condition that's not all that uncommon in bodybuilding circles. It can be caused by taking anabolic steroids. It's a simple enough procedure to correct it."

"Done in a doctor's office as an outpatient procedure?" John asked.

"With Lido-Morphone?" Ryan added.

Dora replied, "Most certainly."

Tammy's fingers were already flying over the screen of her tablet. "There are two plastic surgeons in Leland's area who specialize in that procedure. I have their numbers here if you want them."

Dirk hurried over to her and jotted the numbers down on the pad he carried in his pocket. A moment later, he had the first doctor's office on the phone. He identified himself and then said, "In the past month or two, have you noticed any shortages in your medical supplies? Specifically, a Class A drug called Lido-Morphone?"

His eyes gleamed as he turned to the others, who were holding their breath, and gave them a thumbs-up. "You have. Okay. Would you happen to know the exact date when that drug went missing?"

He scribbled down the date, still smiling. "And one more question. I wouldn't ask this ordinarily, but I'm investigating a murder. So please don't make me have to get a subpoena, okay?"

He drew a deep breath. "The day that medicine went missing, did you happen to perform a breast reduction on a patient named Leland Porter?"

He, and they, waited for what seemed a stretch in Purgatory as the office assistant checked her records. Finally, she returned and spoke to him.

"Of course not. This is strictly between you and me. I'll get the subpoena and make it all legal down the line. This is just for investigation purposes." He paused, listened. "Okay, thank you," he said. "Thank you very much."

He turned off his phone and stood there, saying nothing, his face blank.

Savannah reached over and thumped him on the shoulder. "Well?"

"Leland Porter had his procedure done there. Ten days ago. And that just happens to be the same day the drug went missing."

The room erupted in cheers.

A moment later, a nurse charged into the room, a stern look on her face. "Okay, that's it!" she said. "I told you people that you weren't allowed to have this many in this room at one time. And you certainly can't make a disturbance like that."

Dora stood and, along with the other nurse, started to shoo them out. "Go," she said. "I'll stay here with Tammy. The rest of you go home and get some rest."

But when she tried to shove Waycross out, he wouldn't budge. "I've got a better idea," he said. "I'm gonna stay here with my girl, and you're gonna go home with the rest of 'em. You've done enough, Nurse Jones. Now it's my turn."

As Savannah drove the Mustang down Leland's tree-lined street in Rosado yet again, she said to Dirk and Richard, "We've been here so much lately, it's starting to feel like home."

Dirk, who had given his father the front passenger seat, spoke up from the rear. "Hopefully, this'll be our last trip out here. The uniforms say he's there. They're waiting for us halfway down the block."

Out of an abundance of caution and kindness, Savannah decided not to point out this new trend of Dirk's to have backup along when they arrested one of these bodybuilders.

She had heard a lot of "regular" guys talk about how useless all those muscles were, how slow and muscle-bound those ripped dudes were. But she noticed that most fellas, including her own, had a healthy respect for bodybuilders and didn't want to tangle with them if they could avoid it.

Hence, the squad car that was waiting for them when they arrived on Leland Porter's block.

Savannah pulled in behind them, and everyone bailed out of their vehicles and walked the half block to Leland's house.

"I'd like you guys to wait here for us," Dirk told the patrolmen when they reached the sidewalk in front of the house. "Keep sharp and come in if we call you. We want to try to talk to him first."

Richard said, "I'll wait, too. But we're here if you need us."

"Great. Thanks," Dirk said, as he nodded toward Savannah, and they started up the driveway, heading for the front porch.

Savannah kept an eye on the living room curtains as they started toward the door. But they had gone only a couple of steps when Dirk said, "Hey, listen. Do you hear that?"

She did hear it. The sound of an automobile running. "Yes, it's a car. So?"

"It's coming from the garage."

It took her two seconds to realize why he was alarmed. They both started running toward the building in the back. The patrolmen and Richard followed close behind.

She smelled it even before they reached the garage—the strong, pungent odor of vehicle exhaust fumes.

But she knew that the real killer inside that garage, present in those fumes, was itself odorless. And for all they knew, it had already done its deadly work.

Dirk reached the building first. He grabbed the garage door, gave it a hard yank, and sent it flying upward.

There was the Cadillac limousine, shiny and beautiful, its powerful motor idling.

She could hear the sound of music coming from inside it. Some sort of country rock.

"Leland!" Savannah yelled. "Le-land!"

She knew he wouldn't answer. She could see the garden hose that had been adhered to the exhaust with duct tape, that led around the vehicle and into the rear driver's side window, which was down about an inch.

Leland Porter had meant business. If he were still conscious, he didn't want to be found.

If he wasn't conscious anymore, it might not matter if he was found. They could be too late.

"Try not to breathe!" Dirk shouted to everyone. "Hold your breath as much as you can!"

Savannah filled her lungs, then rushed in with everyone else.

Dirk jerked open the limo's rear door.

Savannah was relieved to see that it was unlocked. But the moment Dirk opened it, the stench in the garage became far more intense.

As the fumes billowed out, her eyes burned, and they all began to cough and wheeze as the gasses attacked their respiratory systems.

Savannah saw past Dirk's shoulders inside the car, where Leland Porter lay sprawled across the floor of his own limousine, unconscious, his face a hideous and unnatural shade of pinkish red.

"Get him out," Dirk yelled, as he, one of the other patrolmen, and Richard jumped inside the limo and grabbed the limp body.

It was no small feat, dragging him to the door. Savannah and the other cop each seized a leg and pulled with all their might. But Leland Porter was no lightweight.

She thought he was dead, but when they managed to pull him from the vehicle, his body hit the cement floor with a thud and it seemed to stir him to consciousness.

"What?" he gasped, looking around him. "What's going . . . what're you . . . ?" Like everyone else, he began to cough and gag.

"Outside," Dirk shouted. "We've all gotta get outta here!"

Savannah jumped into the front seat of the limo and cut the ignition. Then she joined the others in grabbing Leland's various limbs and pulling him across the floor toward the door.

Once they hit the driveway, they continued to drag him until they were all the way to the sidewalk.

Leland started to thrash around, muttering incoherently. He couldn't seem to focus, and to make things worse, he began to vomit.

"Roll him onto his side," Savannah said, as she knelt and tried to push him over, but she couldn't budge the big man.

The others joined in and got him onto his side. After a minute or so, the heaving stopped, and he seemed to be settling down a bit.

She stood and dusted the dirt off her hands and knees. She saw that Richard was calling 911 and requesting an ambulance.

Savannah hurried over to Dirk, who was standing next to a tree, leaning with one hand on its bark. His face was flushed, and he was breathing hard.

"Are you okay, sugar?" she asked him.

He nodded. "You?"

"I'm all right."

She glanced back at their suspect on the ground and the limo in the garage. "Good catch," she said. "I never would've noticed the sound of that motor running if you hadn't pointed it out."

"You'd have gotten to him, once we didn't find him in the house."

"Maybe, but I'd probably would've been too late. He was on his way out."

"Yes, he sure was. A couple more minutes . . ."

"We'd have been calling the coroner's wagon instead of an ambulance."

"Exactly."

Dirk's phone started to ring, playing the theme to *The Good, the Bad, and the Ugly*.

"The chief," they said in unison.

He answered, grunted, "Yes" and "Okay," then hung up. He grinned at Savannah as he stuck the phone back in his pocket. "It's official," he said.

"What is?"

"I caught the case."

She laughed. "That's the chief. Always on top of things."

Chapter 27

As Dirk removed the crank and pulled the aluminum canister out of the bucket, sloshing salted water and ice on the patio, everyone cheered. The homemade ice cream was ready at last!

Savannah handed him some dishes, and with a little help from Ryan, he began to scoop up generous portions for all those who had waited and taken turns cranking the wonderful stuff until it was finally firm.

Usually, the get-togethers at Savannah's house were celebratory. And tonight was no different, as she and Dirk entertained their friends and family.

Savannah passed the dishes among their guests, Ryan and John, Dora and Richard, Waycross and—yes, the queen of the evening's festivities, Tammy, who had just been released from the hospital that morning. And as she served each one of them, she realized that, with this group, the line between friend and family was blissfully blurred.

Some families were created by the mixing of biology. Others by the blending of hearts. And as far as she was concerned, this group was as deliciously blended as this ice cream, made with Granny's best recipe.

Once everyone else was served, Dirk handed her a bowl and whispered, "That one's for you, babe." She looked down at it and saw that the bowl contained a bit more than the others.

She glanced around, saw that everyone was distracted, their noses buried in their own bit of heaven. Grabbing the scooper, she added some more to the helping and handed it to him. "Nope. That one has your name on it."

Mickey the schnauzer danced at Savannah's feet, begging for a bite. She laughed and told him, "Yes, yes, I'll see if I can find a bowl with your name on it, too, you little twerp."

Across the patio, on a chaise next to Tammy's, John raised his dish and said, "Here's to the strong biceps that cranked this wonderful concoction and to our Tammy, who has returned to us, like the first ray of sunshine after a black and stormy day."

"Here, here" were the echoed replies as dishes were raised.

Tammy blushed, reached down, and pulled the begging Mickey onto her lap. "I'm just happy to be back. I've missed you all, and, of course, I've missed out on all the best gossip. What's going on with Leland Porter?"

"He's recovering," Savannah said, taking a seat near Tammy and offering the schnauzer his own small bowl with a spoonful of ice cream in it. "He'll be able to stand trial. That's all that matters to me."

"He confessed, right?" Tammy asked.

Dirk sniffed. "He did. It was sorta a moot point, considering the suicide note he'd left behind there in the limo. In the letter he spelled it all out, what he'd done, how, and why."

"It was just jealousy, pure and simple," Ryan said, his voice tight and somewhat bitter. "He couldn't stand seeing his old friend become wildly successful when he was hitting bottom. His wife says she never did anything inappropriate with Jason, and I believe her. It was all in Leland's mind."

John nodded in agreement. "He spiked that pain patch,

waited there in the hotel until Jason died, and then took it off him. He thought we'd never figure out what he'd done."

"And we wouldn't have," Richard added, "if Savannah hadn't had one of those special overnight revelations of hers about the patch."

The group fell silent. Then Tammy snickered. And Dirk cleared his throat. Ryan and John laughed outright.

"Next topic," Savannah said.

"Fabio Garzone," Tammy offered. "Did he have anything to do with Jason's death?"

"No," Savannah told her. "He was afraid Jason was going to expose him for all the illegal builder drugs he was pushing there in his gym. And he'd threatened Jason."

"That's why Jason was jumpy there at the movie, right?" Waycross asked.

"Yeah," Dirk said. "Nico told us that Fabio said he'd kill Jason, and Jason believed he might try."

"Sad, isn't it," John added, "how Jason was afraid of those scoundrels, when it was his own chum out to get him?"

"That is sad," Dora said, contributing to the conversation for the first time as she took the last bite of her ice cream. "It's often those you love the most who hurt you the worst."

Tammy gave the older woman a smile and said, "Yes, but I'd like to think that more often, they do you good."

As she spoke, the moon slipped from behind a cloud, and its light fell on her face, beautiful and serene, with the bruises all faded. Savannah thought she looked like some fairy creature with moon-silver shimmering in her hair.

"And sometimes," Tammy continued, as she looked around, one by one, at each person present, "if you're really, really lucky—the way I was—those people closest to your heart can even save your life."

* * *

The next morning at 5:30, Savannah was sitting in her comfy chair with a cup of coffee in her hand, Diamante in her lap, and Mickey the mini-schnauzer on the ottoman at her feet. At that ungodly hour, her chair was as far as she could force herself to venture into the world.

Heck, even Granny Reid slept in until 5:45.

Dirk was puttering around in the kitchen with his mom, helping her get the food supplies ready for their trip back home. And Savannah felt bad about that. Her upbringing dictated that she, the hostess, should be performing that chore.

But when she'd heard that they were washing disposable dishes and folding the used paper towels they'd hung up to dry the night before out on the back porch, her psyche had rebelled.

So she sat in the living room, sipping coffee, and visiting with Richard, who was sitting in Dirk's usual spot on the sofa. He even had Cleo in his lap and was giving her a behind-the-ear rub.

"I'd say the visit went pretty well overall," he said, dropping his voice a bit and stealing a glance toward the kitchen. "I know Dora's a little chatty for some people's taste. Hope she didn't get on your nerves too bad."

"Not at all," Savannah said, resisting the urge to cross her fingers behind her back.

"My wife's a really good person," he said, still keeping his voice low. "She had it really hard when she was a kid, and some things you just never get over."

Savannah knew about "some things."

She nodded. "I understand."

"Her mom gave her away when she was just eight years old. Dumped her on their elderly neighbors' doorstep and took off with some guy. Dora took care of those old people, mean as they were. She did everything in that house. Waited on them hand and foot, like a slave. The state even gave them custody of her. She called them 'aunt' and 'uncle', though they weren't."

"That's awful. I'm so sorry."

"They never talked to her or allowed her to talk. That's why she's so chatty now. It's like she never got over the joy of being able to talk as much as she wants."

Savannah looked at Richard and saw into his soul. She saw the love and respect he had for his wife, and she understood why he tolerated her prattling with so much grace.

"They were poor, too," he said. "Always drilled it into her to save this and not waste that."

Ah, Savannah thought, *the mystery of the dried, reused paper towels solved*.

"We met at a school dance," he continued, "and it was love at first sight. We had to sneak around to see each other, because they didn't approve. And when they found out—you know, about Dirk—they threw a fit. They didn't want her taking care of a baby. They wanted her just taking care of them. So as soon as he was born, they took him away from her. They told us that they'd found a good home for him with a nice couple. They told us to forget about him."

Richard paused, and Savannah's heart went out to him as she watched him struggle with his emotions.

"I never even got to see him. We did get to name him, though. I was called Dick back then, so we put Dick and Dora together and named him Dirk."

Savannah bit her lower lip and nodded. "That's sweet. I know he's a little conflicted about his last name. He did get adopted by a guy named Coulter, and he's been Coulter most of his life. It'd be hard for him to change it now. "

"Oh, I understand completely. I don't expect him to change his name. There are enough Joneses in the world already." Richard gave her a searching look. "Is that why you're keeping your last name?"

She nodded. "Reid was my grandfather's name. He was a fine

man, and I loved him very much. And Savannah Reid is who I've been my whole life."

They sat in companionable silence for a while, listening to Dirk and his mother chatter in the kitchen. Once in a while they laughed, and the sound of it went through Savannah, directly to her heart.

She thought of all Richard had said about Dora. She recalled how Dora had crawled into the wrecked Buick and helped them save Tammy.

No, Dora wasn't so bad, after all.

Finally, Richard said, "Your grandfather was a good man, and you were close to him. How about your dad?"

"No. Unfortunately not."

"I'm sorry to hear that."

"It's okay. I'm all right with it." She shrugged. "Might as well be, huh?"

"True."

He hesitated, and she wondered what he was going to say next. He seemed to be having difficulty getting it out.

"If you want," he said at last, "and only if you feel comfortable with it . . . you can call me 'Dad.' I know I could never take the place of a real father for you, but I'd sure like it if you could maybe think of me that way. Once in a while. 'Cause I'd sure be proud to have you as a daughter."

Savannah looked down and noticed that tears were dripping onto Diamante's head. But Di didn't seem to mind, so neither did she.

"I'd like that," she said in a wee, soft voice that sounded like that of a seven-year-old girl. A little girl in a dirty, tattered dress and uncombed hair, who lived with a negligent mother and a passel of siblings, without their absentee father, in a wide spot in the road called McGill, Georgia. "I'd like that a lot . . . Dad."

* * *

An hour later, Dora, Richard, and Mickey were pulling out of the driveway, their Jeep filled with the food goodies Savannah had prepared for them the day before, the freshly cleaned dishes and cutlery, and their colorful "California" shirts.

Savannah felt her heartstrings tug as she and Dirk waved vigorously and watched until they had disappeared down the road.

She looked up at her husband anxiously, thinking he must feel at least as sad as she did, if not more.

But he was looking down at her with a sweet, peaceful, contented expression on his face that told her that, at least for the moment, all was right with his world.

"That was great. But it's just you and me now, kid," he said, as they turned and started back up the sidewalk to the front door. "Imagine that."

"Whatever will we do with ourselves?"

"We can run around the house naked. Hooters and dickey-do abob."

She giggled and poked him in the ribs. "We could fool around in our own bed and not worry about how much noise we're making."

"Now you're talking." He opened the door, and they walked inside.

The house seemed so very, very quiet. Deliciously, miraculously quiet.

She whispered, "We could just sit in the living room and not say a single word to each other."

"Ah-h-h! Lovely."

"Or . . . you could go up to your man cave, shut the door, and watch some Navy SEAL videos, and I can order a romantic, girlie flick and watch it down here by myself."

His face lit up. "Really? Could we do that?"

"Sure we could. Why not? A little solitude once in a while's a healthy thing."

"That's a wonderful idea—if you don't mind, that is."

"Grab a cold beer and Cleo and go."

"Van, when it comes to wives, you are the *best*!"

He headed for the kitchen, then paused and looked over his shoulder at her, a concerned look on his face. "Does this mean the honeymoon's over?"

"Naw. When it comes to you and me, darlin'—the honeymoon's just begun."